I0788425

GOLDI'S GRUMPY COWBOY

COWBOYS OF SUNRISE RIDGE RANCH BOOK 1

NIKI J. MITCHELL

GOLDI'S GRUMPY COWBOY

Cowboys of Sunrise Ridge
Book 1

Niki J. Mitchell

CHAPTER 1

GOLDI SUMMERS

Southern California

No matter how much magic I whisked into my recipes, it was never enough for this cafe—or my boss. But this dish would be different, especially with the added goat's cheese and raspberries from the farmer's market.

I dusted the top of the porcelain ramekin with powdered sugar, sending a puff of white into the air.

Sweet perfection.

Mr. Creativity-Terminator stomped across the kitchen like a man personally offended by flavor. His unibrow quivered. "What have you made, Goldi?"

"Raspberry soufflés." I flashed him a smile.

"I told you—we never change the menu—ever," he barked.

"Don't you get tired of those same boring pancakes?" I sure did.

"Stick to our recipes or find another job."

The guy should be saluting me for my ingenuity—not reprimanding me.

"Clean up this stuff. Now." He motioned toward the counter. "And get back to work."

That was it. The final straw. "You're such an idiot you can't even see what an asset I am. I quit."

Staff members stood frozen in shock. Nobody ever talked back to the general manager. Until me.

"You can't leave in the middle of your shift," he bellowed.

I tossed my apron onto the counter, yanked off my hairnet and flung it at him. "Watch me."

"Don't expect a recommendation."

"I won't." Instead of leaving out the back door like I usually did, I headed through the restaurant. The espresso machine seemed to sputter in surprise. Patrons glanced up from their plates, forks paused midair. I marched through and out the door.

The sunshine hit me like a blessing. Despite having no job and no plan, somehow… I felt amazing. Quitting a job that I'd never liked gave me a sense of power.

This was the first step to something better. A bakery of my own with no managers. No rules. Just me and carbs and maybe a stand mixer that didn't talk back.

Mark, my fiancé, had promised he'd talk to the owner of that cute storefront I'd been eyeing. With any luck, he'd come home with a contract today. I didn't walk to my apartment a few blocks away, I ran—giddy with each slap of sneaker on the sidewalk.

I set my keys on the counter and spotted Mark's T-shirt lying on the floor next to the couch. Talk about annoying.

Picking the shirt up, I took a detour into the laundry room and threw it in the basket before heading for the bathroom.

Then I heard it.

Moaning.

Female.

Coming from our bedroom.

Slowly I made my way to the door and pushed it open.

A naked woman moaned as she rode a man. My man.

"What the freaking hell?"

"Shit!" With his eyes wide, Mark practically threw the woman off him and scrambled to put on his boxers.

That's when I saw her face. Our neighbor, Jenny.

My mouth went dry as I struggled to understand. I looked straight at them. "Is this a bad time?" The absurdity of the situation forced a laugh from my throat. "Because I can come back later." My words dripped with sarcasm, even as my hands shook.

"Sugar, wait—I can explain—."

"What's there to explain, Mark? You're screwing Jenny. In our bed. Seems pretty self-explanatory to me."

"It's not what it looks like."

"Wow. Pulling out a stupid cliche? Because it looks like you're cheating. But please, enlighten me." Mockery tinged my voice, but underneath the facade, I was crumbling.

Jenny clutched the sheet to her chest, a cruel grin playing on her lips. "Don't be so dramatic. Mark and I have feelings for each other. You would've found out soon anyway."

"That's not true."

A nervous giggle bubbled up.

"I love you. This was a moment of weakness. We need to talk."

"Talk? Sure, let's talk." I backed away as he approached, my voice rising. "Let's talk about trust. And loyalty. And love."

Jenny's lips curled as she grasped his arm.

Mark shook out of her hold. "We've been together two years. Don't give up on us now, sugar," he pleaded.

I felt a rush of anger surge through me, pushing aside the hurt. "You both disgust me."

Jenny rolled her eyes. "You were never good enough for him. He deserves someone better, someone like me."

I let out a bitter laugh. "As if."

Mark threaded his fingers together as if praying. "Please, sugar, we can work this out."

"You really are deluded. He loves me—not you." Jenny squinted at me and folded her arms.

Lightheaded, the room spun, the reality of the situation hitting me like a knife through the chest. The man I thought I would spend the rest of my life with, and the neighbor who always seemed so nice, had turned against me in the cruelest way imaginable.

His eyes pleaded for forgiveness. "I love you. It was a mistake, sugar. I swear."

"Get out." My voice iced with rage, I pointed toward the door.

Mark and Jenny scrambled to grab their clothes and dress. Tugging the ring off my finger, I threw it at him. It bounced off his chest and landed on the floor.

"Shit. Don't do this." Mark's eyes widened with his plea. "We can work it out."

"Not in a million years."

Jenny picked up the ring and slipped it on her finger. "This should have been mine anyway." She tugged Mark's arm, leading him away with a sickly-sweet tone. "Come on, honey, come to my place."

"You two idiots deserve each other!" I shouted after them.

Staring at the shattered remnants of my life, I refused to let their bullshit break me. I was sick of this baloney. Sick of men like Mark. Sick of being a pushover.

My brain kicked into action—pack, go to the bank, take off for a month or two.

CHAPTER 2

GOLDI

After cramming a few essentials into my beloved 2002 Camaro and getting out cash to last me for at least a month, I took off, letting the wheels guide me. North, south, east, west—it didn't matter as long as it eased the ache in my chest.

I'd had it with my ex. Had it with the idea of owning a bakery dangled in front of me and never coming to fruition. Had it with this life.

Heading to the 10 Freeway, I careened onto the first onramp. A song about betrayal came on the radio, and I turned it up. When the singer called her man a cheating son of a bitch, I shouted, "He sure is," and sang along. With each deep breath, I let go of some of my agitation, but not the betrayal. It still held firmly into my psyche.

I veered on Interstate 15 North toward Barstow. With the cruise control set at 75, my car zoomed along for miles.

Stopping at a liquor store at the Nevada State Line, I

marched inside and armed myself with a full tank of gas, two sodas, a hot dog, a bag of chips, and three candy bars. I took off again. My phone played jazz music. It soothed the soul, for a while, anyway.

Until realization slapped me in the face. I was jobless, homeless and without a clue how to move forward. My life just collapsed like a deflating angels food cake. What in blazes had I done?

I should talk this out with someone rational. I pushed the button on my phone. "Call Hayley."

My sister picked up on the second ring. "Hi, Goldi."

"I quit my job."

"Good for you. Your boss was an ass."

"Don't I know it."

"Come over to my house? I've got a bottle of Pinot Noir with your name on it."

"That's tempting. But I'm on the road close to Vegas."

"You didn't invite me? I haven't been gambling in forever," her voice went up an octave.

"I'm not in the mood to gamble. I just need to clear my head right now."

"You sure do. I've got a custody case tomorrow, so I couldn't go anyway."

My sister practiced family law, which I respected. Unlike my brother, she'd chosen not to work at Dad's corporate law firm once she passed the bar exam.

"Running away is rather drastic even for you. I think there's more to your impromptu trip than quitting your job."

My sister had this uncanny way of zeroing in on my

thoughts. "You know me too well. Umm… I caught Mark with my neighbor."

"What the hell?"

"My thoughts exactly It's weird, too. I was angry at first, but now I'm just feeling… numb. You know? Indifferent."

"You were always too good for him."

"You think?" My mom's voice crept into my mind. *He's the best man you'll ever find.* I'd bought right into her comment.

"Absolutely. I hope you punched him in the nuts."

I laughed out loud. "I should have, but I'm pretty sure I was in shock. Maybe I still am. Can you believe the cheating bastard told me there'd been a misunderstanding? He thought he could talk his way out of it while he put on his boxers and Jenny remained naked in our bed."

"I'm proud of you for leaving."

For the first time, doubt crept into my mind. Had I done something to drive him to stray?

"This isn't your fault, Goldi. Don't question yourself, or the decision to get out of town for a while."

Hayley's voice brought me back from the edge of my ridiculous thoughts. "You're right." At least I hoped she was.

"I always am. That's what makes me a good lawyer."

While my sister thought out her actions, I tended to be impulsive which could get me into trouble. Except, quitting had been one of the best decisions I'd made in a long time. "All the way home, I was thinking, 'Maybe Mark will come home with a rental contract for that old donut shop on Fifth. This could be the perfect time to start up my bakery.' How could I have read the situation so wrong?"

"When it comes to your wants, he seems to have difficulty with follow through."

I'd bet his plan all along had been to placate me into believing he'd help. My hands clenched the steering wheel.

"Where are you heading?"

"Wyoming or maybe Montana. Somewhere with lots of trees and very few people." Preferably as far away as possible.

"It makes sense. As a kid, you loved our summer camp."

"And you hated sleeping on the top bunk."

"I fell off twice. Not that I ever told Mom. She would have sued. Speaking of her, are you going to tell her the truth?"

"Fudge, no." I wasn't ready to deal with her. "She thinks that jerk walks on water."

"Probably because he's a lot like Dad."

I'd never considered they were alike, but my brain was far too frazzled to try to make a comparison now.

"Let's get back to your trip. How can I help?"

I loved that she had my back. "Don't worry about me. I stopped by the bank for cash, so I'll be fine."

"Why not just use your debit card?"

"Because Mark might track my purchases, and I don't want to chance him coming after me.

"Smart move."

The support of my sister meant a lot. After that conversation ended, I put on an audiobook about dragon shifters. Steamy and as far from reality as it could get, it sucked me right into the plot. Hours later, the sun put on a show, burning itself out with a last hoorah of vibrant orange-red hues across the skyline.

Exhaustion washed over me, and at the next sign for a

motel, I exited, got fast food from a burger place, and pulled into the Sand and Sun Inn. A vacancy sign shown in the window.

As if on autopilot, I checked into a room with a king-sized bed. Totally drained, I must've have fallen asleep when my head hit the pillow.

I had no idea how many hours had passed when people talking outside the walls woke me. For a moment, I couldn't remember where I was. Then it all came crashing back—Mark, the apartment, the betrayal.

I checked the clock. Seven a.m. Might as well get up.

I dragged myself into the bathroom to splash water on my face. My hair looked like a rat's nest, and I felt grungy. Maybe a shower would help.

It did refresh me. Drying my hair after, and putting it up into a ponytail, I glanced in the mirror.

Okay. Presentable—ish.

Grabbing my duffle and backpack, I headed downstairs. Thank goodness the place had a continental breakfast. Coffee, fruit, and yogurt would do. While eating, I texted my sister to let her know I was safe.

I dumped everything back in my red Camaro and took off, loving the rumble of the engine. The Camaro had been Nana's. We used to go on road trips to Palm Springs and San Diego. I'd lost her three years ago. She'd be pleased I still drove her Camaro.

Utah's red rock formations became my background. I didn't know where I was going, only that I had to get away. I stopped for lunch at a fast-food restaurant and ate at a table watching little kids play outside on some sort of jungle gym.

Thank God I didn't get pregnant with that jerk.

I took a picture of my burger and sent it to my sister with the text, "Lunch in Utah." She replied with a smiley face.

On the road again, the landscape changed from endless desert to majestic snow-capped mountains in the distance.

You Have Entered Wyoming.

A river ran along one side of the road. I turned at the sign for *Magician Lake* because the name sounded like an enchanting place. As I drove up the dirt road, my tires kicked up a cloud of dust.

A deer darted onto the road in front of me. I slammed on the brakes and turned the wheel sharply to the right, narrowly avoiding a collision with the startled animal, but my sports car fishtailing to a stop on the side of the road."

With the engine off, I just sat there. I could have died. But I didn't. I'm okay. Breathe in and out.

I turned the key, and the engine started. Putting it in drive, I stepped on the gas. The stupid thing didn't roll an inch. "What is wrong with you? Move."

It remained in the same spot, not budging.

"Of all the rotten luck." I slammed my hands against the steering wheel. I got out and popped the hood. It looked okay. What did I know about fixing cars? My specialty was baking, not mechanics.

Nana, if you're up there watching, you have a rotten sense of humor.

Snatching my backpack and overstuffed duffle from behind the seat, I sucked in a deep breath, ran to the top of a hill, and spotted a building. Glancing back at my car, it looked fine. No flames, anyway. I took out my phone to call my sister. She'd calm me down.

No bars.

Now what?

My mom would say, "That's what you get for making an impetuous decision."

I argued back in my head, "But this time, I had good reason."

Dark clouds formed above me. Droplets of rain fell on my head. The precipitation got heavier. Thunder rumbled in the distance. It'd be just my luck to get hit by lightning.

Again, I started running, down the hill and toward the house. My hair stuck to my neck. I stepped into a puddle and water splashed up my legs and soaked my pants. In soggy shoes, I sprinted the last yards and climbed onto the covered front porch. The air smelled clean and a little musky.

I banged on the front door. "Hello, is anyone in there?"

No one answered. Sheets of rain blew sideways leaving me with little protection. It was summer, still I shivered.

No lights shone inside. Was this place deserted?

I turned the doorknob. It was unlocked. I pushed it open. My heart leapt into my throat as I flipped on the lights. "Hello? Anybody home?" My voice sounded small.

No answer came, just the sound of my own ragged breathing.

A ham radio sat on the counter. Relief flooded through me. Nana and I used to fiddle with one, and we'd talked to people all over the country.

I pressed the power switch to ON. No noise came out. I called into it anyway. "Hello. This is Goldi."

Total silence.

I fiddled with the dial. There should at least be static. Darn. Maybe it's the antenna. I played around with the position.

Dead silence.

At least I was out of the rain. I took off my sneakers and socks and placed them against a wall.

The second door to the right turned out to be the bathroom. My reflection in the mirror showed a drowned rat, shivering, cold, and wet.

A shower would be divine, but that would be more than overstepping social boundaries. I mean, I didn't even know who lived here. But surely it would be okay to borrow a couple of towels and change into dry clothes from my duffel?

After I was dry again, hunger pangs made survival mode kick in. Find food, find warmth, survive the night. I made my way to the kitchen, pulled open the fridge and checked its contents. A girl's gotta eat. I'd leave money to pay for what I took.

Bread, cheese, slices of ham, bottles of longneck beer. I grabbed a bottle and made myself a sandwich.

Here I was, breaking all kinds of rules. Not exactly breaking into a ranch house, but entering without permission, eating someone else's food, making myself at home. I pulled out a twenty and left it on the counter.

I finished eating, taking in the kitchen and dining room. Mom would probably call the décor ranch rustic. The faint scent of leather mixed with pine. Hardwood floors with a few rugs. The furniture plain but functional. A landscape painting of Wyoming reminded me of the view when I entered the state.

I continued my snooping, noting the orderliness of the living room, the neat stacks of logs beside the stone fireplace. A bookshelf against one wall filled with titles that ranged from western classics to sci-fi. No frills.

A door stood slightly ajar. I shouldn't look inside but I was doing a lot of crazy things today. Papers were stacked in military precision on a desk. I smiled at the idea of the owner. Compulsive much?

A yawn caught me by surprise, and I retreated into the living room. "Alright, couch. You win this round." The cushions hugged me like long-lost friends. I wrapped myself in a blanket that resembled a cow's skin, let out a sigh and closed my eyes.

Outside, thunder provided the bass to the rain's relentless percussion. I shuddered and reminded myself I was snug and safe inside.

CHAPTER 3

LUKE

Sunrise Ridge Ranch, Wyoming

SWEAT DRIPPED down my back as I galloped along the dusty trail. Hundreds of cattle grazed in the grasslands. A lone calf wandered aimlessly away from the herd.

"Damn foolish critter." Determined to bring the stray back to safety, I nudged Stormy into action and slowly approached the calf. The young animal paused, its big brown eyes blinking up at me.

"There's nothing for you out here 'cept trouble. Now get." The calf shuffled back toward the herd, its tail flicking. I kept pace beside it, making sure it didn't veer off course. As soon as it was reunited with its mother, my brother's stallion galloped over the ridge. So much for peace and quiet. I slowed and called out, "What's up?"

"The south pasture fence is down by the creek. Given the storm that's heading our way, we'd better fix it as soon as possible," Pete said.

"Let's go then." I patted my stallion's neck and kneed him into action. A few minutes later we met up with our youngest brother, Chase, and headed for the field. The afternoon went by quickly, replacing posts and tightening wire. Pete sang off-key as usual.

"You'd better stop that caterwauling, or your tone might start a stampede," Chase snickered.

"They like it just fine." Pete kept on singing. Being the oldest made him stubborn and hardheaded.

"Could use more wire over here." I held up the half-a-foot strand remaining.

Chase tossed me a fresh spool. "Michelle Miller's been asking about you."

"I'm not interested." She'd been a hook up. Nothing serious.

Chase set another post and wiped his brow with the back of his hand. "How 'bout a break?"

"Finish first. Then you can play." Pete used an old familiar line.

"You sound like Pops," Chase smarted back as cattle lowed in the distance.

"The place isn't the same without the old geezer." After losing him almost three years ago, an ache settled deep in my soul. He'd been the one to teach me to ride, teach me to rope, teach me how to ranch. "I miss him."

"I do, too." Chase leaned on the post hole digger.

"Don't slow down now. There's only one more section to go," Pete said.

Dark clouds floated overhead. I secured the last part of wire as drizzle hit the ground. The wind picked up. "I'm done. Let's get out of here."

We mounted and galloped toward the stables. Rain came down in sheets.

I squinted against the storm, my hat doing a poor job of keeping the water out of my eyes. A flash of lightning split the sky, and I counted the seconds until thunder followed. Close. Too close for comfort.

With the stables in sight, each of us took off faster until we were safe inside. I put my horse into his stall. After rubbing him down, I pulled out an apple from my pocket. "Here you go." Stormy ate the fruit in two chomps.

My dog barreled in and stopped at my feet, greeting me with the wag of his tail. "Hey, Charlie." I patted his head.

"Card game tonight?" Chase called out.

"I'm dead tired," Pete said.

"And I've got a six pack calling my name. See you two tomorrow." Heading across the muddy path to the back of the house, I stomped my feet on a mat to get off the mud.

My lab whined as he pawed at the door. "Charlie? What's wrong with you?" He rarely got worked up.

I pushed the door open. "Go on." Charlie bounded into the living room. I followed him, pulled off my hat and coat and hung it on the rack by the door. "Where you headed?"

Charlie stopped by the couch and whimpered.

I stepped closer to a lump where someone slept underneath my blanket. Hair the color of corn spilled over the arm. "Who the fuck are you?"

The woman startled and jerked up. Her eyes popped open as she stared at me. "I'm—I'm Goldi."

"What in the hell are you doing here?" I had no patience for her right now.

She bit her bottom lip. "Um … you see … my car broke down not far from here, and my cell didn't have a signal."

"So, you decided to break into my house?" This was shaping up to be one hell of an evening. Charlie nudged his nose against my hand, reminding me I wasn't alone. I took off my hat and ran a hand through my damp hair.

"I didn't exactly break in. The door was unlocked."

"And that makes it right?" I grumbled.

"Well … no. But I needed to get out of the rain."

"I suppose that makes sense." Still, I didn't like it.

"I tried the ham radio on your counter and couldn't get it to work."

"The old thing died about a week ago, and I haven't had a chance to order a new one." I'd forgotten. To be fair I'd been busy. I pulled off the walkie-talkie clipped to my belt. "But I'll use this to get ahold of my brothers and go from there. Wolfe to all wolves. Come in."

No response.

"Damn." I assumed they were in the shower or maybe in bed. "I'll have to try again later. Look, Miss—"

"It's Goldi … Summers." She tucked a strand of hair behind her ear. "And your name is?"

"Luke Wolfe." I didn't bother offering my hand. "This is awkward."

"You think? I didn't mean to impose."

"But you're here, aren't you? How long has that been?" I

folded my arms.

"About an hour."

"You obviously made yourself at home. What else did you help yourself to?" Shit. I liked my life orderly, and this gal just messed up my routine. My fists clenched at my sides.

"Well … I took the liberty of using a couple of towels to dry off and changed my clothes." Her mouth tipped up for a second.

I tapped my fingers against my leg. "Is that it?"

"I was starving, so I made a sandwich." Color rushed to her cheeks. "And I also snagged a beer."

"Of course you did." I must've glared at her because she flinched.

"Maybe I should spend the night in my car." Thunder sounded outside as she stood.

Okay. Now I felt like a jerk. In truth, I'd helped myself to food in an empty cabin when I got stranded in a storm. I held out a hand to stop her. "Wait, Goldi. You can't go back out there. It's pitch black, and this storm's only getting worse. You'll end up soaking wet again."

She gave me an eyeroll.

"Listen. My mother taught me better than to leave a woman out in weather like this, stranger or not." That should appease her for now.

"You have a conscience?" She scrunched her eyes at me.

"Yes, ma'am."

"Are you sure you don't mind if I stay?" Hope flickered in those pretty green eyes.

"For the time being. But first thing in the morning we'll take care of your car."

"Fine with me."

Charlie wagged his tail and gave me an approving look. "My dog seems to like you, and he's a good judge of character."

"He is pretty cute." She sat back down, and the little traitor jumped up on the couch next to her and snuggled his head on her lap.

"Charlie's a good boy." And my best buddy.

"About my car." She picked up her backpack from the floor and took out a laptop. "Maybe I can get ahold of someone online?"

"It's worth a try. My uncle, Tim owns the auto shop in town. He'll be fair."

"That's good to hear. What's your internet password? I'd also like to get ahold of my sister."

"It's in my office. Let's try my desktop since it's plugged into the modem. Just remember the internet can be spotty at best."

"Just like the phone reception."

"Exactly."

Inside the tight space, Goldi's sweet perfume floated in the air as she leaned over me. I tried the internet and got a no connection message. "Just like I thought. It's down for now."

"It figures." She worried her bottom lip with her teeth.

"Some days are like that." I wrote down the internet password and handed it to her. "You can try this later."

"I appreciate it." She put the paper in her pocket. "Sorry again about, well …"

"It's done. There's no reason to keep rehashing the same things. Anyway, tomorrow, I'll do my best to get your car up and running. If I can't do it, I'll tow it into town for you." We headed back into the living room. I took the recliner.

"Don't go out of your way for me." She sat on the couch.

"I'm not." I almost said 'I'm just being neighborly' except she wasn't my neighbor. "Where you from, city girl?"

"California."

"You're a long way from home. Why'd you leave?"

"I needed to get away."

"And?" She had me curious.

"It's a long story. One I don't care to share."

I caught a glimpse of vulnerability in her eyes before she masked it with a brave tilt of her chin. She scratched Charlie behind his ears. "Aren't you the sweetest dog?"

"Tell me you're not running from the law or an irate husband?" I refused to tolerate any problem that might eventually affect our ranch.

"I've never been married."

"Fine. If you'll excuse me, I'm taking a shower." I turned my back on her.

"How 'bout I make you a sandwich to make up for… everything?" She lowered her eyes.

"Make it two, and you're forgiven."

"You've got it."

After I showered, I found her sitting on the couch reading a Louis L'Amour paperback that once belonged to my father. I devoured the sandwiches and guzzled the glass of milk she'd set out at the kitchen table.

"You can stay in the spare room. It's not fancy, but it's warm and dry."

"That's more than I deserve. In the morning, I can make you breakfast. I'm famous for my three-egg omelet with green peppers, feta cheese, and avocados if you have them."

"I prefer scrambled eggs, bacon, and biscuits. For breakfast anyway."

"Where's your sense of adventure?" She got up to take my plate. Her hand brushed against my arm, and I'd swear heat singed the skin.

"I've got plenty. About tomorrow, I get up at sunrise."

"Which is what time?"

"Six or six fifteen. "

"Okay. Well, goodnight, Luke." She picked up a backpack and duffle, headed for the bedroom with a sway to her step.

This woman was trouble with a capital T.

CHAPTER 4

GOLDI

The next morning, after making breakfast, I followed Luke to his vehicle and stared at the gigantic wheels that came up to my waist. Looking upward, there didn't seem to be any way for my short legs to reach the door. "Your truck is massive. How am I supposed to get up there?"

"With a little effort." He popped the door, and a rather long running board extended down.

"Now that's impressive." Still, I had to stretch my leg to reach the step.

"It does the job." He set his hand against my waist to steady me as I got inside. I looked down at him. Every muscle seemed to flex under his tight black shirt.

"Is something bothering you?"

"Nope." I'd been caught gawking at the undeniably sexy guy. His intense brown eyes flustered me, and my cheeks got warm. I buckled my seatbelt as the engine rumbled to life.

He rested his hands on the steering wheel and pulled onto the road. "Any idea what's wrong with your car?"

"It's starts but won't move forward." I pushed the window button down and took in a deep breath.

"I'm not an expert, but I'm guessing it has to do with the transmission." He looked sideways at me.

"That sounds expensive." The money I took out needed to last awhile.

"Don't worry about it just yet. It might be an easy fix."

In my experience, things were never simple. I focused on the dashboard with various knobs and gadgets. It was free of clutter and any dust whatsoever. For a cowboy, he sure seemed meticulous. We rounded the bend. A fallen tree sprawled across our path.

"Fuck," he grumbled under his breath.

"I'm sorry."

"Blame it on Mother Nature having a warped sense of humor."

I laughed.

"I'm glad you find this funny." His tone came out harsh.

"But it is. I mean I can just see Mother Nature waving a wand at the tree and telling it to fall here." I kept on laughing.

He glanced over at me, and the corner of his mouth ticked up.

Happy to see Mr. Wolfe did have a sense of humor, I gave him a smile. "What can I do to help?" If it wasn't for me and my car, he wouldn't be here today.

"Stay inside. I've got this."

"Fine." At least I wouldn't be breaking a sweat out there.

Hmm. Did that mean Luke would take off his shirt? I wouldn't mind seeing his ripped muscles.

I shook my head, while my eyes remained glued on him. Why hadn't I once thought about Mark at all today? Had I ever really loved him, or had I liked the idea of being in love?

He moved back to the truck, attached a chain through the hitch, the other end around the trunk, and slowly pulled forward bringing the tree to the side of the road. Then he hopped into the cab and used a bandana to wipe away the sweat on his forehead.

"The men I know would hire someone to do that."

"Typical city folk," he muttered.

"Not everyone can be as big and strong as you."

"Why, thank you, ma'am." He grinned at me, flashing straight white teeth.

I really shouldn't be flirting with him. Still my heart skipped, and I forced myself to look away. Around the bend my beloved car sat half on the shoulder and half on the road.

He let out a whistle. "Is that a Z?"

"Yes." Nana had loved the purr of a V8.

"She's a beauty."

"Not according to my mom. To her, it's an old clunker." Which she told me whenever she had a chance to voice it.

"What year is it?"

"2002." I handed him the key.

"It looks newer." He sat in the car and started it up while I watched.

The engine roared but the wheels didn't move. He got out, popped the hood, and shook his head. "This is beyond my capabilities."

"You did your best." The lame response came of its own accord.

He squinted at me. "It's early. Once I get your car on the tow bar, we can head into town."

"I'm betting you have work to do at the ranch."

"My chores can wait. Besides, my brothers already know I'm helping a friend."

"We're friends now?"

"Yep."

In just a few minutes, we made it to the main road. I checked behind us, seeing the dust kicked up by my car's tires.

He turned on the radio and we listened to the DJ say, "The bridge to Silver Creek is down. Local residents must take alternate routes at this time. Be cautious of downed lines or fallen trees. Please stay tuned to news updates for further information."

Luke slowed the truck. "I don't trust the roads right now. We're heading back to the ranch."

Bossy much? Still, I was thankful I had somewhere to go. "I hate being such a bother."

"It's fine." He turned at a wider area at the side of the road.

The truck's engine vibrated as we drove down the winding dirt path. Fields dotted with wildflowers blew gently in the breeze. Cattle grazed, their heads dipping and lifting as they moved through the grass. His hand rested on the steering wheel, tapping his fingers to a twangy song playing on the radio.

We bounced over a rough patch forcing me to grip the sides of the seat until the road evened out. A few horses grazed near the fence, their tails swishing. I found the openness of this place refreshing. The ranch came into view, a cluster of buildings nestled against the backdrop of the mountains.

Luke pulled underneath a wooden sign.

"Sunset Ridge Ranch. That's a great name."

"My great-great-grandfather's choice."

"You're lucky to have this ranch in the family for generations." I found myself blathering. But honestly, Luke could be a little friendlier.

"Uh-huh." Gravel crunched under the tires, as he parked the truck and stopped. "Promise me you'll stay inside the house."

"Why?" Outside seemed safe enough.

"Cause it's a working ranch. Can't chance you getting hurt."

"Okay, I get it. Remain inside and keep away from the animals. What will you be doing?"

"Checking fence line." He stepped around to the side of the truck and helped me down.

"Want me to make you dinner?"

"That's not necessary. Probably won't be back till dark. Since I'm already late, how 'bout making me two PBJ sandwiches and leaving them on the counter?"

"Absolutely." I had a task.

In a flash, Luke left me alone. What to do? Read. There were plenty of books here. But lazing around all day just wasn't me.

Might as well see if the internet worked. I grabbed my laptop Clicking on my Wi-Fi settings for Wolfe Ranch, I entered the house's code and crossed my fingers. The green checkmark was a beautiful sight. "Yes!"

My fingers shook as a I opened a new email and typed in a message to Hayley. Basically, adding, *I'm safe. Staying on a ranch. No phone signal. Internet is spotty.* Not wanting her to worry, I didn't bother explaining about my car. After we heard from the mechanic, I'd tell her the rest— that was if the connection worked. When the message sent, I let out a big sigh.

I considered looking through my emails, but technically I was on vacation. I took in several deep breaths and let in positive thoughts. I was thankful to have arrived at such a beautiful location. Thankful to be away from the chaos in L.A. Thankful nothing bad happened.

Life was good.

I got up and looked in the pantry. Luke kept his stuff neat and tidy. Definitely a neat freak.

The bottom shelf held airtight containers with flour, sugar, beans, rice, oats, cornmeal, and dog food. The dog food seemed out of place. But really, where else would he store it.

Eye level on left side of the middle shelf, canned goods were organized by vegetables, fruits, and soups. Then jars of homemade preserves, pickles, and sauces. Each jar had been labeled with the contents and date of preparation.

I also spotted baking soda, baking powder, vanilla, and chocolate chips and a variety of spices.

What would Luke like? Hmmm.

Everyone loves chocolate chips. I piled the ingredients on the counter. The containers of sugar and flour were too heavy to lift, so I brought in a couple of big bowls and used a cup to scoop out the goodness.

Music was my go-to during baking. Luckily, I'd downloaded plenty of songs over the years. I noticed my phone had only one bar of power. It took me several minutes to find the charger and plug it in and have rock music blaring out of the speaker.

Again, I found myself smiling. Getting to create desserts gave me a purpose.

The next few hours went by in a blur. The sweet scent of vanilla essence wafted in the air, intoxicating me on some primal level. I made four dozen cookies. Yes, I know that's a lot, but I figured Luke could give them out to the other cowboys. I mean, who didn't like sweets?

Once I finished the cookies, I made two apple pies using the bag of apples I found in a bin by the pantry door. The last stick of butter I'd set out to soften called to me to bake bread. My fingertips tingled as I kneaded the dough, sending a warm energy through me.

With minutes to kill while the dough rose, the messy kitchen reminded me there was another job I needed to do. Cleaning could sometimes be as cathartic as cooking.

And with my favorite songs playing, joy filled me with a giddiness I hadn't experienced in years.

CHAPTER 5

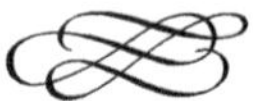

LUKE

As I opened the back door, the sweet scent of chocolate mingled with the warm, delicious aroma of apples and cinnamon. My stomach reminded me I was hungry.

Rock music blared from the kitchen. I spotted Goldi with her hair tied back in a messy bun as she moved in tune to the beat while holding a wooden spoon like a scepter.

"Goldi?"

"Luke?" She startled and turned. Her apron was dusted with flour.

"You were expecting someone else?" I feigned indignation.

"No. It's just I didn't expect you back for a couple of hours."

"I finished early." Glancing toward the counter at cookies piled up on a platter, I also counted two pies on the stove. Something mouthwatering wafted from the oven. "What have you been up to?"

"Baking. I got a bit carried away," she said with a sheepish grin.

"A bit would be a dozen cookies or maybe a pie. I'm thinking you cleaned me out of a month's worth of supplies." Not that it mattered.

"I bake when I'm bored. I bake when I am happy. I bake whenever I can." She crossed her arms and raised an eyebrow. "You did tell me to make myself at home."

"Did I? Because I don't recall saying those words."

"Maybe not, but I know you were thinking that." She leaned against the counter and watched me with a hint of amusement in her eyes.

"You're a mind reader, too? Interesting." I stepped closer, unable to resist reaching behind her and picking up a still warm cookie. Taking a bite, I found it crispy and chewy and loaded with chocolate chips. "These are really good."

"I'm glad you like them."

"I might share some with my brothers and the other cowboys."

"Might?"

"That is if I don't eat them all myself." I crammed another cookie into my mouth and asked around it, "What kind of pie did you make?"

"Apple. I found a whole sack of them near the pantry."

I gave a long laugh. "Those were for the horses."

"Sorry." She shrugged, acting not the least bit apologetic. "I'll give you some money to replace them. Just so you know, Granny Smiths make great pies."

"Is that right?"

"It is. Anyway, we're eating at the main house's kitchen. I'll introduce you to everyone." I questioned my sanity, but the words were out. There was no taking them back.

"I'd like that. How long before we leave?"

Her whole face lit up with her smile. Damn, she was pretty. "'Bout an hour."

"That's perfect." The timer rang and she pulled out two loaves of bread. "Think I should bring these with me tonight?"

"You can take one loaf. I'm making sandwiches with the other one." I snatched another cookie and found myself whistling as I headed off to shower.

Goldi

Music twanged on the radio as I sat next to Luke. "Is country all your radio ever plays?"

"What's wrong with Zimmerman?"

"I prefer rock."

"I noticed that when I saw you dancing earlier."

His comment caught me off guard. "Music inspires me when I bake. And since I assumed I was alone—"

"I didn't mind one bit. Feel free to dance around me anytime." He actually chuckled.

"You're such a guy."

"Why, thank you, ma'am." He glanced sideways at me; his eyes glinting with mischief.

"Modest much?"

"Nope. Never have been good at that."

In the distance, cattle and horses grazed. His truck stopped near a building painted in hunter green with large bay windows. A hitching post stood in front of the place. The covered porch wrapped around the front where several cowboys stood around.

"We're here."

I unbuckled my seatbelt and opened my door.

"Allow me." Luke offered his hand to help me down which was really sweet.

Two men in Stetsons approached us wearing wide grins. My eyes flicked between them, noting how similar they were to Luke—not just in build but in the way they carried themselves.

"Goldi, these are my brothers," Luke's hand settled at the small of my back possessively. "Pete's the old man around here."

"Watch it, little bro. I'm only three years older than you." Pete held out his hand. "Nice to meet you, Goldi."

"Same here."

"And I'm Chase, the best looking of the brothers." His brown eyes twinkled.

These gorgeous cowboys not only had height and muscular bodies, but when they smiled, my oh my. "Your ranch is beautiful."

"Thank you, ma'am." Pete nodded.

"We like it." Chase's grin widened.

Pete lifted a brow. "Luke told me about your car breaking down. Since the bridge is washed out, it looks like you'll be here awhile."

"I just hope I'm not too much trouble."

"You won't be." Luke stood next to me, holding the box of desserts. "Wait till you try her chocolate chip cookies. They're great."

"Let me try one." Chase reached for the box.

Luke slapped his hand. "Later."

Pete offered me his arm. "May I escort you into the dining hall."

Looks and charm and manners. How could I say no? "I'd be honored." I glanced over at Luke, visibly clenching his jaw. Was he jealous? And why did the idea create a fluttering inside me?

In truth, I couldn't remember the last time anyone made me feel this special. Mark had been so consumed with work, he barely noticed me. I should have picked up that something was off between us months ago.

We walked through solid double doors with wrought iron handles that added to the rustic feel. Natural light streamed in through wooden blinds.

I zeroed in on the stone chimney. Luke said the ranch had been in the family for generations. I wondered if this structure had been built by an ancestor—like maybe a great grandfather or uncle.

Luke set the goodies on the table. When he removed his hat, his wavy hair appeared adorably unruly, making me long to run fingers through it. *Stop that. I am so over men.* Except being escorted by a hunky cowboy proved that was a lie.

Luke spoke to a lady with her dark hair in a ponytail, and they walked toward me. "Goldi, I'd like to introduce you to our cook, Mabel."

Not exactly sure what cowboy fare might include, I imagined steak and pickled potato salad.

"I heard you brought apple pie. That's one of my favorites." Mabel's eyes glittered.

Luke and Pete chorused, "Mine, too."

"Have Luke sit you next to me and we can talk recipes." She

scurried off toward a swinging door near the back of the room and disappeared.

Luke asked, "Ready to meet the rest of the gang?"

"Absolutely."

We made our way over to where three cowboys sat at a long wooden table covered in a red and white checkered tablecloth near the center of the room.

"Boys, this here's Goldi," Luke introduced me. "She'll be staying with us for a couple of days."

"I'm Sam, the ranch's foreman. You need anything around here, I'll get it done for you." Lines etched deep into his tanned face.

"Thanks."

Luke introduced me to two cowboys who looked like they were in their teens.

"Go help Mabel bring out the food." Luke motioned to the kitchen. Like magic, the boys hurried to help. He turned to me. "Might as well take your seat now before the rest come in."

"There's more?" The ranch must be bigger than I thought.

"In the summer, we hire on extra people. Right now, we're missing about five of them."

"Amazing. I've landed on a real live cattle ranch." Just like I'd watched on the *Yellowstone* series.

"Yep." He led me to a chair on the end and sat to my right.

Pete scooted in next to me.

"You'd better move down one if you know what's good for you," Luke grumbled at his brother. "I promised Mabel that spot."

"I know better than to mess with her." He moved to Luke's other side.

A couple walked in holding hands. Luke introduced me to Tom and Julie. It turned out they lived next door and pooled their cattle with the Sunrise Ridge animals and helped with the drive in September.

The table filled with cowboys in work-worn jeans and boots. Platters of food were passed around. I let out sigh as I savored each item. The potatoes with a hint of garlic and bacon were creamy because they used fresh milk and butter. The tender roast beef had a hickory smoke flavor. And the corn on the cob tasted simply divine.

"The food is delicious," I told Mabel. "What's the secret to your bread?"

"Fresh churned butter and a dab of local grown honey."

"It works well." I grinned at her. "You know, I make a mean sourdough bread with buttermilk and poppy seeds."

"I bet it's good."

"I think so."

During dessert, I insisted on cutting my own pies and serving everyone.

"Mmm," Luke said, and I think I heard "Yum" from someone else.

Mabel took a bite, slowly chewed, and then put down her fork. "Girl, you've got skills."

"That means a lot coming from you."

The teens passed out the plates to everyone else, and then a platter of my cookies went around.

"Marry me, Goldi," one of the cowboys called.

"No way, she's marrying me," another added.

"Sorry boys." I waved at them. "I'll be heading home in a few days."

"Maybe we can talk you into staying on a little longer." Chase gave a goofy grin.

"That's sweet, but no. My heart belongs in the city." But did it really? "Still, while I'm here I wouldn't mind helping in the kitchen."

Mabel asked, "How about tomorrow at eleven?"

I looked at Luke. "Would that be okay?"

"I'll be busy most of the day." He glanced at Mabel. "Think you could pick her up at my house?"

"Of course."

Once again, I had purpose for the foreseeable future. It felt good.

CHAPTER 6

GOLDI

Sun shone through slatted blinds. I got out my phone and groaned. Eight o'clock. Holy crap. I blew it. I offered to get up early and make breakfast before Luke left. Why didn't I set my alarm last night?

To be fair, I'd been exhausted and fell asleep the minute my head hit the pillow. It must be the fresh air.

I dressed quickly and looked out the window toward the stables. My eyes caught Luke outside near the fence. Good. I could apologize before he left for the day.

Squinting against the sun, I went outside to catch up to him. My sneakers sunk a half inch into the mud as I approached. Yuck. "Luke," I called.

A man turned around, and I recognized him as the foreman. "He left about an hour ago."

"Oh." My heart deflated.

"Can I help you with something?"

"That's okay." I noticed Sam cleaning out what I assumed to be a trough. "I'm sorry to bother you."

"It's fine." He added clean water from the faucet.

I glanced at the fence and a horse stuck its head over it. "Who's that?" I asked.

"Chantilly." He pulled an apple from his pocket. "She can be a real pest. Wanna give her this?"

"Umm." I'd forgotten how ginormous horse's teeth could be.

"Hold your hand like this." He modeled what to do.

I did as shown, and the mare chomped it down in two bites.

"That one will be wanting a treat whenever she sees you." He shook his head. "But don't let her pretty brown eyes fool you. Apples are fine in moderation."

"Why is that?"

"Their stomach can be sensitive and susceptible to colic."

"That's good to know. I've always liked horses, but the only time I've been around them was at camp and occasionally renting horses at a stable."

"We've got plenty of working ones here. Give me a couple minutes to finish up, and I can give you a tour of the stables if you'd like."

"Yes, please." The guy reminded me of Grandpa Summers and his pride when he showed me his workshop. He had died when I was ten. My eyes misted and I shook off the tears. He might be gone, but he'd always remain in my heart—along with Nana.

Sam led the way, his boots kicking up small clouds of dust with each step.

"Have you been with Luke long?" I wondered if he worked for him or was part owner or maybe a relative.

"Close to fifteen years now."

"He seems intense." Especially when it's a stranger who disrupted his routine.

"At times," he said with a hearty laugh.

We ambled past a field dotted with bales of hay. Sam gestured to the towering mountains where pines lined the hills. "If you ever have worries, talk to the trees. They listen good, don't talk back."

"I'll keep that in mind."

"Just to be safe, let someone know where you're going."

"You've got it. I'd hate to get lost out here."

Sam's hand rested on the stable door before he swung it wide open. The scent of fresh hay and horses filled the air, grounding me in the moment.

"Each horse has its own story." He brought me to the first stall on the right and gestured toward a chestnut mare with a white blaze running down her nose. "Take Duchess here."

"What a beauty." The mare nickered softly, eyeing us with interest.

"She's the queen bee around these parts. Acts all regal, but she's got a playful side. Put up your palm and let her sniff it. She's real gentle."

"Okay." Her velvety muzzle tickled my skin, and I giggled. "Hello, sweetie."

We walked past several empty stalls. Sam led me further down the aisle to a gray gelding. "This is Tumbleweed. He's a bit of a loner, likes to be away from the fuss, but he's a good old fellow."

"He's tall."

"Yep." Sam showed me a very pregnant mare. Then a stallion, who looked at us like we were intruders and strode to the food bin.

"I'm helping Mabel this afternoon. Since I might be here another day or two, what can I do around here to pitch in?"

"You could feed the chickens and collect eggs. The wire baskets usually hang on the fence near the coop."

"Okay." I relished the idea of trying new things.

"How 'bout I show you the garden before I head back to work?"

"I'd like that." The wooden gate creaked as I pushed it open. My eyes drifted to a row of tomato plants.

"Feel free to help yourself. The vegetables are for us to eat."

"Thank you for the tour, Sam."

"Anytime." He tipped his hat.

As he walked away, I lingered a moment longer, feeling an inexplicable bond with this land.

On the way to the house, I kept my fingers crossed that the internet would work. I couldn't wait to tell my sister about my day.

CHAPTER 7

LUKE

The idea of Goldi sleeping in the guest room had me tossing and turning most of the night. When I finally did get to sleep, I dreamt of kissing that sweet mouth of hers, until my alarm jerked me out of sleep.

I wanted her, but something inside told me to be wary of the beautiful city girl. I'd been down that road before. Once I took Goldi to town, I'd be done with her.

I got up and tiptoed past her bedroom, happy to see the door closed. Last night, she'd offered to make me breakfast.

I pictured her wearing a nightie as she cooked. *Don't even go there.*

Grabbing jerky, I straightened the canisters on the countertop. Goldi must have done that when she was baking yesterday.

As I rode my horse to the branding area, Chase and Pete were setting up. Hank and his wife were outside the main corral moving the cattle forward.

"Look who finally decided to join us," Pete said.

"Shut up. I'm here." I shot him a glare and grabbed a branding iron. "Let's get to it."

"Yes, sir." Chase saluted me and laughed when I flipped him off.

Hank corralled a calf into the chute away from its mother. The young bovine bawled its protest while Pete and Chase wrestled the calf into position. My job was straightforward: grab the iron from the fire, heat it up to just the right temperature—not too hot, not too cold—and set a clean mark. Branding might not be rocket science, but it required focus.

"Easy there," I kept my voice low and soothing. Pete used a hand to keep the calf in line. It settled down. With a firm grip, I took the glowing iron and pressed it against the hide for a few seconds to sear our SRR mark into her side.

"Only another hundred or more to go," Hank called.

"Which means we'd better get busy. Keep 'em coming." I slid the iron back into the fire. It hissed. Seared hair filled the air as I continued with the process. Calf after calf shuffled through the chute. Sweat trickled down my back. I pulled off my green T-shirt, letting air cool me down.

Blinking several times, I imagined Goldi's eyes—wide, probing, and frigging green. Focus. Quit thinking about the pretty gal and get to work. She belonged in the city not here. I jammed the branding iron into the next calf's hide with a bit more force than necessary. "Shit."

"You twisted the brand," Pete hollered.

"Yep." No sense arguing. I'd messed up.

"Get your head into the job." Pete eyed me sideways.

"Wanna switch? I wouldn't mind a break away from the fire."

"Sure." Pete took the iron out of my hand.

I let out a long breath and got on the other side of the chute.

"Wouldn't mind a couple of those chocolate chip cookies right now. You bring any with you?" Chase tipped his hat back.

"Nope."

"That's a damn shame." He slid a calf into position, and we guided another one into the chute. "She's quite a cook."

"I suppose."

"Pipe down and hold this animal still," Pete called. The bovine shuffled, but I had her head secured, and Chase pressed down gently on her flank. Once again, another animal showed our mark. With the help of Hank and Julie, the flow kept moving.

"Feels like we've been at this since dawn." Hank wiped sweat from his brow with the back of his hand.

"Because we have," I reminded him, trying not to think about Goldi stirring awake in the guest room this morning. "But we should be done soon enough."

A loud crackle split the air. I whipped my head around to find one of the wooden gates splintered. "Son of a bitch. They're getting away." Cattle scattered every which way.

"Secure the herd! Move!" Pete's voice roared over the chaos.

Adrenaline surging, I rushed into action.

"Head them off at the creek!" Julie's voice cut through the air.

"Got it!" I called back, already picturing our land. The creek would funnel the cattle, making them easier to move back. It took us the better part of an hour, all of us pushing our limits, riding hard and whistling commands, but we got the cattle turning. Dust coated my tongue by the time we herded the strays into the pens.

"Last one!" Hank shouted.

A collective whoop came as the final calf, stubborn as the day is long, skidded into the holding area.

"Nice work, everyone." I said, sharing nods as we caught our breath. There wasn't time for more than that. We still had branding to finish.

"Alright, let's get to it." Pete headed to the fire where the irons were heating. We fell into step behind him.

About an hour later, bone weary, we headed toward the stables.

CHAPTER 8

GOLDI

A sense of purpose filled me as I stepped into the main kitchen and set a basket full of vegetables on the workstation next to an industrial-sized mixer. Then, I took in the space.

Ten burners on the stovetop beckoned me closer. Spotting four ovens, I placed my hand over my heart. "This place is cool."

"I rather like it," Mabel said. "When I first came here to work, I insisted on new appliances and a stainless-steel station because that butcher block in the corner didn't cut it."

"I'm glad they listened to you."

"It was either that, or I wouldn't work here."

"I like your style." I tied an apron around my waist.

"I have a feeling we're gonna get along just fine." Her words wrapped around me like a comforting blanket. "Let's get started. What did you have in mind for dessert tonight?"

"Have any suggestions?" I waited, eager for inspiration.

"We should use these lemons before they go bad." She

pointed at a bowl on the counter, and I inhaled the zesty aroma of ripe citrus.

"You can't go wrong with lemon meringue pie." And just like that, we dove into the rhythm of the kitchen, our hands moving with purpose. "What's your secret to a flaky crust?"

"The butter must be cold. The other liquid iced and cold."

"I totally agree. Do you chill your dough before rolling it?"

"Of course. I wasn't born in a barn," she shot back.

"I never thought you were. Who taught you to cook?"

"Grams. She had a knack. Never used measuring cups."

"My Nana was the same way. I lost her a few years ago and miss her every day." I bit my lip to stop my misting eyes. Crying never did any good.

We worked side by side, forming the dough and wrapping it in plastic before setting it in the fridge to rest.

"Have you always worked in a kitchen?"

"Heavens no," she said with a wave of her hand. "Before my husband died, I did the books for our feed store." She paused, her gaze drifting toward the window.

"I'm sorry for your loss."

"Thanks. A drunk driver cut our marriage short." She snuffled softly. "Enough about me. How'd a pretty girl like you end up on this ranch?"

I gathered my thoughts. "I quit my job and wanted to clear my head. And you already know my car broke down near Luke's house."

"Which turned out okay for you."

"It did." I juiced the lemons.

"You have a boyfriend?" This woman was direct.

"Not anymore," I admitted reluctantly. The lemon filling

thickened and bubbled. I removed it from the heat and whisked in one egg at a time, letting it simmer for a couple of minutes while trying to keep my composure.

"Wanna talk about it?"

"He cheated on me."

Mabel set a comforting hand on my shoulder. "I'm here if you ever need an ear." She didn't push, which I respected.

I thought about how Hayley supported me when we talked right after the incident. Last night, I had a chance to read her email. She told me to relax and enjoy myself. I missed talking to her and wished she were here. My eyes got watery again.

Hopefully, my mom hadn't realized I'd left town. If she did, Hayley would let her know I needed to get away after quitting my job. I doubted it would surprise Mom.

How many times did my mom warn me to quit being impulsive and stick things out? I quit cheerleading because I couldn't take a couple of the mean girls. That didn't make her happy. I changed majors from economics to hospitality, which took me off the lawyer track. That upset both my parents. Whatever I did was never good enough. Except for dating Mark. In their eyes, that had been a brilliant move. That must have been why I accepted his proposal without much thought. Had I been in love with him? Maybe at first. To be fair, we'd grown apart.

And I wasn't ready to tell them about the cheating.

I concentrated on adding butter to the mixture to make it glossy. Using a saucepan, I combined sugar, cornstarch, and a bit of salt before gradually stirring in water and lemon juice. The mixture swirled together.

The afternoon went by quickly. The aroma of baking crusts filled me with a sense of euphoria. Yes, I was weird like that.

"Since there are two lemons left over, do you mind if I make blueberry lemon pound cake?"

"Have at it."

The stand mixer whirled as I added the ingredients. And in what seemed like seconds, four loaves of sweet temptation were baking.

"Ready to learn what puts a kick in my fried chicken?" Mabel coated her hands with flour. "I use a blend of paprika, garlic powder, and a little extra chili pepper." She filled the bowl with a mix that could ignite a fire with the tablespoons of deep reds and speckled blacks heaped into it.

"Nothing wrong with a bit of kick."

"True enough." She dipped a piece of chicken into buttermilk, coated it evenly with her fiery concoction, and placed the pieces in the fryer until a golden crust formed.

"You ever try using jalapeno?"

"I have. Chase loves it. Luke and Pete don't. I cook what they like, but I add my own flavor."

My regard for her just picked up a couple of notches. "You're one badass lady." I fixed a salad and made my own recipe for ranch dressing, while chicken sizzled in a fryer.

Footsteps echoed from the hallway. I smoothed down my apron and wished I had a mirror to check my reflection. Ridiculous. It's not like the cowboys cared what I looked like.

"Smells mighty fine in here, Mabel." The foreman strolled inside.

"Wash up outside, Sam. You know the rules." Mabel's hands went to her hips.

"Already did. Anyway, the brothers got held up."

"They said to start without 'em," another cowboy said.

"Thanks for letting us know." Mabel nodded as she set a platter of spicy fried chicken onto the side counter.

My heart sunk a little at the news. I'd been looking forward to seeing the brothers again, especially one in particular.

Knock it off. He's not for me.

Mabel addressed the men, "Well, boys, grab a plate and dig in. There's plenty to go around."

I focused on the laughter filling the kitchen, the sense of belonging that came naturally here.

"You make any more of those cookies?" A younger cowboy asked as he plopped opposite me.

"Not today."

"Darn." He bit into a chicken leg.

"Don't worry. There's a special dessert waiting." I sampled a piece of chicken breast. Juicy and tender, the extra kick of chili pepper made the flavors sing. "Mabel, this is delicious."

She beamed.

I brought out slices of pie on plates and set a basket of cut lemon-blueberry cake on the table.

The door flung open to Pete and Chase but no Luke. After only three days, I gotten to know the brothers. Pete, tallest of the three, gave an almost shy grin. Chase's lips quirked up, wide and friendly. Both brothers tipped their hats in my direction and hung them on a hook.

Then I saw Luke's tall frame as he walked in with confidence. Taking off his Stetson, he pushed a dark wave of hair off his forehead. Our eyes locked in a lingering gaze, and I forgot to breathe.

CHAPTER 9

LUKE

Dog tired after working since sunup, I finally dragged myself into the hall for supper and spotted Goldi sitting with all the cowboys at the table, laughing and chatting like she'd been here all her life.

Those pretty green eyes of hers gazed directly at me, and her lips quirked into a small smile. That made me want to rush over there and join her. Good thing my stomach growled. Like any rational cowboy, I chose food at the sideboard.

"Goldi's fitting in well." Chase nudged me with his elbow.

I glanced back at her. She leaned forward as she listened intently to Sam.

"Yeah." I tried not to sound too interested. "She's making herself right at home."

He smirked but didn't push it.

"All right, boys," Mabel said, standing and motioning toward the younger cowhands. "If you two are done stuffing your faces, help me with cleanup." Her voice cut through the room like a whip cracking.

"I can do that, too," Goldi offered, hopping to her feet.

Mabel raised a hand in protest. "You're our guest. Relax and spend time with the Wolfe brothers."

"All right." Goldi hesitated before easing down into her chair. "Do you need my help tomorrow?" She flashed Mabel a wide grin.

"No need. I'm off on weekends—always have been—and around here that means everyone fends for themselves."

"It's been that way for as long as I can remember," Pete said.

"Which means you get a chance to enjoy the ranch." Chase gave her a lop-sided smile.

"I bet the bridge will open soon, and I'll have my car towed to town." Goldi took a bite of pie.

Which would be for the best in so many ways.

"Maybe. Maybe not." Sam shrugged.

It was time to stop hovering by the sideboard. Plate balanced in one hand, I dropped into the empty seat beside her. "Hi."

"Hey." She gave me a smile.

"Thanks for the desserts," one of the younger cowboys called out as he carried his plate to the kitchen.

Goldi's face lit up, clearly pleased by the compliment. "Mabel and I made the pies together."

"Well, everything's delicious," Sam chimed in as he stood to leave. He tipped his hat in her direction before heading out after the others.

"Appears you've found yourself a fan club," Pete said, as the room emptied out around us.

"I'm surprised none of 'em have proposed yet." Chase's arms crossed behind his head in mock indifference.

"One of the cowboy's did last night," Goldi said.

The idea irritated me. I chided myself. It was plain loco to be attracted to another city girl.

"I'm just here on vacation," Goldi said. "I almost forgot dessert. Be right back." She disappeared into the kitchen and brought us plates with pie and cake.

Pete dug into his pie immediately. "This lemon meringue is outstanding."

"I'm usually more of a pie guy," Chase admitted between bites, "but this cake might've just converted me."

I scraped my plate with my fork. The woman could bake.

"Thank you," Goldi said.

"You're welcome." Pete grinned before turning back to his food.

Seeing an opening—and maybe wanting some time alone—I stood and extended my hand toward her. "Ready to head out?"

She glanced up at me in surprise but nodded. "Sure."

I threw a glance over my shoulder at Chase and Pete. "And you clowns can take our plates to the kitchen."

"Yes, boss." They both saluted me, which made Goldi chuckle.

Minutes later, I had her to myself in my truck. And damn if I didn't like her there. Which was wrong for way too many reasons.

She sat next to me, her hands folded neatly in her lap, gaze fixed out the window. "That kitchen is a baker's dream."

"Mabel made sure everything was top-notch. We're lucky to have her here."

"I like her."

"Good. I assume you were a big help."

She shrugged one shoulder as if brushing off the compliment. "I prefer to stay busy." I heard something deeper in her tone—a hint of weariness, maybe even restlessness.

"I've noticed." Figuring she ought to see some of the ranch before she left, I said, "I'm free tomorrow afternoon. Would you like to go riding?"

"I'd love that."

"Are you a good rider?"

"I've rented horses from the local stables and can hold my own. Although it's been forever since I've gone." She spoke in a wistful tone.

"I think you'll like our horses better than those poor overused ones from rental stables. I'll put you on Honey. She's a real sweetheart."

"Just like you." She smiled.

"I wouldn't go that far."

CHAPTER 10

GOLDI

There was one measly egg in the fridge. How hard could collecting eggs be? After all, I'd seen it done on YouTube. It looked easy enough.

Grabbing a wire basket off a hook in the fence, I strode toward the coop. As I opened the door, the chickens greeted me with squawks, flapping their wings and making me jump back. "Whoa there, girls." I faked confidence because I didn't want to be pecked to death.

The feed bag sat against the fence. I scattered scratch on the ground and the chickens pecked with enthusiasm. I tiptoed through the straw, careful not to disturb much. Reaching for my first egg, nestled snugly beneath a particularly fluffy hen, I heard a loud cock-a-doodle-doo.

I turned and met the fiery gaze of a feathery tyrant. His red comb flopped to one side, while his eyes promised a world of pain for just being there.

"Look, buddy." I tried to reason with him. "I just want a few eggs. You've got plenty."

He responded with an indignant squawk and fluffed his feathers, making himself appear even more intimidating. Not that he needed any help. Those talons looked sharp.

"Easy now..." I reached for another egg while keeping one eye on the rooster. As my fingers closed around the second egg, he pecked at my wrist. "Stop that, you, you Roostifer." The name—a combination of a rooster and the Lucifer—fit him perfectly. Too bad I dropped the egg. It splattered on the ground.

The insane fowl crowed his victory while he strutted back and forth.

"Okay, you win this round." My wrist might ache, but no way would I be defeated by a bird with an attitude problem. I rolled up my sleeves and darted left, feinting toward an imaginary egg. The demon rooster took the bait, charging with fury. I pivoted and scooped up an egg from the right.

"Ha! I tricked you." With a screech the rooster landed a solid peck on my shin. I stumbled, clutching my wounded leg. "Ow! That hurts!" I hopped on one foot and glared.

He seemed to puff up with pride. I'm sure if he could laugh, he'd be cackling like a villain.

"Alright, you little feathered fiend. It's on."

I'd read somewhere that animals respected confidence—or was it fearlessness? I straightened up, squared my shoulders, and met his gaze head-on.

"Listen here. I'm taking these eggs, and you're going to let me because deep down, underneath all those feathers, you're a reasonable... rooster." To my utter amazement, he twisted his head as if considering my words. Or maybe he sized me up for his next assault. Regardless, I seized the moment and snagged two more eggs while I could.

Under a white hen with a red comb, something warm and fuzzy brushed against my hand. I yelped and jerked my hand back, nearly dropping the basket of eggs. Peering into the nesting box, I came face to face with a fluffy yellow chick, chirping happily. Deciding to leave the chick alone, I continued my egg-collecting, keeping watch for the rooster until I had nearly a dozen.

"Thank you." I backed away slowly. And then, with a basket of hard-won eggs, I beat a hasty retreat from the coop.

"Looks like you survived." Luke leaned against the fence. His lips twitched with amusement.

"Survived? I conquered Roostifer." I carefully hid my battle scars.

He laughed. "That name suits him way better than Spike."

"I know. Right?"

"Let me help you with that." He took the basket from my hand, and his muscles flexed under his short-sleeved T-shirt. Talk about buff.

"You finished early today." His dog nudged my hand. I scratched him behind his ears.

"I did. We'd better eat first. Then we can get riding whenever you're ready." He eyed my outfit.

I'd chosen jeans and my pink *I'm a Bakeaholic* T-shirt with images of cupcakes, cookies, and pies.

"I like your shirt." He winked, and darn if my heart didn't do this silly little dance. Inside, he set the basket gently on the kitchen table.

"I've got a joke for you." My sister and I used to tell them growing up and I had tons in my head. "What do you call a hen who counts her eggs?"

"Enlighten me."

"Mathema-chicken." I giggled.

Luke groaned. "That was terrible."

"You have to admit, it cracked you up."

He picked up a spatula and pointed it at me. "No more egg puns or you're sleeping in the barn."

"Truce." I raised my hands in surrender. "I'm making a ham sandwich. You want one?"

"As if you have to ask."

It didn't take long for our stomachs to be filled. After, I washed the dishes and Luke dried. Glancing down at my sneakers, he said, "Your shoes aren't practical for riding. Pick yourself a pair from the women's boots in the closet in your room. I'm betting one set will fit you."

This man's protective side was hot.

Why not see where this attraction went? I mean what would it hurt. It wasn't like we'd fall in love.

I walked into the bedroom anxious to act like a real cowgirl. Since I'd stayed in the guestroom, I hadn't opened the closet door—yet—because in my mind that would have been spying. Although, when I first entered the house, I glanced around his office. But to be fair, it had been opened … a crack … as if inviting me in.

Inside the closet, there must have been at least a dozen boots in a variety of sizes. I pulled out three pairs that looked like they might work.

The pink pair too tight. The red pair were too big. Last, I

tried on the gaudy black and white cow print boots that matched the blanket in the living room. They fit like a glove.

Rushing into the other room, I held up one boot. "What do you think?"

He laughed. "They suit you."

I quirked a brow at him. "Who used these?"

"My sister. As Miss Whispering Pines, she wore them in a parade one year. Afterwards, she told mom to burn them."

"Then I'd better not wear these in front of her."

"She's got a good sense of humor and would probably laugh."

I wouldn't mind meeting his sister. She sounded like fun. I petted his dog. "Will Charlie be joining us?"

"Nope. He's getting on in years. Unless I really need him on the range, he tends to stick around home and the stables."

The way this man cared for his dog. Just—Wow.

CHAPTER 11

LUKE

"I can't believe I get to see the ranch on horseback." Goldi bounced as she walked in denim jeans that hugged her ass. Damn sexy.

"With me as your guide. Things don't get much better than that." I fought the urge to wink. It would be overkill.

"We'll see about that, cowboy." Her mouth tipped up as she eyed me sideways.

Stepping inside the tack room, I grabbed two bridles and halters, and we made our way to the field. One shrill whistle and Stormy came galloping over.

"How'd you train your horse to do that?" She studied me with an intensity that made my pulse quicken.

"Don't remember. I was ten when my grandfather got him as a gift for me."

"Well, he's beautiful!" She reached out to stroke my horse's nose. "Is he a quarter horse? You never said."

"Good eye. He's half quarter and half thoroughbred."

"I bet he's fast."

"He is. He won his share of races over the years."

"You should have named him Black Beauty."

"Which would be a cliché."

"Maybe. But it still suits him."

"Tell you what. I'll think about naming the next black horse I get Beauty."

"The cowboy can compromise." She grinned at me, and damn if I didn't long to kiss that pretty mouth of hers.

"When necessary." Pulling an apple out of my pocket, I pointed at a mare trotting toward us. "That's Honey. Wanna give her this?"

"Yes. You're gorgeous," Goldi cooed. The horse nodded her head in agreement. "And you know it, don't you."

I haltered the mare, gave Goldi the reins and got my stallion ready. "We're bringing the horses to the post outside the stables." Once the animals were tied, I handed her a brush.

"It must've been nice growing up on a ranch."

"I'm sure there were perks to living in the city." None that I could think of since I preferred small towns.

"A few. I do like the variety of shops. And going to the best ice cream shop ever."

"No way can your place compete with Dreamy Scoops. In case you want to know, I'm a rocky road kind of guy."

"That suits you. A little bit grumpy, a little bit sweet."

"Don't let the sweet part get out. I've got a reputation to uphold."

"You're secret's safe with me." She placed a finger against her lips. "Anyway, I'm a cake batter ice cream kind of girl. That's creamy vanilla with rainbow sprinkles."

"Fancy that."

"Are you mocking me?" She placed a hand on her hip.

"No, ma'am. All ice cream is sacred."

"You're crazy." She rolled her eyes.

For you flashed through my mind for a nanosecond.

"Can you guess my first job in the city?" Sun glinted off her golden hair as she flipped her long braid behind her back.

"A barista at one of those high-end coffee shops." I added a pad and saddle onto her horse and tightened the cinch.

"Nope. Dog walker."

"I can picture it now. You trying to control a bunch of pampered pooches down a busy sidewalk."

"It takes skill to manage six leashes at once." She stroked Honey's mane.

"I guess it's like herding cattle."

"That's where you're wrong. How many cows chase every cat they see?"

"None that I know of." I chuckled. "You want help mounting."

"Yes, please."

I lifted her and didn't mind putting my hands against her butt. The only problem was the touch lasted only seconds. I focused on adjusting her stirrups. Then I mounted Stormy. "Ready?"

"More than."

"If you're up for a longer ride, I've got a place I'd like to show you."

"I can handle it, cowboy. I'm tougher than I look," she said, sitting tall in the saddle.

"I don't doubt that for a minute, city girl." From what I'd seen, she could do anything she put her mind to.

We set off at an easy trot, riding side by side with the thud of hooves as our companion. I stole glances at Goldi. She had a big smile on her face, and pink in her cheeks.

As we reached a flat path leading up into the hills, she called "Race you to the water tower," and nudged her horse into a gallop.

"You little sneak," I shouted. When I caught up to her, I called out, "You cheated."

"I like to win."

"I do, too."

She squinted at me while we walked our horses at a slow pace. "Next time, I'll let you beat me."

If she thought I'd let her best me twice, she was wrong. "No way, sugar." I figured being a baker the nickname suited her.

"Don't ever call me that." Her shoulders tensed and she glared at me.

"Why?" Obviously, I'd hit a nerve.

"Because I said so."

"Come on. You can tell me."

"Well… um… because my ex used to call me that."

Okay. She had an ex. I wondered if she ended up here because of him.

"Where are we going from here?"

"We're taking that trail. Trust me, it'll be worth the climb." I led her up a narrow path that wove through wildflowers and lush green knolls.

"This is awesome."

"Wait until we reach the overlook at the top of that hill."

We stopped at a secluded meadow and dismounted. Below us to the south, the ranch sprawled across the land, stitched together with fences and dotted with cattle.

"Luke, this is beautiful."

"Not as beautiful as you." Our eyes met and she gazed at me with an intensity that made my breath hitch. As if drawn by an invisible force, we inched nearer to each other. Before I could second-guess myself, I closed the distance between us, tugging her closer and breathing in her vanilla scent.

Her hands slid up my chest and our lips met. She arched her back and pressed her luscious curves against me.

I whispered her name.

Our tongues glided against each other, tasting, exploring and lighting a slow-burning fire deep within me.

The snorting of a horse barely registered over the pounding of my pulse. With her hands roaming over my back, tracing my muscles, setting every nerve ending in a haze of fierce intensity, my cock strained against my pants until I finally broke away, gasping for breath.

"Goldi," I said, my voice rough with desire. "I—" No words came to mind.

"Shh," she pressed a finger to my lips, silencing me.

Whatever this was, it had knocked my world off-kilter. I brought my mouth back to hers, kissing her hard and long, exploring every inch of her mouth with my tongue.

"We should head back to the house," she whispered, her cheeks flushed with a rosy glow.

"If that's what you want." I wouldn't mind staying longer but honored her wishes.

CHAPTER 12

GOLDI

On the ride back to the ranch, I tried to figure out what the fudge just happened. I mean, one moment I was enjoying the incredible scenery. The next, Luke's mouth crashed against mine, ravenous and commanding. Even now, the ghost of his kiss, hot and intoxicating, lingered on my lips.

Based on how quiet he'd been, I wondered if he was as confused as me.

When we arrived at the stables, I dismounted with wobbly legs and brushed off my jeans. "I had fun."

"So did I." He held my horse's reins. "I'll take care of the horses. Go ahead inside and relax."

"I appreciate it." I made my way to the back door of his house and went inside. How could a simple kiss be so intense? Needing a distraction, I snagged the closest novel on the bookcase.

It turned out to be about tractor repair. I plopped into the overstuffed chair and flipped to a diagram of the working parts of a tractor. The clutch and gear shift seemed normal. Air stacks were kind of weird. Small tires in the front, large on the back. Did this have to do with stability or traction? The term 'crank case' reminded me of the grumpy cowboy I'd first met.

Why did he have to be such a good kisser? I liked him, but a new man in my life was a bad idea.

The back door slammed closed, and I dropped the book.

He picked it up and squinted. "You're into repairing tractors?"

I shrugged. "The book makes for interesting reading."

He laughed. "If my tractor breaks down, you'll be the first one I call to fix it."

"Good to know."

I caught the flicker of something raw in his expression when he said, "The bridge is open. I can take you to town."

"That's great. Give me a couple minutes to get my stuff and we can leave." Why did the thought hurt so much?

"Take your time."

As if time would make a difference. I took a deep breath and hurried into my room, sat on the bed, removed the borrowed black and white boots, and lined them up neatly outside the closet. They weren't my style anyway.

Packing my meager belongings into my duffel bag, I picked up my backpack and walked out, refusing to look back at the room that had been mine for only a few days. It felt like longer.

"Need any help?" Luke's head turned as I entered the living room.

"No, got it," I said, avoiding his gaze. It was safer that way. If I looked into his eyes, I might act recklessly and kiss him.

Outside, he'd already attached my car to the tow bar. I

managed to hop into the truck and tossed my bag behind the seat with a dull thud.

Luke started driving.

"What's the name of the town we're going to?"

"Whispering Pines."

"Is it nestled between conifers?" What a lame comment. To be fair, my mind reeled with so much happening.

"Yep. There's plenty of ponderosa pines in this state."

The way he gripped the wheel, he must sense tension between us. I focused on the repaired bridge which marked the line between my past and future.

"Are there any good hotels in town?" Since the likelihood my car would be fixed today was practically null, I might as well figure out my options.

"There's a motel right off the highway. It's clean enough. If you'd rather be in the center of town, you should stay at the Buckshot Bed and Breakfast."

"That sounds good."

"Built in 1890, it's been remodeled. Still, it's said to be haunted." He waved one hand in the air in a squiggle.

"Really. I love a good ghost story." I'd been on ghost tours in both San Diego and Los Angeles. They'd been a blast.

"Supposedly there's a woman in red who can be seen pacing the balcony. And it's been said that the piano plays in the wee hours of the night."

"That's pretty tame."

"Well, I don't want to scare you." His teasing tone was back. "Only the bravest souls stay in room two-eleven on the second floor. According to local history, the owner caught his wife in bed with his partner. He shot them both dead, then turned the gun on himself."

"Okay, that could happen. Do all three spirits appear?"

"Usually, it's the owner who holds a gun and points it at whoever is sleeping in the bed. Then he pulls the trigger."

"I'm getting that room. I've never seen an apparition myself. But there's always a first time."

"Then I hope it works out."

"Me, too. I find paranormal activity fascinating. My sister and I have dabbled with a Ouija board."

"Did you gals hear from the spirit world?" He eyed me sideways.

"We did."

"And?"

"It told us this guy named Ben Caruthers had been in love with our Nana when she lived on a farm in Illinois and moved to California. Knowing my sister, she might have pushed the planchette to the letters and made up the story."

"Speaking of your sister, did you ever get a hold of her?"

"I've been emailing Hayley. Everything's fine. I'll call her once I check into a hotel."

"Is she older than you?"

"Two years."

"Like me and Chase." He glanced over at me and his mouth quirked up.

The man was disarming. "Pete said he's three years older?"

"He is. Thinks he's smarter and wiser than the rest of us."

The road became windy, and he concentrated on driving.

"You guys seem to get along well."

He snickered. "Not hardly. We've thrown plenty of

punches over the years. Pete even knocked out one of my teeth. I've got a fake one to prove it." He pointed to a tooth on the bottom.

"What'd you do to earn that?"

"Gave him a black eye." Luke's smugness showed in his grin. "But the three of us have mellowed over the years and hardly ever come to blows anymore. Especially since we have a ranch to run."

"So let's get back to the spirit world. Do you believe in ghosts?"

"Maybe? Not that I've experienced an apparition myself, but my little sister did."

"Really, tell me more."

"Peggy had been riding at dusk when a man in a sombrero came out of nowhere and walked straight toward her. She called out and he disappeared, so she raced as fast as she could to get home. Her hands were shaking when she told us her story."

"This is the same sister with the funky boots?"

"The very same."

"Where does she fit in the family?

"She's thirteen months younger than Pete."

"So Chase is the baby?" I had assumed that already.

"He is. I wouldn't say he's spoiled but—." He laughed. "He has his moments."

We reached the Whispering Pines city limit, and my phone started pinging.

"You're pretty popular."

"The cell service must be kicking in." Not in the mood to deal with any of this in front of Luke, I didn't bother taking the device out of my bag. "Like I said before, all this can wait until I'm in my hotel room."

We turned off the interstate onto Main Street. "Do you ever go dancing at the Boot Scoot?" A handful of cars were in the parking lot of the two-story building.

"More times than I can count."

"You like to dance?" Most men I knew did only when necessary.

"If I have the right partner." He grinned at me, and my whole body tingled.

He slowed to the posted speed limit of 25, allowing me to check out the residential neighborhood. "These houses remind me of Old Town Stardust." They even had sidewalks lining both sides of the streets. A couple of blocks further, we reached the gas station and Rocky's Burgers.

He pointed to the building on the west corner. "Peggy manages the general store. Maybe you'll run into her."

"I hope I do."

Making a quick right, he pulled into Wolfe's Automotive Complex and parked near a shop where a light flashed in Timber Wolfe's Auto Repair window. He pointed to the clock on his dash. "It's ten to five. We just made it."

"Thank goodness." I got out quickly. The sign on the door said they were closed on Sunday. Just my luck.

Luke held the glass door open. As we made our way to the counter, the air reeked of gasoline and engine grease. Shelves were stacked with tools, cans of motor oil, and more car parts.

A gruff voice called from the back, "Be right with ya!" Footsteps on concrete preceded a lanky man in overalls, wiping his hands on a rag. He shook hands with Luke. "It's been too long."

"That it has, uncle. How's the family doing?"

"Well." He turned to me. "You must be the lady who broke down by Luke's place?"

"Uncle Tim, this is Goldi Summers," Luke introduced me.

"Hi," I held out my hand and he gave me a firm shake. "Think you can help me?"

He glanced at the clock on the wall. "I won't be able to look at your car until Monday afternoon."

"It's fine." I wish I had money to throw at him so he'd get it done earlier—like my father would do--but since I didn't all I could do was smile.

"Move the car into this spot," he told Luke, and handed me a clipboard and a pen. "Write down your name and phone number."

I filled the paper out and handed him the keys to my Camaro, ignoring the twinge in my chest. "Thank you, Tim."

"You're more than welcome."

Luke backed my car into the spot with ease and unhooked the tow bar.

"See you Monday." It was as if I left a part of my heart behind. I pivoted to Luke. "Let's go."

"How bout I buy you dinner?"

"No way. It will be my treat for towing my car."

"We'll see."

"Black Bear Diner's only a few doors down. You okay with walking?"

"Sure am." This quaint little town reminded me of a Hallmark movie with Luke as the leading man. We passed a sports, trophy, and phone shop, which sort of made sense. "Hairway to Heaven—that's classic." I chuckled at the Led Zeppelin play on words. The outside walls featured brightly-colored, painted flowers and peace signs.

"Arrow Jones, a self-proclaimed flower child, bought the place in the 70's. She retired a few years ago, but the name stuck."

"I bet she has great stories. Does she still live in town?"

"Nope. She moved to Florida and is living it up."

"Well. Good for her."

A life-sized statue of a bear stood outside the diner. I got out my phone and handed it to Luke. "Take my picture. I'll send it to my sister."

He snapped the shot. "Come on, little tourist, let's go inside." He held the door for me.

I admired a hand-painted wall mural of a bear fishing in a stream. The glass display at the counter showcased hundreds of bear figurines in all shapes.

A woman wearing the diner's logo on her T-shirt came strolling in from the back. "Good to see you, Luke." She eyed me and picked up two menus.

"Goldi, this is Betsy. We went to school together."

"Nice to meet you." She led us to a booth with a window view.

I opened up my menu. "What do you recommend?"

"My favorite's meatloaf, still you can never go wrong with a bacon cheeseburger."

My stomach growled reminding me I hadn't eaten for hours. "A cheeseburger, fries and Coke would be lovely."

"I'll take the same," Luke added. "But make my drink a chocolate milkshake with extra whipped cream."

"You've got it." Betsy hurried off.

"I like your town. It's quaint." I got out my phone. "I better make a room reservation. Is the place called Buckshot Bed and Breakfast?"

"Sure is."

I clicked the button. "Done. Fingers crossed I get room 211."

"You're crazy."

"And proud of it." The food came out. I took a picture of the plate and sent it with the bear photo.

Me: I'm bear-y happy with my food.

Sis: Looks good. Call me.

Me: Later tonight. I promise.

I had one hundred and twenty-three unread text messages. Deciding to go through them later, I put my phone away.

"Do you always take pictures of your food?" Luke raised a brow.

"Just when I'm out of town. It's something my sister and I started years ago."

"That's different." He ate a fry.

I concentrated on my burger. "This is really delicious."

"It should be. The beef comes from local ranchers, including Sunrise Ridge." He sat up a little taller when a man came up to our table.

"Hey, Luke! How are things at the ranch?"

"Busy as usual."

"Good to hear." He turned to me. "Heard you caused quite a ruckus out there."

"If you mean I helped Mabel in the kitchen, then yes, I did." I flashed him a smile. "I'm Goldi."

"How's Mabel doing? I haven't seen her in ages."

"She's well, as usual," Luke said.

"It's been a pleasure, Miss Goldi. Luke, tell Mabel I say howdy. I'll leave you two to your meal."

"He likes Mabel," I said when he walked away.

"He's not the only one. But she's never gotten over her husband."

"She told me her story. It's so sad." I couldn't imagine such loss.

"It's life." His lips pinched together.

We finished eating, and the waitress brought the check. Luke snagged it first.

"You sneak."

"Yep." He got out cash and left it inside the bill holder.

"Thanks for dinner."

"You're welcome." Once on the sidewalk, Luke offered his arm which I gladly accepted. It didn't take long to reach his truck, and we headed down Main Street. I liked the brightly colored awnings, especially the ones above the toy and candy shop.

"This is the place. There's a saloon on the corner, left hand side."

Large arched windows adorned the three-story brick building. "Is that a hitching post out front?"

"Sure is. People still use it."

Gravel crunched under the truck's tires as he pulled into the parking lot with a total of six cars. He took a space near the front door. "Goldi—"

I turned to him. "Yes."

He leaned in and pressed his lips to mine in a whisper of what might have been. All too quickly his mouth was gone. "I should be in town again on Tuesday. If you're still here, I'll take you to lunch."

"Only if I get to pay."

"Not likely."

I wished for more time with him. Wished I could have stayed at the ranch a little longer. Wished he'd kiss me again. Too bad my wishes never seemed to come true. "Thanks for everything." I placed my hand on the door handle, feeling the cool metal against my skin.

"You're more than welcome. Have fun with the ghost."

"If I'm lucky." Carrying my duffle and backpack, I headed for the front door and glanced back, waving at him as he drove away. My steps were heavy as I went inside.

And just like that, I closed the door to the best adventure I'd ever experienced.

CHAPTER 13

GOLDI

A board creaked under my feet as I made my way toward the front desk where a gray-haired woman greeted me with a warm smile. "Welcome to the Buckshot Saloon Bed and Breakfast. Checking in?"

"Yes. I booked online. Is two eleven free?" Luke's words about it being haunted ricocheted in my mind, and I was more than ready for the experience.

"It is. You're a brave one. Most folks steer clear of that room." She eyed me sideways.

"What's your take on the ghost?"

"To be honest, I've never seen him myself. But he's scared plenty of guests over the years."

A couple walked in the door and stood behind me.

The clerk scooted a skeleton key across the counter. "We'll talk more later."

I read her nametag. "I'd like that, Carol."

Once I got settled, I'd come back and explore the bar. I made my way up the creaky stairs to the second floor. The narrow hallway lined with framed black and white photographs depicted the town's history. My favorite was the one where firemen in suspenders stood in front of an old horse-drawn fire engine.

Inside the small but neat room, I made myself at home, taking maybe five minutes to put my clothing into the antique dresser. I opened the window allowing the lace curtains to flutter in the breeze. Picking up my cell, I fell back on the bed's patchwork quilt and scrolled through my messages.

One was from my old boss. Even if he begged, I'd never work for him again. Several were from Mark. He wasn't worth the effort.

Then I read my sister's text.

Sis: Call me.

I pushed her name. "What's up?"

" Mom knows you and Mark broke up. Can you believe he called her to see if you were there?"

"Of course he did." I let out a huff. "I'm not ready to talk about the cheating with mom or dad. I'd rather do that in person." Something I dreaded. "Still, I can't miss my weekly phone call with Mom." I sucked in a deep breath and made a mental list of what I wanted to say. "Wish me luck."

"You'll be fine. Text or call me later and tell me what happened."

"Will do." My stomach clenched as I pushed Mom's number.

One ring.

"Sweetie, I've been so worried about you."

"I'm doing great. I quit my job a few days ago. Mark and I broke up." I paused before saying, "I needed to get away for a few weeks and found a nice quiet town in Wyoming. It's beautiful here and just what I needed.'" Should I tell her about my car? Fudge no.

"Honestly, Goldi, you didn't have to run away. Mark isn't mad at you."

"You're cutting out. The signal around here is pretty bad."

"But—"

"Love you." I hung up. A teeny tiny bit of me felt bad, but honestly, I didn't want to hear about the virtues of Mark. Turning off my phone and setting it on the end table, I let out a huge sigh.

What a day.

I opened my laptop, opting to FaceTime my sister. "Hey."

"How's Wyoming treating you?"

Holy hotcakes, it was good to see her smiling face. "It's been great so far. Right now, I'm in Whispering Pines. The town's cute."

"Let me see." Knowing my sister, she had just looked it up on her computer and already ran a background check on crime in the area. "Why didn't you send a selfie with your hot cowboy? I'm dying to see what he looks like."

"I didn't take any of him."

"Well, that's a shame." She sighed. "Why are you in town?"

"The highway's open now, and Luke towed my car. Since the auto shop owner won't look at it until Monday, I'm staying at a bed and breakfast."

"You really liked being on the ranch."

"I did." Like usual, she picked up on my thoughts. "But look at this room." I showed her with my cell. "The hotel was built in the 1800's."

"It's perfect for you." She flashed me a grin. "Now for the big question. When do you think you'll be coming home? Mom's driving me nuts with questions. Which I refuse to answer."

"I called her and kept things brief."

"That should help."

"Well, she's not happy with me. You know her. She thinks I'm running away." I couldn't help wincing.

"But you're doing it for a good reason."

"Which I'll explain to Mom and Dad when I get home."

"That's a great plan." She gave me a thumbs up. "If you need me, I'm here."

"That means a lot. Look, I'm exhausted. I'll check in with you tomorrow."

"You'd better."

Once my head hit the pillow, I closed my eyes and dozed until the faint banging of keys on a piano came from below in the Saloon. Might as well check out the entertainment.

It was as if I stepped back in time to the Wild West. Whiffs of whiskey and wood polish filled the air. Antique lamps cast dancing shadows along the walls and illuminated the space with a warm, nostalgic light. The spacious room featured high ceilings and tall windows. On the shelves behind the mahogany bar, glasses and bottles sparkled. Several people took up the bar stools, their conversation barely audible.

I strolled up to the bar.

The bartender, wearing a white shirt, black vest, and bow tie, poured shots. "What's your poison?"

"Your finest draught."

"That'll be Buckshot Gold. It's made at a local brewery."

"Works for me."

He poured the drink into a mug and slid it down the bar without spilling a drop.

"That's impressive." I picked up the mug and left a five in his tip jar.

Carol, the clerk from the front desk, waved me over to a table near the bar. "Goldi, join us."

"Okay."

She introduced me to Amos the local banker, Silas the blacksmith, LeRoy the general store owner, and Carol's husband, Ned.

I shook each one's hand. "I've heard there's rich history in this area."

"Sure is. This town's survived fires, droughts, even Prohibition," the banker said. "We've got ghosts, too, if you believe in that sort of thing."

I played along. "Supposedly, I'm bunking with one of them tonight."

"You're the one who picked Old Tom's room." Amos' lips turned up at the corners.

"That's him and his wife right there." Jed pointed to a sepia-toned image of the couple.

I stared at the long-passed couple. "Look at his stern expression. The way he's practically frowning. He looks intense. But she has a softer edge to her mouth and eyes."

"Older photos are like that. It's because people sat still forever," LeRoy said.

"About this ghost friend of mine. What should I be watching for?"

"Don't rightly know. Never seen him." Silas pushed a strand

of his dark hair out of his eyes and grinned at me. The guy was cute. Not flashy like my ex. Not sexy like Luke.

"What other sightings can you tell me about?"

"When Ned and I inherited the place and first moved here, I heard footsteps outside our bedroom," Carol said.

I hadn't realized she was the owner.

"Once when I went down to the cellar to bring up a case of whiskey, the door at the top shut, and I was locked in for a few hours," Ned spoke slowly.

"Supposedly, around dusk a lady of the night peers over the balcony." Amos lowered his voice.

"Enough with the stories. We don't want to run Goldi off," Carol scolded.

"I don't scare easy. Not even during a horror movie." Which was true enough. "How long have you owned this place?"

"Twenty-two years. Ned's great-great-great-grandfather built it in 1890. Someone in the family has run it ever since."

A man sat down at the piano.

"You're in for a treat. Frank's played here on Saturday nights for years. Enjoy." Ned held out a hand for his wife. On the small dance floor, he twirled her under his arm. Two other couples joined in.

"Care to dance?" Silas asked me.

"I'd like that." He was nice enough, with a boyish charm and an easy grin, but he lacked the raw intensity and quiet strength of a certain cowboy.

The song ended and the next one began. I found myself dancing with several other men, gliding across the floor. I'd never two-stepped before. Silas ended up teaching me. I only tramped on his toes twice and another man's once.

"Alright folks, it's midnight. Finish up your drinks and call it a night," Ned's voice boomed across the room.

People trickled out, and I walked toward the stairs.

Carol caught up to me. "Don't forget we serve breakfast from seven to nine. If you're interested, you're more than welcome to join us for church afterwards. It's right across the street."

It had been eons since I went to church. Why not? This was Wyoming. People were friendly.

And since I didn't have a kitchen to experiment in, I could use something to do. "I'll be there."

CHAPTER 14

LUKE

Sunday, the old rooster crowed and woke me up. I hadn't slept worth shit. All night, my mind refused to stop thinking about Goldi.

Why the hell did I kiss her? I didn't need to get involved with another city girl.

I mustered the will to get up and dress. The guest room door was ajar. I knew I shouldn't, but I stepped inside.

Charlie trotted in next to me and whined. Even my damn dog missed her.

The faint scent of her vanilla perfume reminded me of the cookies and pies she baked. The neatly made bed appeared as if it'd never been used. Then I spotted those ridiculous black and white boots. They had suited her.

I told myself Goldi had been nothing serious. Nothing lasting. Nothing worth fretting about.

I downed a strong cup of coffee, fixed two slices of toast

with peanut butter and headed out to the stables. "Hey, boy." I brushed my stallion. "What do you say to a nice long ride?"

He snorted his agreement.

"Or you could go with us to the Triple H Ranch to check out their newest acquisition." Pete stood outside the stall door, holding his horse by the reins.

"Sounds good. I'd been meaning to go over there this week but never got the chance." I saddled Stormy.

Behind him, Chase walked out with his mount. "How'd it go taking Goldi to town?"

"Fine. Can you believe she wants to stay in the haunted room at Buckshot?"

"You'd never catch me doing that." Pete shuddered. "Messing with the dearly departed is plain loco."

"Are we going or not?" Chase hopped on his horse.

Pete and I followed suit, and the three of us took off at a gallop. The boundary between our ranch and the Triple H was marked by sagebrush and rugged fence posts and barbed wire. Mule deer spread out along the distant meadow. A red-tailed hawk soared above. We crossed a shallow creek giving us a view of cattle grazing in a pasture.

I got down and opened a metal gate with the Triple H logo embossed on it.

We rode a short distance and dismounted by the paddock. A stallion's nostrils flared as he caught our scent and pawed the ground lightly.

"Looks like somebody's got an attitude," I said.

Our neighbor, Roy walked out of the stables and held out his hand, his grip as firm as ever. "Diablo's strong-willed. Auburn is determined to train him herself."

"Knowing her gift with horses, she'll tame him," Chase said.

Pete huffed. He'd been competing with her for as long as I could remember.

"Where'd you find Diablo?" I asked.

"A ranch in Colorado. It took some convincing to get the owner to sell, but I knew he'd be worth it."

"He's got good lines and conformation." I stepped closer to get a better look.

"Gonna breed him with Daisy. I figure their opposite temperaments should make for a good mix." Roy placed his hand on the railing.

"You interested in studding him out?" Pete asked, and I knew which horse he'd pick. Duchess.

"Maybe next season. First, I need to get him settled."

"Fair enough."

Roy brought us to his stables. Horses poked their heads over the stall doors, watching us with mild curiosity. "That's Stolen Promise." He pointed to a sleek, chestnut mare with a white blaze down her face.

"She's a beauty," Chase whistled. "Is she fast?"

"You bet. She's even better at cutting. Got the instincts for it."

We moved further down. Fresh straw mingled with the musky smell of horses. Each stall was neat, the horses well-groomed. He pointed out a gray mare, and a young bay gelding just starting to come into his own.

A horse whinnied and Roy stopped at the stall on the end, his grin widening as he pulled out an apple. "I'm coming, Outlaw." As Roy opened the door, the white stallion pranced forward.

"You've got a good bunch," Pete said.

"I'm happy with them. Why don't you boys join us for lunch? Gladys is making meatloaf."

"I'm in," I said.

Chase and Pete nodded.

We sat around the long table in the dining room. "Tell me about that visitor staying at your place?" Gladys stared directly at me.

"Goldi's car broke down near my house. She's in town getting it fixed."

"Mabel raved about her baking skills. I'd love to catch up with that girl and get a couple of her recipes."

I shrugged. "She'll be there until at least Monday afternoon, but after that who knows?"

The click of boots on the wooden floor had me looking up.

Auburn came over. "Well, if it isn't the Wolfe brothers," she drawled, blue eyes scanning us before landing on Pete with a frosty glare.

Pete's jaw clenched for a second and he quickly replaced it with a wide smile. "Hello, Red." He offered his hand, but she ignored him and took a seat on the other side of her father.

"Did you boys come to see Diablo?" Her eyes went to mine and Chase's.

"We sure did," Pete answered for us.

As the others launched into training techniques, my mind wandered to Goldi and her night at the saloon. Did she like staying there?

"What do you think, Luke?" Auburn asked.

About what? I had no clue. "It's hard to say." I opted for indifference.

"You're not much help." She sipped her tea.

"Never said I was."

"We'd best get going." Pete stood. "Thanks for the tasty lunch, Gladys."

"When will you share this recipe with Mabel?" Chase asked.

"I won't. This gives you an excuse to come visiting more often." Gladys just grinned. "You boys are welcome here anytime."

I stole a glance at Auburn. She still glared daggers at Pete. He stood with his arms folded, the tension between the two crackling.

Would these two ever just admit they like each other and quit the foreplay?

CHAPTER 15

GOLDI

I dreamed of galloping through hills, my horse going faster and faster as the wind whipped my braid back. "I'm winning, cowboy," I called back to Luke.

"Not today, city girl." His mount got closer. But he couldn't catch me.

"Wake up, lass."

"What the—?" Disoriented and still half-asleep, I shot up in bed. Rubbing my eyes in the dimly lit room, I squinted at the foot of my bed. A translucent figure of a man shimmered as if he were a mirage.

Every instinct screamed to move, to run. Instead, I blinked hard, certain that sleep played tricks on me. There had to be some logical explanation for this.

"Has a cat stolen your tongue, lass?" The unnerving voice seemed to hang in the air.

Talk about impossible. I gripped the blanket, my fingers numb, staring at the spectral image. "You can't be real." Yet here he was, hovering over me, not a trick of shadows, not a figment of sleep.

"Aye, that I am. Flesh no more, but truth all the same." A chilling draft wrapped around me. His Irish accent added an eerie melody to his words. He stayed, hazy yet unmistakably present, with eyes that seemed to peer straight through me, filled with a haunting intensity.

"What are you doin' in my sleepin' chamber, then?" The voice sounded calm, almost too controlled. Each precise and measured word sent prickles across my skin.

"I rented this room for the night from Carol and Ned, the owners."

"It is balderdash you speak. You ought to know—I built the finest hostelry in Whispering Pines. I am the master here, and the watchman." He held up a pistol and swung it around his finger.

"There's no reason to get upset, Mr. Ghost." Thank goodness the gun looked as translucent as the apparition. Still, I couldn't take any chances the weapon might work. "I asked for this room because I hoped to see you."

"Did you now?"

"You're quite a legend around here. Your photograph still hangs downstairs in the saloon." I figured I'd play on his pride. "Like you said before, you are the reason this place exists."

"That is true enough." His body seemed brighter somehow. His grin widened.

"Would you mind if I stay here for a few days? It is a rather nice room."

"Indeed, that would suit me fine, lass, since you asked with a fair tongue."

"Thank you, kind sir." I reached out to shake his hand, but my fingers went straight through him. Right, I forgot for a moment he was a ghost.

He remained standing. "Beware of any fella you might be keepin' close, lass. He will be your undoing, sure as rain."

Which sounded like the story I'd heard last night. What was the man's name again? Toby? Tim? Todd? "Are you talking about your wife, Tom Devlin?"

Right before my eyes, he vanished into thin air.

My whole body trembled as I remained under the covers, totally freaked out. Did I just have a conversation with a ghost?

I do believe I did.

I turned on the lights next to my bed. When the guy didn't show again, I got up and looked down the hallway. Not a single person in sight.

The grandfather clock downstairs chimed six times. "So much for sleeping until eight," I muttered under my breath.

Wide awake, I got out my phone and looked up ghost hauntings. Several stories featured bland and basic sightings—until I came to the Place d'Armes. The hotel burned down during the Great New Orleans Fire of 1788. In the vicinity, several guests reported having conversations with a bearded man.

Meaning I wasn't the only one who talked to ghosts.

What happened to me might be weird, but Tom seemed harmless enough. Except in life, he'd killed his wife, lover, and then himself. I shuddered at the thought.

"Just so you know, Tom." I spoke like he still occupied the room. "Killing your wife wasn't the best way to deal with her infidelity. My ex cheated on me, and I came here. It's a much better alternative to murder."

The curtains fluttered.

He must exist because that explained this crazy encounter. "I'm getting dressed," I said out loud, "but you'd better not be watching. That would be creepy."

Nothing happened. I took that as a good sign. Not sure what people wore to church, I opted for a silky blouse, black pants and sneakers. I mean, why not be comfortable while I explored the town afterwards?

The echo of chatter filled the bottom floor. When I entered the dining room, Carol waved at me. "Hope you slept well."

I shrugged, deciding to tell her about the ghost later. Taking a plate from the sidebar, I added scrambled eggs, bacon, and a chocolate chip muffin. The smell reminded me of making chocolate chip cookies for Luke.

Knock it off.

I filled a mug with rich, dark coffee and generous portions of cream and sugar, walked over to an empty table and sat down.

"May I join you?" Carol asked.

"I'd love the company. I had an interesting guest this morning," I said.

"Do tell." She eased into the chair across from me and folded her fingers together.

"I met Ghost Tom. He thinks he's still the proprietor of this place."

"As long as he doesn't try to hurt anyone, I can live with that. Did he try to shoot you?" Her brows furrowed.

"No, but he spun his pistol."

"Were you scared?" Her eyes widened.

"Who wouldn't be? But for the most part, he was nice. He warned me to be careful about the men I associate with."

"That's odd."

"It made me think he might have been talking about his wife and how she cheated on him. Anyway, when I called him Tom Devlin, he just… disappeared. Poof!" My voice dropped to a whisper.

"That'll be a first. He usually scares off guests."

"Actually, he seemed sad." I bit into a dry muffin. A little more butter would make it moister.

"Or he suffers from melancholy. He did have a tragic death." She sipped her coffee. "I can't wait to tell Ned. He's gonna flip."

The morning went on. Church was filled with friendly people asking questions about how long I planned to stay in town. If only I knew.

Needing a little solitude after the service, I peered into the window display for Fur and Feathers Pet Shop. Dog toys, treats, bones, and food were arranged next to a dog statue. The animal looked like Charlie wearing a red collar. Luke's sweet dog.

Time to move on.

A closed sign hung in the flower shop.

Crossing the street, an empty gazebo in the town square called to me. Perfect. I sat inside and breathed in the fresh mountain air.

In the park, a group of girls played with dolls. Other people spread out blankets and picnicked. The water fountain trickled and splashed. A car drove by slowly. Everyone smiled and took things in stride and appeared to enjoy the day.

I got up and walked along Main Street. The scent of sweetness wafted from the candy store. A couple of kids played with a wind-up dinosaur on the table outside the toy shop.

Cattle Call Clothing featured jeans, cowboy boots, Stetsons and calico dresses. I kept on walking.

Based on the window, Saddles & Sage Gifts showed some cute knickknacks inside. I should find a gift for my sister.

The bell chimed. "Hello," a young clerk greeted me. "Can I help you?"

"I'm just browsing."

"Give a holler if you need anything." She went back to her bead working.

The store was organized in rows. The mugs, bowls, and plates in earthy tones appeared handmade. I ran my fingers along the woolen blankets draped over a wooden ladder. Soft as velvet. The bold geometric designs would look great on the back of Luke's couch or spread out for a sunset picnic.

Quit thinking about him.

At a center table, hand carved bears were placed next to a moose and deer. On a corner shelf, dozens of snow globes drew me to them. I picked up one with a castle that reminded me of Disneyland. Another globe had an intricate snowy owl perched on a branch. My sister would love this for her owl collection.

"A local artist designed these." The clerk stood next to me. "She's quite talented. You've gotta see this one." She handed me a frosted globe with a couple riding horses in the hills.

This would make a perfect Wyoming souvenir. Thirty dollars apiece was a steal, and I'd be helping support the town. "I'll take both of these."

With the packages tucked away in my bag, I stepped out onto the sidewalk and did a silly victory dance.

CHAPTER 16

GOLDI

My hand tapped the side of my leg as I waited in the tiny office of Timber Wolfe's Auto Repair Shop. My stomach churned while I breathed in motor oil and gasoline and stale coffee.

"It's the transmission, Goldi." Tim's downturned mouth didn't bode well. "We have two options. Rebuild it for anywhere from two to three thousand depending on the extent of the damage. Or put in a new transmission for about four."

Shit. Panic rose in my throat. This would mean using up most of the cash I brought with me. Desperation clawed up my spine. This was my Nana's car. "I'll come up with the money."

Mom's words popped into my head. *Impulsivity will one day be your downfall.* Her point had me grinding my teeth. "What would you do, Tim?"

"Rebuild it. My son's excellent. He does all the work in town. His shop is just next door."

"Okay. How long do you think it will take?"

"Three, four weeks. Possibly more."

"Would the crate transmission be faster?"

"Possibly, but it's on backorder right now."

"And I assume you have no idea when they will be restocked?"

"Exactly."

"Then I'll hire your son."

"I think there's three cars ahead of you. He'd talk to you himself, but he's out of town today," Tim said. "If you'd rather, I could have your car towed to White Ridge. They have more mechanics and work a lot faster. I'll call them if you'd like?"

"No thanks." I'd figure this out. I wanted Nana's car somewhere local. "How much do I owe you?"

"Nothing yet. Just sign this agreement and I'll give it to my son."

I penned my signature. He gave me a copy. Another issue hit me. With suddenly-limited funds, I'd better find somewhere cheaper to stay and see about a job to help with the repairs.

"Is anyone around here hiring?" My voice actually tremored.

He rubbed his chin. "The general store."

I'd met Leroy, the owner, last night at the saloon. He seemed nice enough. "Thanks, Tim. I'll go talk to him."

I marched down the sidewalk. People waved or said hello as I passed them. Did I know any of their names? No, but I waved anyway.

I crossed at the corner. The building looked as old as the saloon. A 'Help Wanted' sign hung in the front window.

I took a deep breath, plastered on my best smile, and approached the counter.

A youngish dark-haired woman grinned at me. "How can I help you?"

"Is the owner around?"

"Sorry. He's stepped out and should be back any minute."

I read her nametag. Peggy, Manager. She had to be Luke's sister. Should I say I knew her brother? Not yet. I'd tell her if I got hired. "I'd like to apply for a job."

"It's only part time." She grabbed a clipboard from underneath the counter and gave it to me.

"That's fine."

"You're welcome to fill this out at one of the chairs near the dressing room."

"Thanks." I made my way past canned goods and animal supplies including chicken feed. A chuckle escaped thinking about my run-in with Roostifer. It amazed me how much my life had changed in the last few days.

Exposed wooden beams stretched across the ceiling. I kept on walking until I reached a small rack of clothing. Who knew plaid had been made into not only shirts, but skirts, shorts, dresses and hairbands? Actually, the pink and white skirt was pretty cute. I nixed that idea and said a new mantra in my head. *No spending money unless necessary.*

I plunked into a chair and clicked the pen to add in my name. No way would I use my address with Mark. I opened my phone to check for my sister's address.

As far as previous employers, instead of the manager at my last job, I opted to use my prep chef friend as a reference. With the application finished, I headed to the front of the store.

"Hey, Goldi." The owner greeted me. He turned to Luke's

sister. "Can you believe she's staying in the haunted room at the saloon?"

"Really? You're way braver than I am."

"More like curious." I lifted one shoulder.

"Or a bit crazy. But aren't we all, in one way or another." He shook his head. "Peggy says you're looking for work."

"I am." I handed him the application.

He glanced it over. "Heard your car won't be fixed for weeks."

"You're right." Small town gossip sure worked fast.

"Wait." Peggy squinted her eyes as if trying to figure me out. "Are you the one who stayed with my brother?"

"That's me. I hope that won't be a problem." I crossed my fingers behind my back.

"Not at all." The owner scanned over the application once more. "You up to stocking and ringing up customers? It's minimum wage."

"I'll take it." Relief soared through my veins. Money was money. And he didn't even check out my references.

"When can you start?" he asked.

"As soon as possible." I could use the hours.

"How about today?" Peggy said. "Right now would be even better."

"That'd be great."

"Follow me." She gave me an apron and brought me to a grocery aisle with boxes on the floor. "I'm glad you're here. As you can tell, there's plenty to do."

We fell into an easy rhythm, stacking cans and boxes on the shelves.

After a while, Peggy said, "I still can't believe you were at Sunrise Ridge. I'm assuming you also met Pete and Chase."

"I did. They're nice."

"They're better now. As the little sister, I got my ponytail pulled and the heads taken off my dolls. Usual brother stuff."

"My brother's five years older than me. When I pestered him, he'd just shut his door." We'd never been close, which made me a little sad.

"That's better than being locked in the pantry."

"Who did that?"

"Chase. Of the three, he's the one most likely to pull pranks." She sighed. "Once he came back from college, he stopped with the craziness. I think he's trying to be a role model for my little girls. Trying is the key word."

"I bet they're all great uncles. How old are your kids?"

"Six. They're twins."

"I always wished I'd been a twin." I tended to be a loner in school.

"Having them can be tiring." She opened a box with a cutter. "Back to Luke. Did you really break into his house?"

"A thunderstorm hit, and I found the door unlocked."

"I wish I could have seen his face when he found you. I love him dearly, but he doesn't do well with surprises."

"At least Charlie didn't mind. He's a good dog."

"The best. We have two cats. The kids want a dog. With the hours my husband and I keep, we're not around enough to do a good job training one."

"What does your husband do?"

"He's the sheriff. Unlike big cities, most of the crime here tends to be vandalism or teens tipping cows."

"Is that really a thing?" I tore open another box and continued to stock the shelf.

"It is. I never saw the fun in it."

"It is kind of weird."

"You've got that right. I heard you're from California?"

"Near L.A."

"I'm going to Disneyland next summer with my family and can't wait. I've never been any farther than Vegas."

"It's a great place. The Matterhorn is my all-time favorite." I stacked more cans on the shelf.

"Do you live near the park?"

"It's in Orange County, about an hour from where I live. Or more, depending on traffic."

"You're lucky to be so close."

"Maybe. But this town has plenty of charm."

"Thanks."

We continued working for the next few hours, until a male voice announced over the speakers, "We're closing in ten minutes, folks."

I finished up the last open box.

"You're a fast worker." Peggy stood next to me eyeing the empty cartons. "Can you come back tomorrow, say around nine, to work the register?"

"I'll be here."

CHAPTER 17

LUKE

The day had been busy, just the way I liked it. After visiting the Triple H, I took Stormy for a long ride. Then I brushed him down, mucked out stalls, washed up, and came in for dinner.

Helping myself to biscuits and gravy at the side bar, I called to Mabel, "You're the best."

She waved at me, filled a container with tea, and went back to the kitchen. A part of me expected to find Goldi back there cooking, but I knew better. I sat on the end across from my brothers and several cowboys. Taking a bite, I enjoyed the creamy, beefy flavor. The crackle of a walkie-talkie made me pause.

"Hey y'all. I've got some news," Peggy's chipper voice burst through the static.

My stomach clenched. Peggy calling during dinner usually meant trouble.

"Does it have to do with the girls' recital next month? Because we're all going." Pete spoke.

"Nope."

"Then what's up?" I tried to keep my voice level.

"Guess who's working at the store with me?" she asked in a singsong tone.

"Who?" Pete asked.

"Goldi Summers. The same woman who stayed at your house, Luke."

The idea of Goldi working with my sister threw me.

Peggy went on. "Why do you think she took a job in town?"

"Her car repairs won't be cheap," Chase chimed in.

"Bingo."

It must have been her transmission. "Did she say how long that would take?" The damn words came out before I could think about it.

"At least three weeks. Maybe more."

I asked, "That long?"

Peggy laughed. "I'm not complaining. Goldi's a hard worker. I haven't had decent help in months."

"That's not surprising. You should have seen how many cookies and pies she made when she had nothing to do at Luke's place." Pete snickered.

"She bakes, too?"

"Like a dream." Mabel marched out from the kitchen, obviously eavesdropping on the conversation. "I appreciated having her help me."

"I wish the store could offer her more hours, but part-time is the best we can do."

Pete tilted forward, a glint in his eyes. "You know, we can afford to pay her, what, three hundred a week."

"If she'd make cookies every night, I'd be willing to add another fifty," Chase said.

"Deal." Pete shook Chase's hand.

"Hold on," I gulped down water. "Goldi's a city girl." The words tasted bitter on my tongue, but I forced them out. "It'd be better if she stayed put until her car's fixed."

Mabel wagged a finger at me. "Don't give me any of that 'city girl' nonsense. That girl's got grit."

Pete shrugged, a knowing grin on his lips.

"I'm with Luke. I hate to lose her," Peggy said. "But it's her choice."

"*Mooo-oom! Susie took my doll and won't give her back,*" one of my nieces whined in the background.

"Gotta go. Let me know what you decide." Peggy ended the call.

I focused on shoveling food in my mouth. My mind raced with memories of Goldi's lips against mine.

Pete and Chase chattered on about the benefits of having Goldi. The traitorous part of me wondered if maybe it wouldn't be so bad.

"She needs a place of her own," Chase said.

"The cottage by the dining hall hasn't been used in about a year." Pete glanced at me.

I shot him a glare.

Did I want her to stay with me?

Hell, no.

Maybe.

"It wouldn't take much to clean the place up. I'll get started in the morning." Mabel beamed at me. "You can head to town and talk Goldi into accepting our offer, right, Luke?"

"Fine." My brothers' knowing gazes bored into my back as I walked out.

CHAPTER 18

GOLDI

"You're still here." Someone whispered in my ear.

"Not again. Shut up and let me sleep." I pulled the pillow over my head.

"'Tis eight o' clock. I kept me word, I did."

"Shoot. Why didn't my alarm go off?" Because I forgot to set it. So Tom did me a favor. Not that I'd tell him. "What do you want now?" Without coffee, I was in no mood for this. I sat up and glared at the translucent man standing next to my bed.

"A wee bit o' company, is all. You *are* in me chambers."

"I don't have time for this. You know, it's a little creepy that you just show up unannounced."

"I'll take that under advisement." He spun his gun.

"Put that weapon away. It's annoying."

"Aye." His form brightened. "Just so you know, this day you have a matter to settle." He disappeared.

"Really? You're gonna leave now." Irritated, I closed my eyes and imagined myself at the top of a mountain. Breathed in and exhaled slowly.

I could handle staying here. Last night, my sister offered to send me money, but I was okay for now.

A glance at my phone showed it was a quarter after eight. Knowing I'd better hurry, I showered, helped myself to coffee downstairs in a to-go cup, snagged a muffin, and rushed out the door.

I strolled along Main Street U.S.A.

No traffic. Nice.

The shops' colorful awnings were pretty.

"Howdy, ma'am." The man from A. Wolfe Realty stopped sweeping the sidewalk. "Beautiful morning, isn't it?"

"It sure is." Everything in Wyoming seemed brighter. Fresher. Healthier.

I went through the general store's back door and headed for the front.

"Morning, Goldi." Peggy greeted me from the check stand. "Let's get you set up. Knowing this town, it's going to be busy."

"Why?" Tuesday didn't seem like it should be crazy.

"Because people are nosy, and they're anxious to see the newcomer for themselves."

"At least the day will fly by."

"I'm counting on it." Her golden eyes twinkled in the same shade as Luke's. "The register's simple but you need to press extra hard on the five because it can stick. The price of produce is on this sheet." She pulled out a cardstock paper. "Any questions?"

"Not at the moment." I'd worked a retail job for about six months in high school. This looked similar.

"Show time." Peggy unlocked the front door. Several folks marched in.

"Hi." A brunette about my age placed an apple and sandwich on the counter. "I work at the library. You should stop in."

"I might just do that."

More locals stopped by, each one eager to introduce themselves and offer their own brand of small-town hospitality. Several men flirted with me as they bought their supplies. These people appeared genuine. How long before they realized I was running from my mistakes?

I pushed the thought aside, focusing on the task at hand.

A woman in a bright pink work shirt burst in, her dark hair piled high on her head. "I'm Tiffany, the hairdresser. You simply must let me work my magic on that gorgeous mane of yours."

I'd braided it earlier. I pictured her contorting my hair into a blonde beehive or putting it in pin curls. "Maybe later this month I'll let you trim it."

She rubbed her hands together. "Since you're new, I'll give you a special discount. Everyone should look their best, don't you think?" She flounced out of the store.

Lost in thought, I failed to notice a woman with a fluffy poodle in her arms standing before me, her eyes bright with excitement. The poodle yipped and jumped out of her arms. A blur of fur streaked past me, followed by a crash and a yelp.

I whirled around to see a cat darting along the aisle with the dog in hot pursuit. The poodle yapped as it knocked into a display of cereal. Boxes tumbled like dominoes.

"Fifi, no!" The woman chased after her dog. "Come back here, you naughty girl."

I rushed to help, trying to corral the animals. The dog

barked in a non-stop high-pitched tone. The cat hissed. And the woman shouted at the top of her lungs for them to stop.

Peggy came out of her office, hands on her hips. "What the heck?"

The cat went through her legs, the dog in hot pursuit. "Oh, no you don't Fifi." Peggy snatched the end of the dog's leash and picked her up. "Got you."

"I'm so sorry." The woman rushed up, huffing for breath.

"It's fine. If I were a dog, I'd probably chase Taffy." Peggy turned to me. "He's our store cat."

"That's cool." This job kept on getting more interesting.

I surveyed the damage. Except for a few dented boxes, it could've been worse.

"I'll help you tidy up. It's the least I can do after causing such a ruckus." The woman picked up a box.

"No need." Peggy gave back the dog.

"We've got it covered," I added.

With the help of Peggy and an older man who pitched in, we had the store back in order in a few minutes.

I'd just caught my breath when the bell above the door jingled. Luke walked in. Seeing his handsome face, my heart may very well have stopped.

"Hey, Luke." Peggy hugged him. "What brings you here?"

"My favorite sister."

"I'm your only sister." Peggy stepped back.

"The best sister ever."

"You're never this nice. I'm assuming you're here for Goldi." She gave a knowing look like the two of them shared some secret.

"Do you have a minute?" he asked me.

"I'm working." I fought off the memories of his lips against mine.

"It's important."

"Take your break. You've certainly earned it." Peggy shooed me out from behind the counter.

I followed Luke outside, my nerves on edge.

"Sorry about your car."

"The expense sucks but I'll get over it." The comfortable relationship I'd had on the ranch with Luke turned awkward. If only I knew how to make it better.

"Let's sit here." He motioned to a bench. We kept at least a foot between us. "I've got a job offer for you while your car's being fixed." His words rushed out. "Working with Mabel in the kitchen for breakfast, supper, and dinners. $350 a week."

I blinked, ready to say yes immediately, but I already liked this man way too much. And working with him would make it harder to leave. Still, the pay was more than double what I made at the general store. "I can't ask you to give up your guest room again."

"I won't have to. Mabel's cleaning up a cottage not far from the dining hall. It's small. Nothing fancy. But it'll be yours for as long as you stay."

"Umm." I bit my lip. "It's a generous offer, but I don't want to cause any trouble."

"You'd be doing us a favor." He gave me a lop-sided grin. "Plus, Mabel will tan my hide if I can't convince you."

"She can be quite a force."

"You've got that right." He smiled at me. "So, it's a yes."

The offer was too good to turn down. "I'll do it. After I finish my shift."

"Thank you." We got up and headed toward the store. "When is your shift over?"

"Two."

"I'll be here."

I'd get to spend the next few weeks on the ranch watching the sun set over the mountains and baking to my heart's content. Could it get any better than that?

CHAPTER 19

LUKE

Sneaking a peek through the front window of the store, I spotted Goldi laughing with Peggy behind the counter. It surprised me how easily she fit in. I pushed open the door, the bell jingling.

She glanced over, green eyes bright as they met mine. "You're right on time."

"Thought we might grab a burger before heading back."

"Good. I'm starving." Goldi untied her apron and hung it on a hook.

"If your job doesn't work out with this yahoo or my other brothers, you're always welcome back."

"I'm standing right here, Peggy."

"Just saying." She smirked at me.

After more hugs, mostly between Goldi and my sister, we climbed into my truck. I turned the key, and the engine rumbled to life. "How'd you like working with my sister?"

"She's great. Stocking the shelves yesterday, she pitched

right in. And you should see her skills wrangling a wayward dog named Fifi."

"Let me guess. Taffy was involved?"

"How'd you guess?"

"Because those two have been at odds for years. I'm surprised you didn't have everything under control, Miss I Can Walk Six Dogs At Once."

"That little dog is fast."

I pulled into Rocky's Burgers. "Should we eat inside or do drive through?"

"Drive through. I'm anxious to see the cottage." She tucked back a wayward strand of hair.

We reached the order speaker. "Single or double patty?"

"Double. Can you have them add grilled onions and extra pickles? And a strawberry milkshake?"

"Yes, ma'am."

As soon as we got our bags, I pulled into the parking lot space and passed out the food.

"I'm surprised you allow eating in the cab. You are kind of a neat freak."

"They did give us paper placemats." I took a big bite.

Goldi dug into her burger. "My god. This is really good."

"I know." I drank my soda. Ice cold, just the way I liked it.

It didn't take long to finish our meals, and we were on the road.

"Did you enjoy the town?"

"Staying at the saloon, I got to dance with several of the locals on Saturday night."

"Is that so?" I gripped the wheel tighter, trying to focus on the road and not the growing tension in my gut.

"Are you jealous, cowboy?"

"No." I barely knew her, much less did I have any claim to who she was with, but the idea of another man holding her in his arms didn't sit well.. I switched topics. "Did you see the ghost?"

"Tom's a pain in the neck. He woke me up by whispering in my ear."

My eyes widened in surprise. "What'd he say?"

"That I should be wary of cowboys."

"You're funny." I turned up the radio. Brett Young's, "You Ain't Here to Kiss Me" came on. I'd best remember the words. This city girl wasn't for me.

About ten minutes later, we reached the ranch's driveway. Gravel crunched beneath the tires. We stopped in front of the cottage and the front door burst open with Mabel waving. "Welcome back, Goldi. Come on inside."

Goldi hopped out. "I can't wait to see my new place."

I grabbed Goldi's duffle from behind the seat and followed her inside. Mabel had placed fresh flowers on the table. It smelled nice.

Goldi's eyes widened as she looked around. Her fingers trailed the back of the plaid couch. "Not bad." She went over to the kitchen, tried out one of burners, which lit, turned it off, and opened the oven. "This place is perfect."

Mabel beamed. "I'm glad you like it. I've packed the fridge with essentials and added snacks in the pantry."

"You thought of everything. Thank you."

"It's my pleasure."

"When do I start tomorrow?"

"Five-thirty should be fine."

"I'd best get going," Luke said.

"Wait a minute, Luke. I almost forgot about the quad for Goldi to use." Mabel smirked at me. "Would you show it to her?"

"Of course." As if I could say no.

"See you tomorrow." Mabel left.

"I can't believe I get to ride a quad. My friend use to have a Banshee. I loved how it took the hills. Can we go now?" She walked to the door, and I followed her.

"You might be disappointed. Chase rode the TRX90 as a kid until he stepped up to a Renegade. Your quad's reliable and will get you around the ranch but it's not that fast." I opened the single garage. "This is it.

"Yes." She pumped her fist in the air. "This is almost as good as my car."

"It'll be fixed before you know it." And then she'd leave. Why did that idea bother me? I handed her the helmet. "See if this fits."

She set it on her head and tightened the straps.

I pushed the quad outside. "Always check the fuel. I'd hate to see you run out." I showed her the switch under the seat. "It's full and should last for a couple of weeks. The extra can is right over there." I picked it up. "It's full, but when it gets low bring it to the shed by the stables to top it off."

"You guys are self-sufficient."

"We have to be out here." I moved closer. My hip brushed against hers, creating a spark that coursed right through me. Not good. Not good at all. "The controls are straightforward. Hop on and turn the fuel valve to ON."

"Got it." She leaned forward and her shirt rose, showing a strip of bare skin.

Did she have to be so sexy?

She pressed the start button on the handlebar, twisted the throttle, and took off. "Woo-hoo," she shouted and did a double circle around her cottage before stopping inches from my feet. "I just found my favorite new toy." She got off and flung her arms around me. "Thank you, cowboy."

"For what?" I backed away from her, refusing to look into her eyes. If I did, I might be tempted to kiss her.

"Offering me a job and my own place to stay. Plus, the quad."

"You're welcome. I've got chores to do, and I figure you'd like to get settled into your new place."

"See you around." She walked toward her cottage.

There went trouble with a capital T.

CHAPTER 20

GOLDI

As I walked outside, I breathed in the scent of prairie grass and sagebrush. A band of gold and pink and pale blue lit the horizon. If getting up early meant waking up to such a beautiful sight, who was I to complain?

I could have walked to work, but what would be the fun in that? Hopping on the quad, instead of going straight I looped south around Luke's house. A dog barked from inside.

Uh-oh. I might have woken the cowboy. I pressed the throttle to full on and headed for the dining hall. I parked by the back door, hung my helmet on the right handlebar and stepped inside.

Mabel enveloped me in a warm hug. "It's good to have you back in this kitchen."

"I'll only be here a few weeks."

"Unless we talk you into staying longer."

The idea held plenty of merit. Conflicting thoughts ran through my head. I loved it here. But my home wasn't in

Wyoming. Though I didn't have a home in California, either. My sister would let me use her guest room. Probably.

"Help yourself to coffee." Mabel motioned to a large stainless-steel dispenser. "I've already drunk two cups."

"Bless you." After adding real cream and sugar, I sipped the rich flavor.

"I've started on eggs and bacon. You wanna make flapjacks?"

"How many should I make?"

"About fifty should suffice. Better warn you, breakfast is pretty crazy. Everyone is in a hurry to start their day."

"No problem. I'm used to busy." I tied my apron strings and dug in. Bacon sizzled as I mixed batter and poured round circles onto the skillet.

"People should start drifting in soon."

"Does the whole crew come for breakfast?"

"Most of the time."

I hoped I'd see Luke again. Things were off between us, and I hoped to make them right. I filled a platter with pancakes, set it on the counter, and started on the next batch.

Mabel carried in eggs and bacon.

Then the stampede came in, or at least it felt that way. The place filled with cowboys chattering. Forks and plates clattered. As I set out pitchers of orange juice, I spotted Luke, waved, and rushed back into the kitchen.

An hour later, tired in the best of way, I joined Mabel at the table with a fresh cup of coffee and a muffin. Sipping the rich flavor, I glanced out the tall windows facing west. The meadows led into pretty thickets of trees. This was way better than my last job in the city where the windowless kitchen gave me a view of the dishwasher or the double-doors that led into the restaurant.

"How do you feel about taking over most of the baking? I'll let you know what help I need with the meals."

"I'd love that." Unbelievable. I'd get to create my own recipes.

"You already know the boys love cookies and pies and cakes, so it will be easy enough to please them. Anyway, we're down to our last loaf of bread. Make about two dozen loaves. That will last us two to three days."

I finished my coffee. "I'll get right on it." A surge of excitement bubbled within me.

"You don't fool around. I like that about you."

She liked my work ethic. I stood a little taller as I headed to the pantry, taking inventory of the ingredients. Flour, sugar, yeast, even a sourdough starter. Eggs in a basket on the counter. Spices on a rack.

I measured out flour and dissolved yeast in warm water and thought about Luke. We'd gotten close before I headed for town. Holy hotcakes, we'd even kissed. But now he acted distant.

"You okay?" Mabel's drawl snapped me out of my reverie.

I nearly dropped the ball of dough clutched in my hands. Heat crept up my neck as I met her gaze. "I'm fine. I just got lost in my work. Did you say something?"

"I asked how you enjoyed being in town."

My fingers kneaded the dough, centering me. "It was interesting. I saw… a ghost."

Her knife paused. "A what?"

"A spirit or apparition." The dough's texture became smooth and stretchy.

"You've gotta be joking."

"It's true. Not only did the ghost wake me up at six a.m., but he whispered in my ear."

"What'd he say?"

"That he owned the place."

"Did you stay at the Buckshot Bed and Breakfast?"

"I did, and asked for room two eleven."

"I can't believe you saw the infamous murderer, Tom Devlin." She shook her head. "You've got guts staying in his room."

Really? I hadn't before I came here. Thinking back, I tended to go along with whatever Mark wanted because it made him happy, while never considering what I might need.

Her eyes widened. "Did he say anything else?"

"To be wary of men." I figured that summed up the conversation. "I called him Tom. Then poof, he vanished. Like he was never there." I finely chopped rosemary and added it to the dough along with a sprinkle of sea salt. "But he did show up again the following morning."

"That's incredible. From what I've read, he built the hotel to impress his wife. You can find blueprints in the archives of the library."

"I wonder what the original stove looked like?"

"Probably cast iron, heavy as hell, and used a firebox."

"I imagine it took skill to bake in it. Still, I'd like to try. I bet I could get the hang of it."

"That's not for me. I prefer self-cleaning ovens."

"Good to know." I put a towel over a bowl for the dough to

rise. "I'd better get started on desserts. Are you saving the jars of peaches in the pantry for anything?"

"No. What are you thinking?"

"Peach cinnamon turnovers."

"The cowboys will love them."

"I'm counting on it." Blending butter with flour and water, half an hour later, I had the turnovers filled, folded, and placed in the oven.

"How'd you like working with our Peggy?" Mabel chopped carrots and potatoes and added them into the pot of stew.

"We hit it off right away. I felt bad about leaving, but she couldn't match the pay or give me free rent." The timer dinged, and I pulled out the golden-brown pastries.

"Those smell delicious."

"Thanks. You'll have to try one when they cool."

"Like I said before, you fit right in."

I fit in here better than with my own family. At home I was the oddity. My father worked as a high-powered corporate lawyer. My brother was a junior partner in the same firm. My sister was a top-notch divorce attorney. I'd been expected to go to law school. But it had never been my goal, much to the disappointment of my parents. At least my sister understood my desire to start my own bakery.

Looking at Mabel, I kept my thoughts about working at this ranch to myself. This job was only temporary. "Do you have specific menus for each day?"

"It's pretty routine. Breakfast with bacon, eggs, and either biscuits and gravy or flapjacks. Lunch is the heaviest meal and consists of meat, potatoes, beans, bread or rolls, vegetables, and dessert. Dinner might be leftovers, sandwiches, chili, and whatever else I throw in."

I got into the rhythm of making sourdough bread and set the loaves in the oven. "Mind if I take a break? I'd like to step outside for a moment."

"You don't have to ask."

Snagging a soda from the fridge, I popped the top and sat on the step sipping the cold, bubbly drink. This ranch went on forever. In the closest field, horses chased each other and kicked up their heels. Cattle marred the other fields like little black dots.

A cowboy rode off in the distance, and I wondered if it was Luke.

CHAPTER 21

LUKE

Goldi had been on the ranch for three days so far, and except for a little small talk at meals, I avoided making contact with her. Which was for the best. She'd be leaving soon.

Breakfasts were easy, being the busiest meal of the day with her running in and out of the kitchen. I assumed she took her meal either before or after we ate.

Lunch was a tad slower.

But dinners tended to be more casual with Goldi and Mabel joining us. People drifted in as they finished working. For the last few evenings, I noticed how friendly she acted with everyone, smiling, joking. Every so often she'd look my way. I had the hots for her, even when I knew I shouldn't.

Tonight, I came in with my brothers. After filling our plates at the side counter, Pete and Chase took the spots on the end, leaving the only seat right across from her.

"Hi," she said to me. "How've you been?"

"Good." I took a bite of my ham sandwich. I really should

have made lunch at my place. It would have been less tense for me. Still, I figured I should be polite. "Is your cottage okay?"

"Absolutely. The place is perfect."

"Got any plans for the weekend?" a cowboy asked. His smile was wide, easy, and way too familiar for my liking.

"I need to go to town tomorrow. That is if I can get someone to take me."

"I'll do it," a younger cowboy cut right in.

My gaze lingered on her. She looked even better than the first sunshine after a long winter.

"You can't. We're supposed to paint my sister's house. She did promise pizza," his friend said.

"I forgot."

Gritting my teeth, I warred with myself. Taking her meant being alone with her. But then I chimed in before another cowboy did. "I'll take you."

Bad idea. A very bad idea.

But then she grinned at me and my resolve crumbled. "That would be great."

I turned to her. "Where exactly do you plan to go?"

"The general store for staples, and maybe a little clothes shopping—if that's okay with you."

"As long as I'm back before two." I'd keep my time with her short.

"Works for me. Think we could leave at around eight or nine?"

"8:30 is fine."

"Deal." She headed toward the kitchen with an easy grace.

I tried to focus on finishing my dessert, but as each cowboy brought his plate to the kitchen, an irrational prick of annoyance hit me, as if each one were making excuses to talk to her again.

"You've got a date." Pete wiggled his eyebrows.

I shot him a glare. "It's a favor. Nothing more."

"Sure it is," Chase said.

The room became warm, the buzz of conversation too loud. I pushed back from the table, my chair scraping against the wooden floor. The screen door creaked as I stepped outside, the cool evening breeze a welcome respite from the stuffy dining room. I walked a few steps into the yard, my hands clenching and unclenching at my sides.

What the hell had I gotten myself into?

CHAPTER 22

GOLDI

Heading toward town, the truck's engine growled, reminding me of the owner. I glanced at him, taking in his rigid jawline and the deep furrow between his brows. "Are you scowling at me?"

Luke's eyes flicked in a mix of annoyance and something else I couldn't quite place. "I'm concentrating on the road."

"Oh, my mistake." A piece of hay stuck to his shoulder. I reached out to brush it away, my fingers grazing the rough fabric of his shirt. I let my hand linger, feeling the warmth of his skin through the material. "Can't have you looking like you just rolled out of the barn."

Luke's lips quirked into a reluctant smile. "I reckon not."

I reached into my bag, pulling out a small container of homemade chocolate chip cookies. "Want one?" I held the tin out to Luke. "Freshly baked this morning."

Our fingers brushed as he plucked a cookie from the tin. A jolt of electricity shot up my arm. I'd never experienced this kind of chemistry before. If he lived in L.A. I would go out with this hot cowboy. But here … I wasn't sure.

He took a bite. "You ever think about opening up a bakery?"

"My ex and I were supposed to invest in a shop." He'd even said he'd write up the contract. I'd envisioned a glass display with cupcakes, muffins, cookies, and specialty donuts. There'd be free WI-FI along with scattered tables where people could hang out. Now that he was out of the picture, my bakery dreams vanished.

"Why'd you leave?"

"It's complicated."

"Good answer," Luke said.

Maybe I should tell him my story, but I wasn't ready to talk about it yet. "Wanna play a game?"

He raised an eyebrow.

"Yeah. 'Would You Rather?' It'll be fun."

He grunted, which I took as a yes.

"Alright, cowboy. Would you rather... muck out stalls or listen to rock music?"

Luke actually chuckled. "That's not even a choice. Give me mucking any day."

I gasped in mock offense. "What's wrong with rock?"

"It's not country." He glanced my way for a second. "Would you rather go riding or bake cookies?"

"Ride."

"Really."

"Yes. As much as I love baking, I rarely get to ride. But I hope to remedy that while I'm staying on the ranch." With a bit of luck on my side, I'd do it later today since I didn't have work. "I'll ask Chase. He's very helpful."

He strangled the wheel with a white-knuckled grip. Okay, did that mean I'd unnerved him? Well, he could've offered to take me himself.

We crested a hill, and the town of Whispering Pines came into view. "Think Peggy will be working today?"

"Nope. She took the twins to a dance competition in Cheyenne."

"And you guys didn't go?"

"It's all day and lots of waiting around. After their first competition, the three of us opted for recitals only."

The Wolfe brothers were sweet to take an interest in their nieces. "That makes sense."

I opted to turn on my phone and send my mom a quick text that I was doing well and not to worry. Then I turned the cell off.

We turned off the highway, passing the Boot Scoot. "Do you guys ever go out dancing?"

"Occasionally." He shrugged and parked his truck near the back of the lot.

I used the step at the side to hop down, but Luke was there to offer his arm.

"Ever the gentleman."

"Yes, ma'am." He gave me a lop-sided grin.

We made our way inside the store and squeezed through the crowd, finding ourselves wedged into an aisle with canned goods and bags of flour. "I stocked that shelf with the help of Peggy."

"Did you now?"

I nodded. "Think you can add five bags of flour into the cart?"

"No problem." His muscles flexed as he hefted the twenty-five-pound bags into the bottom of the cart like they were as light as a candy bar.

"Show off." I longed to run my hands over those big strong biceps.

"If it ain't Luke Walker!" A burly man with a thick beard strode toward us.

Luke managed a nod.

"You must be Goldi. Heard you're quite the cook."

"She is." Luke's arm snaked around my waist, pulling me close. "If you'll excuse us, we've got things to do." He steered me away.

I blinked in surprise. I kind of liked having him close. On the next aisle over, I grabbed a hat off a mannequin. It was a pink cowboy hat with 'Princess' written in rhinestones on the brim. I plopped it on my head and struck a pose, grinning at Luke. "What do you think?"

"This one would match your boots." He handed me a child size hat covered with cowskin.

"Too bad it's not in my size. I'd so wear that." I bumped my hip against his.

"Maybe we can find one in the western shop down the street."

"I hope so. I'd like to buy a pair of boots and maybe a top while I'm there."

"We'd better hurry. The clock's ticking."

Going through my list, we walked through the store with a mission as I added cans, bags, and boxes. Soon, the cart was filled to the brim. "We're done."

Luke stashed the supplies in the back of the truck with ease. "Where to first?"

"The western store."

His hand hovered near the small of my back.

My boot heel caught on a loose plank, and I stumbled forward. "Shoot."

"Whoa there." His arms wrapped around me as he steadied me against that broad chest of his. "You all right, darlin'?"

"Fine, thanks to you," I purred, my hands resting on his biceps. With our faces inches apart, and his eyes intense as he stared at me, I waited for his lips to brush against mine.

But he stepped back, clearing his throat. "We should, uh... get going."

And just like that, the moment disappeared.

We entered Cattle Call Clothing. "I love your shop's name," I said to the clerk.

"Thanks. My grandmother came up with it. Can I help you with anything?"

"Boots. Maybe in pink or red or even black." I sat down and she measured my foot.

"Calf or full length?"

"I'd like to try both."

Luke went over to the hats and tried on a black Stetson. I fanned my face. Holy smokin' moly he looked good. "You have to buy that."

"Okay." He grinned at me.

The clerk brought out five pairs of boots. I tried on hot pink ankle ones with fringe and rhinestones.

I walked to the mirror and turned to the side. Too gaudy for my taste. "What do you think, Luke?"

He whistled. "You'd definitely make a statement in those."

"But they're not very practical." I tried on full length red ones, primrose ankles with rose embroidery, even a red and white pair. None of them seemed right. Then I slipped on calf length black boots with white embroidery along the top and sighed. "These are really comfortable." I walked to the mirror and checked them out. "They're perfect. I'll take them."

"I've got a hat to match." She grabbed one from a display.

I put it on and called, "I look like a real cowgirl."

"That you do." Luke stood behind me, flashing his dimples. "Put those on my bill."

"You don't have to do that."

"Consider it part of your salary." He pulled out his credit card.

"Thank you."

While the clerk rang up the sales, I browsed through the woman's western shirts. When in Wyoming, I might as well fit in. I picked out three tops, grabbed three pairs of wranglers in my size and paid for my purchase with some of the cash I'd brought with me from California.

"Ready to head back," Luke said, holding the door for me.

"You just made my day." And he had.

Shopping with a cowboy. Check that off on my Wyoming bucket list.

CHAPTER 23

LUKE

Saturday morning.

Taking Goldi to town yesterday had been a huge mistake. I'd come damn close to kissing her. The more I was around her, the more I wanted her.

I decided to take Tumbleweed out for a walk. He might not be as fast as he used to be, but he had a smooth gait.

As I entered the stables, I heard a feminine voice. "Hey, handsome. I bet you think you're the king of the place."

Rounding the corner along the stalls, I came to an abrupt halt. Goldi fed Tumbleweed oats out of her hand.

I should announce myself. Instead, I pressed against the wall and watched her.

"And you'd be right," she said, filling the barn with a calming hum. "You might not be impressed with a city girl like me. But you know what?" She paused, stroking his head. "You're secretly into the attention."

The stallion snorted, and she laughed.

"I can see right through you. Big, tough, and untouchable. You remind me of someone I know." She scratched behind his ear. "You're lucky. No schedules to keep. No family expectations. Just wide-open skies and fresh hay. Honestly? I'm a little jealous."

Goldi reached out, letting her hand hover near his neck. "We're not so different, you and me. Both trying to figure out how we fit in." She lowered her voice as if sharing a secret. "Between you and me, though, I think I like it here more than I should."

She might stay for a while, but I knew full well she'd leave—eventually.

The stallion nudged her shoulder gently, and she laughed again. "Okay. I'll stop being sappy. Just don't go telling anyone, alright? Can't have the whole ranch thinking I'm a softie."

I lingered in the shadows.

"One of these days, big guy, I'm going to talk Luke into letting me ride you."

"Is that right?" My voice echoed in the otherwise peaceful barn, sharper than I'd intended.

Goldi startled. "Luke, I didn't hear you come in." Her cheeks flushed pink as she brushed her hands on her jeans.

I should keep a distance from this woman, but Goldi always managed to draw me in. "You want to take Tumbleweed out?"

"I would." She put her hands on her hips as if challenging me.

"Hmmm. He is a lot taller than Honey," I said, seeing if she'd change her mind.

"Which would give me a different perspective of the ranch. Do you think I can handle him?"

"Probably. This fellow's getting on in years and is usually mellow on the trails. Still, I'd like to see how you handle him in the arena first."

"Is that an offer?"

I should tell her I was busy, but the hopefulness in those pretty green eyes of hers made it hard to refuse. "Yes, ma'am."

"Thank you. Should I grab the saddle I used on Honey?"

"Nope. I've got a different one for him."

Inside the tack room, I handed her the bridle and saddle pad and hefted the saddle on my shoulder. She sauntered toward the stall, and I tried not to watch how her—but failed.

"It's really nice of you to let me ride him?"

I opened a latch on the stall and led him out. "Keep away from his back legs. He been known to kick."

She hurried ahead of me. "What else should I know about him?"

I respected the fact that she asked. "His mouth is sensitive so be gentle with the reins."

She set the saddle pad on his back.

I added the saddle. "Watch his ears. If you're doing something that bothers him, he'll pin them back."

"Does that happen often?"

"Nope. Need a boost up?"

"Yes, please." She wiggled as she brought her leg over him. "I'm on top of the world."

I shook my head. "Are you a Titanic fan?"

"Who isn't?" She tossed her long braid behind her.

"Me." I shrugged. Over the years, Peggy and Grams had forced me to sit through plenty of romance movies. And to be fair, some of them weren't bad.

"I'm gonna lead you to the ring. It's safer that way."

She walked Tumbleweed around the arena, then shifted to a trot and finally a gallop. The damn woman looked way too confident.

She reined up, smiling. "How am I doing?"

"Okay."

"I'm better than okay. Come on, admit it. I'm ready to take him out on a trail."

"I don't know." I folded my arms.

She stopped near the gate and fluttered her eyelashes at me. "Please. I'll make you a batch of cookies. Whatever you like."

"You play dirty." The double innuendo made me think about sex and I diverted my thoughts to mucking out stalls.

"I make a mean peanut butter blossom or coconut macaroon." She glanced at me. "Or just plain old chocolate chip if you prefer."

My mouth watered at the idea of her cookies. "Make mine chocolate with chocolate chips and you've got a deal."

"You're on."

Dammit. I shouldn't be spending more time with her, but I couldn't help myself.

CHAPTER 24

LUKE

"Where's Stormy?" Goldi asked as I rode up to the arena on Duchess.

"It's his day off. He's most likely kicking it up with his friends."

She laughed. "Good for him."

I opened the gate, and we walked our horses to the trail. "Let's head for the water tower."

"Race you there?" She urged Tumbleweed into a gallop. Her body was in sync to the gait. My cock twitched. I concentrated on nudging my horse faster.

The water tower loomed tall. I tugged the reins, bringing my horse to a stop as Goldi dismounted ahead of me.

She was up to something.

"I bet the view is fantastic. I'm going up." She stood at the base of the tower, one hand gripping the ladder.

"Don't do it," I warned, my voice sharper than I intended.

"Relax. I'll be fine." She glanced over her shoulder with that damn grin of hers and put one foot on a rung. Metal groaned under her weight.

My chest tightened, and I swung off my horse, striding toward the base. "Please stop. It's not safe."

"There's a story here."

I hesitated, debating what to say. Since lying wasn't my style, I sighed and scuffed my boot against the dirt. "If you have to know, I broke my arm falling off that exact spot."

She turned to me. "Really."

"Yep. Pete dared me to climb to the platform."

"And you couldn't back down from a dare?"

"Not then. At ten, I thought I was invincible." Even now I hated to admit I'd been wrong. "Anyway, about halfway up to the platform, the rung I'd been holding onto snapped along with the one under my feet, sending a shower of rust cascading to the ground. My other hand scrambled for purchase, but it was too late."

"Did everything happen in slow motion?"

"Nope. Time sped as I hit the dirt with a bone-jarring thud." I took her hand. "Do you get why you shouldn't go up there?"

"Absolutely. Which arm?"

"The right."

She ran her fingers up and down and gave an extra squeeze for good measure. "It's healed just fine."

My breath hitched. I liked having her touch me a little too much.

"Did you get in trouble?"

"Nope. When I told my grandparents I'd fallen, they assumed it'd been from my horse."

"And you didn't bother correcting them."

"Hell, no. It was bad enough to be stuck with a cast for most of the summer, but I refused to get grounded for acting like an idiot."

"Good point." She pushed a stray lock of hair behind her ear. "I kept plenty of things away from my mom and dad."

"Like what?" She had a sneaky side. Who knew?

"Any assignment less than an A. Hanging out with a friend Mom didn't like. Breaking a family heirloom vase and gluing it back together." She glanced down at the ground. "The list goes on."

"So, the city girl isn't perfect." I bumped her shoulder.

"Not even a little bit." She seemed small and vulnerable, and a part of me longed to pull her into my arms and say everything would be okay.

But I didn't.

GOLDI

The next week flew by. If only I could FaceTime my sister but at least we could email. I even sent Mom an email saying I was staying on a ranch and loving it.

On my day off, I visited the stables and talked to each of the horses. I wouldn't mind riding Honey today. Except I couldn't just go out and get her. Not without asking permission.

I headed inside the tack room and breathed in the musky scent. Saddles were set on wall-mounted racks. Pads and blankets were neatly folded on shelves. Bridles hung with reins looped over the hooks. Bits were in labeled bins, with brushes, curry combs, hoof picks, and detanglers stored in cubbies.

In the back corner, I spotted an ornate women's side saddle on a wooden stand, its seat adorned with rich burgundy velvet. I ran my hand over the leather skirt and sides as I traced the tooled design of roses. "Whoever designed this saddle had talent." A board creaked, and I jumped.

"Sorry." Luke's tall form was silhouetted in the doorway, his saddle and bridle slung over one muscular arm. "Just putting these away." His muscles flexed as he lifted his gear in place.

I shouldn't stare, but holy hotcakes. This man's body made my core tingle. What would it be like to run my hands up and down every inch of that sexy body?

"Goldi?"

Shoot. He'd caught me gawking. What was I looking at before he came in? Right. I gestured toward the sawhorse. "What's the story behind this saddle?"

Luke's brow furrowed. "I think it belonged to my great-great-grandmother. She lived in New York City before marrying and moving out West."

"It's pretty. I just don't get how women rode sidesaddle."

A ghost of a smile flickered across his face. "I bet Great Grammy quit using it and rode astride the minute she arrived here."

"Works for me. Do you have any photos of her?"

"Probably somewhere around here." He turned to leave. His jeans hugged his butt. His shoulders filled out his flannel shirt. I shook my head.

Luke clearly wasn't interested in anything beyond basic politeness. Too bad because I wouldn't mind something more.

I walked toward the exit. The tip of my foot kicked a hard object, which moved, followed by a bang as the door slammed shut. "Oh." I jumped back, my heart beating a million times a minute.

He came over in two long strides, brushing past me to test the door. Grasping the handle, he gave it a firm tug. It didn't budge. He tried again, yanking harder. "Damn it," he muttered under his breath. "The latch must've caught."

"Sorry."

"No worries." He reached for the radio clipped to his belt and fiddled with the dials. "Damn. It's not working. Battery must be dead."

I pulled my phone out of my pocket. "There's not even a single bar." I tapped at the screen. Nothing changed. "Looks like we're stuck for a while."

"Appears that way."

"What will we do?" I wouldn't mind sharing another kiss.

He jiggled the handle again. "Wait until someone comes. It might be a while." His eyes locked onto mine, intense and steady. "This isn't my first rodeo being locked in here."

"Really?"

"Yep. Chase loves a good prank." He snatched a blanket and spread it on the floor. "Have a seat, and I'll tell you all about it."

"Okay." I lowered myself to the ground, and he eased next to me.

"Well ... I was playing hide-and-seek in the stables with my brothers and came in here. Chase was counting to ten when the door closed on me. I called out. Thinking back, I'm pretty sure Chase peeked."

"How long were you stuck?"

"It seemed like hours, but I don't know. Anyway, Sam found me. I said blame it on Chase, and he just shook his head."

"I like Sam. He's nice."

"We're lucky to have him." He took my hand in his.

"As a kid I also liked to hide. Behind the curtains, in the closet, under the bed."

"And?" He raised a brow.

"I'd been about four or five when I took the toys out and

climbed into an old toy chest. I couldn't get out because of a latch."

"Obviously, someone found you."

"My mom. I can still see her scowl." I shivered, rubbing my arms to generate some warmth.

"You cold?" He sighed and scooted closer, draping an arm around my shoulders.

I leaned into his warmth. "Not anymore."

"You're pretty special." His voice came out like melted chocolate. Rich, smooth, and sinfully tempting. His eyes darkened as he gazed at me with a shattering intensity. "I can't fight this thing between us anymore." His hand cupped my cheek. His lips collided with mine, warm and inviting.

My fingers curled into the fabric of his shirt, drinking in the heat of him. His tongue traced the seam of my mouth, sweeping inside. He stoked a fire burning within me. I became a mass of blazing embers, sizzling and hissing with a desperate desire.

Footsteps sounded from outside.

He pulled away, leaving me longing for more. "Shhh." Pressing his lips against my earlobe, he breathed hot air onto my skin. Shivers made me squirm against him. "Looks like the cavalry just arrived." His tone came out a bit harsh as he helped me to my feet.

The door opened with a thwack and banged against the wall. "Luke? Goldi?"

"We got stuck in here," Luke said.

Pete just smirked. "You guys all right?"

"Just peachy."

"Good to hear."

"I'll walk you out," Luke said, his hand on the small of my back and led her away. "I like you, Goldi. More than I should."

"Back at you cowboy." Something fundamental had shifted between us. This wasn't just attraction or a fleeting spark. This was the beginning of something deeper, something that both thrilled and terrified me. After what happened with Mark, I was surprised at how easily I'd moved on. Which proved to me that we had never been a good match from the start.

"You interested in having steak dinner at my place?" His thumb traced my cheekbone.

"Yes, please." If I were lucky there'd be kissing and more. "What time?"

"Four?"

"Perfect."

He tugged me back toward him, crashing his lips onto mine as if staking a claim on me and my heart. "I'll pick you up."

Instead of overthinking what happened, I opted to just savor this moment.

CHAPTER 26

GOLDI

Seated outside on the patio at Luke's place eating dinner, I could see the entire valley. "I love the view." I crossed my legs and my short sundress inched up.

Luke's gaze flicked to my legs, lingering for a heartbeat before he snapped his eyes back up to meet mine.

"Like what you're seeing?"

"Yep." He sipped his beer.

I wanted him. Wanted to kiss him. Wanted to see where this night might go.

"You aren't hungry?" He motioned to my plate.

I am for you, I almost said. Instead, I took a bite of steak letting my eyes flutter closed as I savored the flavor. "Yum. Is that hickory I taste?"

"I used hickory chips in the grill. Have you ever done that?"

"Not yet. You'll have to show me how." And show me other sexy things like kissing me senseless.

A rooster crowed in the distance. "I think Roostifer's calling you," Luke said.

"As long as he doesn't greet me with his talons, I'm fine with him."

"I'll remind him to be nice when I see him tomorrow morning."

"Good luck with that." My voice came out huskier than I intended.

"I'm curious. Did you inherit your baking skills from your mom?"

"Nana. She had a knack for mixing ingredients together. As a little girl, I thought she mixed magic into her dough. Later, I learned the freshest ingredients made the difference."

"You were lucky to have her."

"I was. I wish I'd spent more time with her. But she knew I loved her." I found my eyes tearing up.

"What about your sister? Is she as good as you at baking?"

"Not really. She's more analytical. Which makes her a great attorney."

"I get the feeling you two are close."

"We are. She's my best friend." I finished the last bite of my food and set my napkin on the table. "Thanks for the delicious meal."

"It's my pleasure, darlin'." His gaze lingered on me, causing warmth to shoot straight to my core. I shifted in my seat.

We moved inside. "Wanna watch a movie? I've got DVDs and some old videos."

"Okay."

"Pick whatever you like."

"From westerns, actions, or horror, right?"

"There's a couple of Peggy's chick flicks along with a few of my nieces' movies."

"I can't see you watching Disney."

"I'll have you know I've seen my share of princesses." He stared at the floor. "I've also been known to wear a tiara on occasion."

A snicker slipped out.

"What?" He shrugged. "The twins can be quite persuasive and not just with me. Once they talked Pete into wearing wings and forced him to attend a pixie tea party."

"But not you?"

"Luckily, I was out of town."

"Meaning you would have joined them." Luke was an enigma wrapped in a flannel shirt and faded jeans. "Have they talked you into doing anything else?"

"I've already given up my man card. Isn't that enough?"

"Fine, but in exchange for dropping the subject, make popcorn. And snag me another beer?"

"Or." He inched in closer. "I could pour you a shot of whiskey."

"Are you trying to get me drunk?"

"Would that be wrong?" His eyes darkened to a smoldering shade of rich honey.

"Not at all. But make mine a whiskey sour."

"You'll have to help me with that one. What's in it?"

"Whiskey, lemon juice, sugar, water."

"Sweet but not too fancy. It sounds good."

His deep voice caused my body to quiver. "I'll fix our drinks." I got up and found two jelly jar glasses that were the perfect size and set a bottle of whiskey next to them. "Can you find me a pitcher?"

"Sure." He handed me a decanter, the brush of our skin igniting sparks which danced up my arms. He retrieved an air popper from a cabinet.

"Most people use a microwave."

"I'm not like most people." He added kernels and got a large bowl to put under the machine.

"You're not so bad, cowboy."

"You're not either—for a city girl."

Snatching three lemons from inside the crisper drawer, I juggled them to show off. I lost my flow and dropped two.

"I saw that."

"Nothing gets past you, does it?"

"About that you're wrong. You see this lady snuck into my house ..." He bumped my shoulder. "But she turned out to be really pretty."

"Aww." Squeezing lemons through a strainer into the pitcher, I added water and several spoons of sugar, stirred with a spoon, tasted it. "Now for my secret ingredient."

"What is that?"

"Promise you won't tell anyone." I placed my hand on his shoulder as he melted butter on a burner.

"I promise."

"A dash of egg whites." I cracked an egg, separating the whites from the yolks. "Would Charlie like this?"

His eyes traveled down my body. Then he took the shell from me and poured the yolk into the doggy bowl. "Here you go, boy."

A man and his dog. The way he cared for him made me sigh.

Adding whiskey and the sweet lemon mixture, I topped the glasses off with a zest of lemon. "You're gonna love this." I set the drinks on the coffee table. "About the movies."

"In the drawer under the TV."

This was different. I'd gotten used to streaming everything. "*Pride and Prejudice* or *Barbie*?"

He groaned.

"Here's an oldie. What about *Jerry Maguire*?"

"Fine." His pinched mouth said it wasn't one of his favorites. As a kid, I'd seen it countless times with my dad because he loved the line, "Show me the money!"

I slid the DVD into the player, pushed play, shifted close to him on his couch, and crossed my legs. I could have sworn I heard him growl.

He took a sip of his drink. "This is good."

"Told you." I patted his thigh, letting my hand linger on the solid muscle beneath denim. Cowboy, through and through.

His arm slid around my shoulders, pulling me closer. I scooted forward, reaching for popcorn, trying to distract myself from him.

"Goldi?" His voice broke through my thoughts.

"Shh." I pretended to be enthralled in the movie. It was safe, familiar, and required absolutely no emotional investment.

"Admit it, you're not even watching this."

"It's the part where she realizes she loves him but won't admit it. Classic." As if I had a clue what just happened.

"Sounds complicated." He shifted to face me, his knee brushing against mine. His thumb lifted my chin urging me to meet his gaze. He edged nearer, his mouth hovering close to mine as if drawn by an invisible force

The heck with this. I pressed my lips against his and flicked out my tongue, running it against the seam of his mouth. He tasted like sweetness and whiskey.

"Yum." He tugged me closer, igniting a fire that spread warmth through my entire being. Our kisses grew more heated in a deliberate and intoxicating dance. Without missing a beat, he pulled me onto his lap. I craved his touch and arched my back.

He pulled back, his eyes glazed with desire.

I found myself panting. "Holy smokes. That was…" More than I'd ever expected.

He took my hand in his. "I think it's best we stop now."

"What if I don't want to stop?"

"It's getting late." He pressed a kiss to my forehead.

Darn sensible cowboy.

"Have any plans for tomorrow afternoon?"

"Besides collecting eggs, and picking vegetables, nothing. Why?"

"Wanna go riding?" His lips quirked up in a sexy grin.

"Absolutely. Are we heading for the same place?"

"Nope." His grin widened. "I know somewhere where we can swim."

Luke with water dripping off his abs. That's a show I wouldn't mind seeing.

"Bring your swimsuit."

"I don't have one."

He brought his lips to mine again for a brief kiss. "You're welcome to check the dresser drawers in the guest room."

CHAPTER 27

LUKE

Sunlight glittered off Goldi's hair as she walked toward the stables wearing black jeans and a tight-fitting T-shirt.

"Hey, beautiful." I tipped my hat, trying to play it cool.

She placed a kiss on my cheek.

"You can do better than that." Closing the distance between us, I snaked an arm around her, tugging her against me. Capturing her soft lips, I kissed her until she melted into me, hands fisting my shirt. When we finally broke apart, breathing heavily, her eyes glazed with desire which sent my blood racing south. I liked her way more than I should. "Ready to ride?"

"Absolutely." She ran her tongue along her lips, tempting me to bring my mouth back to hers. "I'm more than ready for that swim."

"So am I." Did she have any idea what she did to me? Soon, she'd be in a swimsuit—preferably a bikini.

I assisted her to mount Honey, my hands lingering a moment longer than necessary. Then I swung up onto Stormy.

With a click of my tongue, we set off on an easy trot into the pastures, side by side. We took the path to the east and veered north.

"Who owns that house?" She pointed at the two-story home on the other side of the barbed wire fence.

"Roy Hood and his family."

"I love the mix of natural stone, wood, and picture windows. It must give them a view of the whole valley. Are they nice?"

"They're great neighbors. Andy and I used to compete in junior rodeo. We're the same age."

"Do you see him much?" She continued along the path.

"Not very often. He went pro and is on the rodeo circuit most of the year."

"It must have been wonderful growing up on a ranch." Her voice sounded wistful.

"Most of the time—except for the chores every day when I'd rather be out riding or fishing or just fooling around."

We galloped north along the trail through fields dotted with wildflowers and cattle.

"This is incredible," she called. "What breed are those cattle?"

"Black Baldy. It's a mix of Hereford and Angus."

"What's the reason for crossbreeding?"

"Better meat quality."

"If your steaks are anything to go by, I totally approve." She gave me an impish grin.

We crested a hill. I pointed out the cove nestled in a grove of cottonwood trees. "That's our swimming hole."

And with that, she urged her horse into a gallop, leaving me in the dust.

Letting out a whoop, I kneed my mount forward. My heart

pounded with the thrill of the chase. I passed her and slid off my saddle. "Even though you gave yourself a head start, I won."

"Your horse might be faster." She rubbed her mare's neck. "But Honey is sweeter."

"You're right about that. She's the perfect match for you." I stretched out a hand and helped Goldi dismount.

She kicked off her boots and wiggled her toes in the grass. "This feels amazing." Then she stripped down to a bright pink bikini.

I couldn't take my eyes off her. "You're so fucking hot."

"You coming in?" She glanced over her shoulder at me.

Shaking myself out of a daze, I got down to my swim trunks and waded until I was chest deep.

Goldi dipped under the surface and came up with a gasp. Droplets streamed down her body. Then she dove back under and swam across to the other side of the cove.

I went under and popped up a few feet in front of her.

"You scared me." She scooped water in her hands and splashed me.

"You're gonna pay for that." I would have dunked her, but she squirmed away and glided through the water.

We swam around each other. I closed in on her, caging her with my arms. Water droplets clung to her lashes and slid down her pink cheeks. "Goldi," I rasped, pushing a damp curl behind her ear. "You have no idea what you do to me."

Her eyes darkened, lips parted. "Show me."

Unable to hold back, I brought her body flush against me, lowered my head and captured her lips in a slow, sensual kiss. She opened for me. Our tongues tangled as the kiss grew more heated.

I forced myself to slow down, to savor each moment, as I traced my mouth along her jaw, tasting her. She tipped her head back, giving me better access. I trailed open-mouthed caresses down the elegant column of her neck before finding a sensitive spot below her ear. She whimpered.

Crashing my lips against hers, I was hot and desperate and aching for more. My hands roamed her body, memorizing every curve, every dip, as if I'd been waiting my entire life for this very moment.

She arched into me, whispering my name.

I broke the kiss, panting as I stood in water up to my chest, staring into her eyes. "What do you want, darlin'?"

"More."

My fingers found their way to the back of her bikini top. I untied it, unveiling her perfect breasts. Gently cupping one in my hand, I took the discarded top and tossed it carelessly onto the grassy shore.

Her hands traced patterns on my back as she pressed closer to me. The heat of our kisses intensified. I pushed my hardness against her, showing her the effect she had on me.

She shivered. "I need you."

I scooped her up in my arms and we stumbled onto the bank, our lips glued together.

"Hold on a second." With my mind in a haze, I moved away from her toward our horses who munched on grass. I grabbed a quilt out of the saddlebag and tossed her a towel.

"You always so prepared?"

"Yep. Earned my Eagle Scout badge." I grabbed my jeans and found a condom in my wallet.

"Of course you did." She laughed a little huskier than usual.

I spread the quilt over the grass and pulled her down beside me, drinking in every inch of exposed skin. "This doesn't seem real."

"Kiss me again and find out."

Lowering my mouth to hers, I poured every ounce of pent-up longing into our kiss. She returned my passion with her own.

My hands ran along heated skin. I couldn't get enough of her taste, her scent, her very essence. I eased down her bikini bottom and slipped a finger inside. Holy shit, she was warm and ready.

Goldi moaned into my mouth, her nails digging into my back.

"You like that." I added another finger.

She squirmed. "Please, Luke."

I smiled against her mouth. "Just relax and enjoy."

"Patience isn't one of my strong suits."

"That's not true. You've already proved you can be very patient with Roostifer. And that's not an easy skill." I feathered kisses against her neck.

"It's more like self-preservation, and you know it."

"I suppose. You're so sexy. I have to taste you." I went back to her mouth, kissing her.

I knelt between her legs. My tongue went against in her slit, savoring her. The little sounds and moans of pleasure she made drove me on, and my thumb hit her clit. "Come for me, darlin'."

She let go. Her body shook as wave after wave of pleasure washed over her. And I continued watching her until her breathing slowed.

Gripping her ass, I ground my erection against her, the swim trunks the thinnest of barriers against my intention.

She grasped my shirt. "Don't stop now."

"Tell me what you want."

"You, inside me, now."

"Who am I to argue with such a pretty lady?" I tore off my swim trunks. My dick sprung to attention like it had a goddamn mind of its own, hard as steel and throbbing.

She eyed me appreciatively and licked her lips. "Yum."

"Like what you see?" Full of need, I fumbled with the condom.

"Let me." The wrapper crinkled as she tore it open, rolling the latex down my shaft with a maddeningly light touch. I groaned, my hips bucking forward involuntarily, desperate for more of her.

I grabbed her by the hips and flipped her onto her back, plunging into her mouth to claim her. Her moan vibrated against my lips, and I was already lost in her taste.

Positioning myself between her legs, my cock brushed against her slick folds, and I paused just for a moment, enjoying the way she shuddered beneath me. "Ready for me, darlin'?"

She nodded.

"I like a woman who knows what she wants." I got lost in the pleasure soaring through my body.

"Faster," she cried.

My hips snapped forward, driving myself deeper into her. I couldn't think, couldn't breathe, all I could do was fuck her like my life depended on it.

"You feel so good." I slammed into her harder and deeper.

Her inner muscles clenched around me. My fingers found her clit and rubbed it in tight circles.

"Luke!" She screamed my name, her body convulsing around me as she came, her pleasure intensifying my own.

I wasn't far behind, as I buried myself deep inside her and let go, filling the condom with my release.

I rolled to the side and pulled her against me, my chest heaving, my cock still twitching inside her. "That was—"

"Phenomenal," she whispered, her breath hot against my ear.

"Yep," I agreed, my arms tightening around her. She'd be leaving in a few weeks, but right now she remained here with me. "Stay at my place tonight."

"Okay." She nestled into my side with a contented hum. I wrapped my arms around her, holding her tight, determined to keep her with me for as long as I could.

CHAPTER 28

GOLDI

The alarm went off and I awoke with a start. A warm body pressed against my backside. Holy sugarplums. I'd slept with Luke yesterday. A lot.

At the lake. Against the back of his living room couch. His bed. The man was insatiable, and I loved every minute.

"Morning, darlin'." Luke nipped the sensitive part of my ear, making me squirm under his touch.

"I have to go home and change before work." I tried to pull away, but he wouldn't let go.

"You can be late. I know someone who won't mind."

"Not Mabel."

"Shower sex then? I'll make it worth your while." Luke's voice came out all gravel and heat, eyes dark and predatory.

Honestly, I wouldn't mind another orgasm. "Fine."

The man didn't waste a second. He scooped me up like I weighed nothing. The tile might be cold when he set me down, but his hands were warm as they skimmed my hips, my waist, trailing up to my breasts as if he memorized every inch of me.

"You're sexy, city girl." His lips nibbled along my neck. My core quivered, my pussy already slick and aching for him.

The water came on, steam rising around us as Luke reached for the soap. His hands were everywhere, slick and slippery as he lathered up my body. He started with my shoulders, kneading the tension from my muscles before sliding down to my breasts. My nipples hardened under his touch, and he pinched one lightly, making me gasp.

"Like that?" his voice dripped with smug satisfaction. His hands slid lower, over my stomach, my hips, and then between my legs. His fingers found my clit, circling it with just the right amount of pressure to make me moan.

"Luke." His fingers teased my entrance, dipping inside briefly before retreating, driving me wild with anticipation.

"Patience, darlin'," he purred, his lips brushing against my neck as he withdrew his fingers. I heard the tear of the condom wrapper, then he pressed himself against me, his erection nudging at my ass as his hands gripped my hips.

"I'm going to fuck you hard." He practically rumbled.

"Yes, please." My voice came out like a low whisper.

His cock sunk into me, the heat of him filling me as the water cascaded over us. My moans and his low growls of pleasure echoed off the tiled walls. His hands gripped my hips, sliding between my legs to rub my clit in time with his strokes, each move deliberate and deep.

"Come for me," he demanded, finding the spot inside me that made stars burst behind my eyelids.

And I did, my body tightening around him as wave after wave of pleasure crashed over me.

He wasn't far behind, following me over the edge, pulsing inside me.

We stayed like that for a moment, both of us breathing hard, the water cooling around us.

His hands were gentle now, smoothing over my skin as he pressed a kiss to my shoulder. "What a perfect way to start the morning."

"Cocky much?" I asked.

He responded with a deep, searing kiss.

Needless to say, after changing at home, I ended up twenty minutes late. As I stepped inside, I found Mabel in the kitchen.

She smiled at me. "How was your weekend?"

"Good." I put my apron on, grabbed a cup of coffee, and got out flour and butter to start on the biscuits.

"What'd you end up doing?"

"I took a ride out to the lake." My face heated when I recalled swimming with Luke and what we did. I concentrated on cutting the dough and setting the circles into the oven.

"By yourself?"

"With Luke."

"Oh."

A couple of cowboys strolled in, which meant there'd be little chitchat. Thank goodness. For the next hour, I rushed around, setting out orange juice, making more coffee, and frying up potatoes.

After placing the last plate in the dishwasher, I practically fell into the kitchen chair. Holy hotcakes, I was tired. A wild night would do that to a person.

"Knock, knock. It's Auburn. I come bearing gifts." She strolled in and placed her Stetson on a hook. With her hair up in a high ponytail and the smattering of freckles across the bridge of her nose, I found her strikingly beautiful.

"Come right in," Mabel said. "Have you met Goldi yet?"

"Can't say I have. But your cookies are infamous around here." She held out her hand and gave me a firm grip. "I heard about your car. When do you think it'll be fixed?"

"Maybe this week or next." The idea of leaving made my stomach clench. But I didn't belong here. Not really.

"What'd you bring?" Mabel asked, taking me out of my doldrums.

"Cinnamon twists." Her blue eyes sparkled.

"Perfect timing. We were about to take a break." Mabel motioned us to the table.

I helped myself to a pastry. "This is delicious."

"Cook's secret recipe."

"One she refuses to share. Believe me I've asked." Mabel placed her hands on her hips.

"She's stubborn that way. But I love her anyway." Auburn tilted her head. "Have you heard any good gossip?"

"Besides Old Joe's cow getting loose and wandering into town, I've got nothing." Mabel chuckled.

"This must all seem pretty boring to you, Goldi."

"Not at all. The whole town is charming. What was it like growing up around here? I would have loved the freedom."

"I used to sneak over to this very kitchen and visit with Grandma Wolfe. Peggy and I helped her make snickerdoodles and got to lick the bowl."

"Where were the Wolfe brothers?" I asked.

"Most likely outside working with Pops. Ornery as all get out, but he was a marshmallow underneath. Plus, the man knew horses. The boys learned a lot from him. As much as Peggy liked to ride, she usually finagled a way out of her chores."

"That's our princess." Mabel turned to me. "Auburn, Peggy, and Judy, who lives kitty-corner from here at the Double J, used to cause plenty of mischief."

"We were angels compared to the boys."

Mabel snorted.

"We never snuck into the county fair after hours." Auburn smiled. "And Luke dared Chase to get inside the cotton candy machine."

"His mom and I worked out the sugary residue in his hair using mineral oil." Mabel sighed.

"Do these guys ever turn down a dare?" I asked.

"Maybe now, but as a kid Pete talked his brothers into doing just about anything," Mabel said. "It's surprising they all survived."

"Their mother was a saint. Did you know she used to teach English at the high school?" Auburn asked.

"I did not." I knew little about his life.

"I'd better get going. Training Diablo is turning into quite a challenge." Auburn shook her head. "He's the new stallion we just got."

"If anyone can tame him, it's you." Mabel held admiration in her gaze.

She shrugged. "We'll see."

"You could always ask Pete for some pointers."

"I can handle the stallion myself just fine." Auburn's eyes glinted. "It's nice meeting you, Goldi."

"You, too."

"Both of you have an open invitation to stop over at the Triple R for sweet tea."

"I'll keep that in mind."

Auburn settled her Stetson on her head and flashed a smiled before she left..

"I like her."

"So do I." Mabel stood up. "We'd better get started on supper."

"Yes, ma'am." I saluted her, enjoying her laughter.

CHAPTER 29

GOLDI

If anyone had told me last month I'd be working on a ranch as a baker, sleeping with my ultra hunky cowboy boss, and loving every minute, I would tell that person they were totally certifiable.

But it happened. And I'd never been happier.

Tonight, I rode in the backseat of Pete's crew truck with Luke's arm around me. "I can't believe you're taking me dancing."

"Actually, all the Wolfe brothers are bringing you," Chase said, sitting shotgun.

"Thanks for the clarification." We reached the outskirts of town. My phone screen lit up with the pings of multiple messages.

"You're mighty popular," Pete called back.

"I doubt it." I turned to Luke. "Do you mind if I check them?"

"Have at it."

There were some unknown numbers. Probably spam. I saw a text from Mark and winced.

"You okay?" Luke asked.

"It's my idiot ex."

"Tell him I say to go to hell from me," he whispered in my ear.

"He doesn't deserve the effort." Which was true enough. I'd emailed my sister over the past few days, but it would be nice to get an instant response now that I had a signal. "I'm going to text my sister."

He placed his hand on my thigh, and I reveled in his touch.

Fighting the urge to kiss him, I bit my bottom lip and typed.

Me: Going dancing at the Boot Scoot. Wish you could join us.

Sis: So do I. M stopped by this morning and is driving me bananas. I said you're off at some ranch retreat with practically no reception. How much longer will you be there?

Me: Another week maybe?

Luke tugged me closer and whispered, "I missed you today."

"You saw me in the morning."

"That was hours ago."

"Shh. Let me finish with my sister."

"I don't mind as long as you promise I'll have your attention for the rest of the evening."

"You're incorrigible, Luke Wolfe."

"Yep." He brushed his lips against my cheek.

I went back to my phone.

Sis: Send a selfie of you and your cowboy.

Me: Will do.

"Smile." I told Luke as I held up my phone and put the other arm around his shoulder. I clicked and showed him the picture.

"What do you think?"

"That you're too pretty for words." He brought his lips to mine, warm and oh so delicious.

Sis: You two make a cute couple. Heart shape.

Me: Thumbs up. Gotta go. I'm texting Mom. Email you tomorrow.

Sis. You'd better.

"I'm going to update my mom." I took in a deep breath.

"Relax. It'll be fine." He massaged my shoulder.

Not bothering to read her text, I opened up a new window.

Me: Hey, Mom. I'm still at a ranch. Besides riding horses, I'm baking. For me this is paradise. I'm doing well and plan to come home in a week or two. I love you.

"It's sent." I shut off my phone.

He brought his lips to mine and gave me a slow kiss, reducing my stress.

"We're here," Pete said.

"That's one way to cool the mood." Luke's breath tickled my neck.

We really shouldn't be making out in the backseat like teenagers.

Pete squeezed his crew cab truck into an empty spot in the back of the parking lot.

I took a photo of the Boot Scoot sign and slipped my phone into my pocket. "Will I get to two-step?" I learned that dance at the Buckshot Saloon.

"Yep." Luke helped me out of the truck and eyed me from top to bottom. "You look gorgeous tonight."

"And you're smokin', cowboy." Black button-down shirt. Jeans. White Stetson. His scent a mix of leather and spice.

"Thank you, ma'am. Did you just sniff me?"

"Maybe." I focused on the truck next to us. "Its gigantic tires come up to my shoulders. I would need an extra-long ladder to get inside."

"You know I'd help you up," Luke said.

"Only because you like having your hands on my butt," I whispered to him.

"Can't help it. You've got a fine ass." He showed off those darn dimples and my heart beat a little faster.

"That's Randy's truck. Rampage Renegade competes in monster truck shows," Pete chimed in.

"I picture a burly guy with lots of tattoos. Am I right?"

"He's tall, skinny. No tattoos, but he's got a nose ring," Chase said.

"Point him out if you see him."

"Will do."

We made our way to the front door. I walked into the bar with three hot cowboys. When was the last time I did that? Never.

With Luke's hand in mine, we headed for a table. Ever the gentlemen, he held out a chair for me.

A country western song about a spurned woman played. Weeks ago with the fresh sting of betrayal, it might have bothered me. Now I figured my loser of an ex did me a favor. Thinking back, there had always been something missing in our relationship. I'd been attracted. We had fun at first. The sex decent, but compared to the fireworks with Luke, Mark was a dud.

"Hey, boys." A pretty brunette with long hair tied back in a ponytail came up to us. "Who's your friend?"

"This is Goldi," Luke told her, and said to me, "Claire and I went to school together."

"Nice to meet you." Claire smiled at me.

"Same here." I tapped back the twinge of jealousy that twisted my stomach.

"What would everyone like?" She got out her pen.

"Longnecks." Pete spoke for everyone.

"Got it." She scurried off.

"Is she one of your exes?" I had to ask.

Luke placed his arm around the back of my chair. "Chase's. But now she's married to the fire chief."

Relieved, I refused to let out a sigh. My eyes caught on the mounted moose head above me. "Don't you feel the least bit guilty staring into Bullwinkle's eyes?"

"They're made of glass." Pete chuckled.

"But his head is real. And look over there. It's Bambi." I shuddered.

"This is Wyoming. We hunt. It's really no different than buying beef in a store," Luke said.

"I don't mount a cow's head in my living room."

"We don't hunt cows." Chase laughed.

"Your point's taken. I'll do my best to ignore the walls and enjoy the bar." After all, I came here to dance and let loose.

A gorgeous redhead came up to us and I recognized her as Auburn. "If it isn't the Wolfe brothers. Good to see you guys again." Her eyes darted toward Pete.

He glared at her, which seemed odd. He'd always been nice to me.

"I'd like you to meet Goldi Summers. She's working at Sunrise Ridge while her car gets fixed," Luke said.

"We've met. Great seeing you again." She held out her hand and gave me a rather firm shake.

"Same here."

Chase waved, Luke smiled, Pete folded his arms and squinted his eyes.

"Gotta go." She nodded and left.

"Why don't you like her?" I arched an eyebrow at Pete. "She seems nice."

His lips curled into a tight line as he glanced across the bar at the group of women that included Auburn. "Red can be a real pain."

"Only to you." Luke tilted forward in his chair. "Everyone else gets along with her."

"I'm gonna play pool. You coming, Chase?" Pete rose with a huff.

"Nope."

As Pete walked off, I asked, "What's up with him and Auburn?"

"Ever since they were kids, they've always tried to one-up each other." Chase settled back in his chair.

"I think it started with mutton busting." Luke turned to me. "That's when five-and-six-year-olds ride sheep."

"I've seen the clips on TikTok. Those kids are adorable." I tried to picture Luke as a five-year-old. He'd probably been hot even then.

"Anyway, Auburn won. Pete took third. He was livid."

"Weren't you guys too young to remember?"

"I was almost three. I remember because he threw a tantrum when he got home. In my mind, he was too old for that."

"Gramps used his mutton busting video to show what not to do. I've seen it plenty of times." Chase shrugged.

"That must suck for Pete. But there has to be more to this

rivalry."

"Auburn beat Pete in roping. Pete beat Auburn in barrel racing. They both ran for class president their junior year and Auburn won. Pete became president their senior year. It's gone on like that for years. It doesn't help that he calls her Red, which she hates." Luke chuckled.

"I wish the two of them could make amends." Chase had this faraway look in his eyes.

"Or screw. We all see it coming." Luke snickered.

Chase's phone chirped. "Peggy texted me and said she'll be here within the hour."

"I can't wait to see her again. I like your sister."

Luke twined his fingers between mine. "If you'll excuse us, I owe Goldi a dance." His eyes darkened, igniting a flutter in my chest.

He brought me to the dance floor, sliding his hand along my shoulder while his left hand took mine. The fast tempo matched my heartbeat. He spun me and twirled me back into his arms.

"You're a good dancer."

"So are you." His deep voice sent thrills down my spine all the way to my core.

We promenaded side by side. I waved to Tim as he danced near us. "Is that his wife?"

"Sure is."

"How many of your relatives live around here?"

"More than I can count. Wolfe's Crossing Ranch is north of Sunrise Ride. Other relatives own businesses in town. Most of my mom's family settled in Montana."

"Your family reunions must be wild."

"They can be."

I figured they were way better than the stuffy affairs my sister and I suffered through. Not paying attention to where I was going, I turned the wrong way and stepped on his toe.

"Careful, darlin'." He hauled me closer and whispered into my ear, "This is more like it."

The song ended, and he released me.

"Thank you," I said, slightly out of breath.

"The pool table's empty. Ever play before?" Luke's voice sounded as smooth as whiskey.

"I haven't. But I'd like to try."

"I'll be happy to show you the basics." His intense gaze zapped heat throughout my body. "Care to make a friendly wager?"

"Ten dollars enough?"

"How about the winner decides?"

"You'll regret that." My competitive streak kicked in. "When you lose, you'll be washing dishes all week."

"Not gonna happen." He stood and offered his hand, guiding me to an open table. Arranging the balls inside a form, he lifted the plastic triangle off. The colorful balls stayed in a perfect triangle. "Grab a stick off the wall."

I wrapped my hand around a cue, feeling the weight, and chose it.

He stepped behind me, his body close. Placing his hands over mine, I got caught up in the feel of him. "Keep your grip firm but not too tight. When you take the shot, aim for that solid one."

"Got it." I shot the cue ball, and it hit its target, scattering the others. Two solids rolled into pockets.

He whistled. "Beginner's luck."

Taking another try, I missed. "Your turn. Let's see what you've got."

He snagged his own stick from the top of a rack and took his shot. The cue ball clacked, and three balls found their pockets. He glanced up, grinning. "Not bad, right?"

"Show-off," I muttered, admiring his skill. He was good, but I wasn't about to go down without a fight. During my turn again, I wiggled my hips as I lined up my shot.

Luke groaned softly. "You're mighty distracting."

"That's the point."

The cue ball skipped off the table and smacked into the leg of a guy playing at the next table.

"Sh-sh-sugarplum," I gasped.

A tall, lanky man scooped the ball off the floor. "Luke, did you do that?"

"Nope." He pointed at me.

"Sorry," I said. I had to look way up at the bearded man, who seemed familiar.

"It's no big deal, ma'am."

"Uncle Alex, this is Goldi."

"We've met, but never formally. My shop's next to the general store."

"I remember you. A. Wolfe Realty. What a great name."

"I think so. Next time you guys come in, stop by and I'll take you to lunch."

"You're on." Luke bumped his fist.

"There's a beer calling my name. See you guys later." Alex went back to his game.

Luke stepped behind me and brushed a kiss on my cheek. "I

can't wait to get you home."

"What about the bathroom? I've never had sex in one before." I placed my hand over my mouth. Was I becoming an exhibitionist?

His grin widened. "Neither have I. Come on. There's a private one in back."

I didn't ask how he knew this. Just allowed him to lead me on toward the front entrance and down the hall.

"Luke, Goldi," a woman's voice called from behind us.

I turned to see Peggy waving. She stood next to a tall dark-haired man in a sheriff's uniform.

"Of all the fucking timing," Luke grumbled in my ear.

"You poor cowboy." And walked over to Peggy, giving her a hug. "It's good to see you again."

She stepped back. "Henry, this is Goldi."

"Nice to meet you." I shook his hand.

The guy had the bluest eyes. For such a small town, the ratio of good-looking men was ridiculous.

Peggy glanced at my footwear. "Are those my old boots?"

"I borrowed them from Luke's closet. I hope you don't mind."

"Not at all. I used to hate them, but on you they look good with your black jeans."

"Thank you, I think."

"Achy Breaky Heart" played. Peggy took my arm, and we headed for the dance floor. It was clear that sex would have to wait until later.

CHAPTER 30

LUKE

After getting back around three a.m., Goldi spent the night in my bed, her soft, naked body pressed against my side. I got an eyeful of her incredible tits when I climbed out of bed. I wanted her, but Goldi deserved to sleep in after the long night. And I had chores to do. I dressed, trying to be quiet, and reached the door.

"Come back to bed, cowboy."

"Later, I promise." I made the mistake of looking at her. Feeling like a sailor when a siren called, I struggled to resist her. Besides dancing, we'd been up half the night, and she must be exhausted. "Get some rest for now."

"I can't. I'm awake." She reached for the T-shirt I'd worn last night, snagging it off the floor and pulling it on. Her nipples pressed against the fabric. "Let me make you breakfast."

This gal would be the death of me. "If you insist." I followed her into the kitchen, reminding myself to get my mind out of the gutter. I made coffee while she piled ingredients on the counter.

"Would you rather have chocolate chip or strawberry pancakes?"

"Surprise me." To be fair, whatever she made would be incredible. "Coffee?" I held up the pot.

"As if you have to ask."

I poured her a cup, adding a good helping of cream and sugar.

Taking a sip, she sighed. "Real cream makes my mornings perfect."

"I prefer hot and black." I downed my coffee and poured another.

"Why don't you get out either ham or bacon, and I'll cook it up? The extra protein will build up those sexy muscles of yours."

"You think I'm sexy." I winked at her.

"Like you don't already know that."

"I'll fry bacon. You concentrate on your creation."

"Thank you."

I stood next to her at the stove, well aware that underneath my shirt she was naked.

"What's your favorite dessert?" She minced strawberries and folded them in, before poured the batter into a buttered pan, and folded the sweet mixture into the eggs.

"Chocolate cake."

"So adventurous." She whisked up whipped cream with sugar. "I make a killer chocolate and salted caramel layer cake."

I turned the sizzling strips. "Sounds good. When can I try it?"

She bumped her hip against mine. "One of these days."

"I'll look forward to it." I placed the bacon on a paper towel.

She piled a plate with pancakes and added a big dollop of whipped cream on top. "Here you go."

I moved to the table with her sitting across from me and dug in. "This is good, really good."

"I love playing around with recipes."

"Where'd you work in California?" I knew little of her life there.

"A cafe. My boss was an idiot, so I quit and ended up here."

"It's his loss, and my gain. At least for now." Should I ask her to stay longer? Maybe give us a try. Still, I balked. She belonged in the city and would eventually head that way. "Do you still plan to open your own bakery?"

"Maybe I can get my sister to back me. I know better than to ask my father."

"Why's that?

"After I graduated, I asked him to support me in starting up a business. He said I'd be better off finding a husband."

"You're kidding, right?"

"I wish I were. He told me my future husband would appreciate that I could cook. I think he's stuck in the middle of last century in his idea of where men and women stand." She fiddled with her napkin.

"Your dad's wrong." My fingers brushed against her cheek.

"He sure is." She ate her food and stopped to look at me. "At least I caught my ex in bed with our neighbor before we signed a lease in California." It's still hard to believe I almost married him.

"I'm glad you ended up here."

"So am I." She gave me a half grin, but the sparkle had gone out of her eyes.

"What are your plans for the day?" I rubbed circles along her palm with my thumb.

"I'd love to learn how to rope. You wanna teach me?"

"I'd be glad to—after I muck out the stalls."

"Can I help?"

"You're joking, right? It's messy work."

"Don't care. I'm living it up like a real cowgirl."

"Scratching more items off your bucket list."

"Of course." She got out her phone. "I've already checked off working in a small town, meeting a ghost, horseback riding, getting locked in a storage room, picking fresh vegetables, using locally grown flour, collecting eggs, and dealing with a devilish rooster."

"Don't forget about meeting a handsome cowboy."

"Are you talking about Chase or Pete? Or maybe Sam? He is a silver fox."

"Very funny." I brought my mouth to hers and gave her a quick kiss. "Come on, darlin'. We've got work to do."

CHAPTER 31

GOLDI

"You sure you're up to mucking out stalls on your day off?" Luke asked.

"If you haven't already figured this out, I am a bit crazy."

"But gorgeous." He tugged me in for a kiss.

If I weren't careful, I'd fall for this guy. Charlie pushed his nose against my leg, and I scratched behind his ears. "I always wanted a dog."

"You've never had one growing up?"

"My mom said they were too much work." I moved toward the open stall and ran my hand along the white blaze on Duchess' head. "You're such a beautiful girl. Are we cleaning her stall first?"

"Nope. Tumbleweed's."

"Don't tell him this, but I like riding Honey a little better."

"You're secret's safe with me." He made a pretend zipper over his mouth.

Horses stuck their heads out as we walked by. They seemed to be as curious about me as I was them.

"Back up while I bring Tumbleweed out." He opened the stall on the left and added a halter to lead him.

I stepped away, recalling Luke saying that he might kick. "Was he born here?"

"On this very ranch. My grandfather used to ride him."

"How long has it been since you lost him?"

"Almost three years. This place isn't the same without him. He used to be the glue that kept us together." His tone came out a bit terse.

"It looks like you and your brothers have done a good job."

"We try. Pete and I always planned on running the ranch, but I think Chase wished he could have stayed in college longer."

"Did he get a degree?"

"In kinesiology. He planned to be a P.E. teacher or maybe go for a few more years and become a physical therapist. But he came home because he was needed."

This family had been through so much and had made the best of it. Meanwhile, I'd been complaining to my sister about a cheating ex and overbearing parents. In the scheme of things, I had it pretty easy. I moved to the side and stood in front of the hitching post. "You are such a handsome fellow," I said to the horse. "Be good out here while we clean your room."

"He doesn't live in a house." He smirked at me.

"In his mind, it is."

He chuckled. "Come along, city girl. The stalls won't clean themselves." He snatched a pitchfork from the wall as we went inside.

"Show me what to do."

"Use the pitchfork to sift through the straw. Solids go into the wheelbarrow. Then we add fresh bedding."

"Sounds easy enough." I scooped up a clump of hay, but it fell off the tines.

"Keep the pitchfork tipped away from your body."

"Like this?" I poked and prodded at the hay.

"Almost. Let me show you." He moved behind me, his body fitting perfectly against mine. His hand slipped across my waist, his fingers interlocking with mine on the wooden handle.

I inhaled his masculine scent. "I've got it."

"Not quite." He brought his mouth against the sensitive shell of my ear.

"I thought we had work to do." I attempted to regain some semblance of control over my racing heart.

"We do. But for now, I'd like to do this." His voice came out low and husky, as he pressed a feather-light kiss against my neck, his teeth scraping gently against my skin.

Holy hotcakes. I liked this.

"You make it hard to step away." But he backed up anyway, leaving me longing for more.

I focused on the task. "How old is Tumbleweed?"

"Twenty-two. If we're lucky, he'll live to be thirty."

"From what I've seen, he's pretty mellow. Is there anything that sets him off?"

"Mice. He hates them. Luckily, we have enough barn cats to keep most of the rodents away."

We finished cleaning and I helped him add a straw covering.

"You can walk him back," Luke said.

I liked being useful. I held the lead, and the horse followed.

Once he was in his stall, we moved on to cleaning Duchess' stall. I watched Luke's muscular arms flex and tense. Talk about ruggedly hunky. "I bet you and your brothers were hellions growing up."

"Nope."

"Like I'd believe that. Tell me one crazy thing you did."

He heaped manure into the wheelbarrow.

"Come on. I promise I won't judge."

"All right." He eyed me sideways. "Once we got up on top of the barn, and Pete dared me to jump off."

"Really?" It sounded pretty crazy.

"Give me a break. I was thirteen and dumb."

"Fair enough. Did you get hurt?"

"Nope." He glanced over at me, his mouth quirking up. "I landed on several bales of hay and knocked them over. Then I made Pete restack them."

"Where were your parents when this happened?"

"Gone." His lips pinched together. "Enough with the questions."

I held up my hands. "I can't help being curious."

"Don't I know it."

We cleaned four more stalls.

"Next up's feeding time." His hand went to the small of my back as he brought me past the storage room where we'd been locked in.

I walked by. Inside the feed room, sacks of oats and barley were piled high.

"Use this cup to measure out the portions." He showed me a chart on a clipboard listing the grains and supplements for the horses.

"This is Tumbleweed's mix." He scooped oats from a container. "He's got a bit of arthritis. We add in some glucosamine. Keeps him spry. Stormy gets only hay with a bit of oats."

"How about Duchess?"

He grinned. "No extra treats for her, no matter how much she bats those pretty eyelashes at you. In fact, she kinda reminds me of you."

"I look like a mare?"

"No, but you like getting your way."

"Who doesn't?" A bay gelding nuzzled my palm seeking more oats.

"Looks like you've got yourself a fan club. Jasper's usually standoffish."

"Don't you listen," I told the stallion. "Underneath that bravado you're a softie."

Luke laughed.

"What? I think I've missed my calling as a horse whisperer."

"Keep dreaming, city girl."

I picked up a handful of hay, threw it at him, and sprinted off.

"You're gonna pay for that," he growled.

"No way, cowboy," I ran out the door.

He caught up to me outside the stables and pressed me into the wall. Tipping my Stetson back, his fingers traced the curve of my jaw, and he kissed me long and deep.

"You're not getting out of teaching me to rope."

He backed away and held up two hands. "Fine for now."

Darn. I had hoped he'd carry me up into the hayloft. Maybe later if I had my way.

CHAPTER 32

LUKE

I lugged the wooden horse with the hand carved horns out of the stables and set the makeshift steer in position.

"How cute. Did you come up with the design?" Goldi placed a hand on her oh so curvy hips.

I plucked a piece of straw from her shirt. "If I say I did, do I get a kiss?"

"After you teach me to rope." She picked up a lariat off the sawhorse and snapped the end.

"You can be quite bossy," I shot back.

"I'm just eager to learn from the best."

"The best, huh?" I grinned.

"Please. Like your ego needs any more stroking."

"Well then, listen carefully." I snatched the other rope and held it in one hand. "First create a loop. Hold the knot in your dominant hand. Are you right-handed?"

She nodded.

"Good. Coil the rest with your left. Make the loop big

enough to rope the dummy but small enough for control. Swing the loop above your head slow and steady, and throw." My rope sailed around the horn. "It's your turn." I backed away.

She eyed the rope like a puzzle she was hell-bent on solving.

"Give it a try."

"Okay." Her movements were clumsy. Her grip off. Her stance too stiff. The rope flopped to the ground. "This looked easier when you did it."

I stepped closer, my hand brushing hers as I adjusted her grip on the rope. "Keep your wrist loose, but your fingers firm."

"Like this?"

"Exactly." I stepped back to give her space.

"I missed again. The friggin' rope just won't listen."

"You should have seen me when I first tried. I tossed the whole dang coil over the fence."

"That makes me feel better." She grinned at me and my pulse sped a little faster.

"You'll get it—eventually."

Biting her bottom lip, she swung the loop in an arc. The noose settled over one horn. "Yippee!"

"You're almost there. Move back a few feet and see how you do."

She squared her shoulders and let it fly. The rope spun out and landed dead-on.

"Hot damn, darlin'. You're becoming quite a cowgirl."

"Thanks to your help. Watch this." She hit three out of five.

"Impressive."

She launched herself at me, wrapping her arms around my waist. The press of her body against mine sent a jolt through my system.

"Thanks for being patient with me." Her breath tickled my neck. "I have to take a picture of this day." She snatched her phone from her pocket. "Smile."

My lips twitched up.

She clicked a few times and swiped through several photos. "I like this one best."

"Are you sending it to your sister?"

"As if you have to ask. You're very photogenic, cowboy."

I kissed her, going from cool and collected to turned on in seconds flat. The taste of her ignited a smoldering fire.

Her stomach growled, and she pulled away. "I'm starving."

So was I—for her.

"Come back to my place, and we'll celebrate with fried chicken and mac and cheese."

"It's your day off. How 'bout I take you to a diner a couple miles south of here?" It was the least I could do for her.

"Mind if I go home and shower first?"

I really shouldn't be spending so much time with her. She'd be leaving soon. I told myself I wasn't in love with her. I knew better than to make that mistake again. For now, I'd enjoy myself.

If only I believed what I was shoveling.

CHAPTER 33

LUKE

It might not be wise spending the last week with Goldi sharing my bed. But it felt right with her body tight against mine, her skin warm and soft. I pressed myself closer.

She stirred, letting out this little moan that went straight to my cock. I slid my hand up her side, cupping her breast, my thumb brushing over her nipple until it pebbled under my touch.

"Morning, darlin'," I murmured into the nape of her neck.

She turned to face me. "What time is it?"

"Five twenty." I pulled her closer, happy we'd have an hour before work. Running my thumb along that pouty mouth of hers, I brushed my lips against hers. My hand slipped down her stomach until I got to the wet heat between her thighs.

"Mmm," she hummed, her touch trailing up my chest.

With one hand, I pressed her palm against my chest so she could feel how fast my heart pounded. The other teased her entrance, sliding inside until her hips jerked against me. "I love how wet you get for me." I worked her body, curling my fingers just right to make her cry out. "I want you, now."

"Please."

I flipped her onto her back, spreading her legs wide, and she looked up at me with those big, pretty eyes, and I knew I was done for. Somehow, I managed to remember to grab a condom off the side table and slide it on before I pushed inside, slowly, inch by inch, until I was buried to the hilt. "You feel so damn good." My hips moved in a slow, steady rhythm.

She wrapped her legs around my waist, pulling me deeper. Her nails dug into my shoulders. I loved the way she marked and claimed me as hers.

"More," she gasped, her hips lifted to meet mine.

I gave her what she wanted, harder, faster, determined to make her come first. She cried out, her body tensing, muscles spasming around me my cock. Unable to hold back, I came hard, groaning her name like a prayer, and collapsed on top of her, both of us breathing hard, slick with sweat.

I buried my face in her neck, inhaling the scent of her. I liked waking up with her. Liked it way too much. But I wasn't ready to admit why, not yet. Not when I knew how much it would hurt when this time between us inevitably ended.

Catching my breath, I looked into her eyes. "Are you okay? I was a little rough."

"I'm fantastic."

A serious conversation hovered on the tip of my tongue. We should talk about us, about what this thing between us meant. But hell, I couldn't bring myself to do it. "What's your day like?" I tried to keep my voice steady, tried to pretend like my heart wasn't about to beat out of my chest.

"Pretty easy. I should be done around one or two." She yawned and unwound herself from my arms. "I need caffeine. Make us some coffee, cowboy."

"Yes, ma'am." I was addicted to her. How in hell would I survive this?

As she'd done for the past few mornings, she moved into a spot on the couch and grabbed her laptop from the coffee table and turned it on. "There's a new recipe for blueberry crepes. Maybe I can try them out on you this weekend."

"Sounds good to me."

She kept on tapping as I sat next to her.

"Anything else interesting?"

She scrunched her nose. "I can't believe it. There's a message from yesterday. My car's done."

"Already." I tried to sound casual while my pulse kicked against my ribcage. I set my untouched coffee on the coffee table, fighting the urge to pull her into my arms and kiss her until we both forgot about cars, towns, and everything else.

"It's been over a month. I can't wait to drive my Camaro again." She put her laptop down. "Don't get me wrong. The quad has been great, but—"

"It is rather slow." I told my sinking heart to chill.

"I like dependable Little Quaddy."

"Well, you do look hot riding it."

"I do?" Her cheeks flushed.

"We can pick up your car this afternoon and get dinner in town." If only the sense of dread would quit showing its ugly head. She could leave today, and I'd never see her again.

"Sounds perfect."

I gave her one more lingering kiss and headed for the

stables. My boots kicked up clouds of dust, mirroring the chaos inside me.

Saddling up my horse, I took off. I had to find the right words to show Goldi how much she meant to me. Would that be enough for this city girl, or would she head off like my last serious girlfriend did?

CHAPTER 34

GOLDI

Mabel and I finished up earlier than I'd expected, giving me an hour to kill before I'd meet up with Luke. As I got on the quad, tears filled my eyes. Mabel said I should stay. But this job had been temporary from the start.

Instead of heading straight to the stables, I drove up the trail that led to the water tower and stopped to revel in the fresh air and beautiful view.

I had raced Luke on this trail on horseback. I assumed he'd let me win. Which was sweet. If only Luke asked me to stay. But he hadn't. Why would he? He wasn't serious about me.

I started up the quad and headed for the stables to say goodbye to the horses. In about an hour, Luke would take me to town. My heart pulsed with unease. I told it to stop. No sense dwelling on something I couldn't change.

Parking the vehicle near the front entrance, I glanced over at the field next to the stall, hoping that Honey would come trotting up to me. She didn't. I assumed a ranch hand took her out. A single tear dripped down my cheek. I'd miss that little mare.

Stepping through the stable entrance, I inhaled the wonderful scent of hay and horses. Duchess' head showed over the top of the stall. "Hello, girl." I ran my hand over the white blaze on her nose. "You are definitely the queen around here."

She whinnied.

"I see you approve." I wandered among the stalls, my fingers trailing over the rough wooden dividers. Grabbing some oats from a bin, I let Jasper eat them out of my palm. "That tickles."

He nudged his head against my shoulder.

Tumbleweed came next. He'd been a sweetheart. "Hey, handsome. How are you?" I planned to kiss his nose.

Except he didn't come to me. His snort seemed to mirror my own restlessness. I opened the gate cautiously like I'd done once before with him and stepped inside. Straw crunched under my boots as I approached him.

He snorted again and pranced backward. I noticed an uneasiness about him that I'd never seen before. How odd. This guy was always so mellow.

"It's okay, boy."

Tumbleweed whinnied.

"Shhh, easy now." I kept my voice low and gentle as I reached out a hand and brushed his mane.

His muscles tensed. His eyes fixed on me. "Easy, easy."

He thrashed, bucking against the confines of his stall. His powerful body sent shivers down my spine as he pawed the ground. His nostrils flared as he took a long breath, shook his head violently and paced back and forth.

This half-ton equine might trample me under his hooves.

My nails dug into my palms as I tried to stay calm and move back. Something was off with him.

A mouse skittered right over my foot which made me squeal. Luke had said Tumbleweed despised mice. Was that why he was acting so restless?

Panic rose within me. Instinct said to move, but I had nowhere to go but into the hard wooden wall behind me, or toward the furious beast in front of me. In one swift motion, Tumbleweed reared up on his hind legs, hooves slicing through the air.

"Whoa, Tumble—" His front legs struck out, clipping my shoulder and sending me spiraling backwards. My head connected with the wall, causing such intense pain that stars burst in front of my eyes.

"Luke." His name slipped from my lips as darkness clawed its way in.

CHAPTER 35

LUKE

My chest tightened as I considered Goldi leaving the ranch for good. Once she headed back to California, I doubted I'd see her again. Which would tear me up. She made my life better. Our chemistry and sex life were more than incredible.

No sense fighting the inevitable—I'd fallen hard for her.

I was several minutes from the stables when a gut-deep certainty said something was terribly wrong struck. I kicked my horse to a gallop. Reaching the stables, I dismounted and ran inside. My heart hitched as I heard a high-pitched, piercing squeal combined with panicked whinnies.

I reached Tumbleweed's stall to see his eyes wild as he reared up and his hooves struck out. Goldi stood right in the damn strike zone. "Goldi, watch out."

The horse knocked her against the stable wall with a thud.

"Noooo!" My boots skidded on the straw as I reached her crumpled form. "No, no, no."

"Luke?"

"Listen to me, Goldi, you've gotta open your beautiful eyes for me. You hear?" I shouted, hoping I could get through to her.

The only sound I heard was the shallow rise and fall of her chest.

"Come on, Goldi. Don't do this. Don't leave me—" My words choked off. I gave a silent prayer for her to be okay.

Pete barreled into the stable and must've figured out what happened because he called, "Outta the way, Tumbleweed." His hands grabbed the horse's halter, guiding the spooked animal away from her.

"Radio for a chopper, now!" I hollered without looking up.

"Got it."

My fingers gently probed the back of Goldi's head and felt a bump forming. My heart raced even faster. "Please wake up for me." The silence sat heavy as I held her.

It seemed like forever before the distant thwap-thwap-thwap of rotor blades tore through the air. My thumping heart matched the beat. A helicopter landed in a gust of wind and dust that drifted inside the stables.

Two people in blue uniforms rushed inside and knelt beside Goldi, their gloved hands swiftly assessing her condition.

Please, God. Let her be okay.

The female EMT flashed a penlight into her eyes while her partner held a stethoscope against her chest. "The heartbeat's one-forty. She might be in shock." He placed a mask over her nose and mouth.

I asked, "Will she be okay?"

"Should be." Together, they loaded her onto a stretcher.

"I'm going with her."

The flight was a blur of noise and motion. I held on to Goldi's hand, willing her to open her eyes. My thumb brushed against her knuckles. "You've got to fight, darlin'."

She remained unconscious.

"I'm here for you." If only she'd wake up. I needed her.

Once they unloaded her inside the hospital, a nurse stopped me. "Sir, you can't go in there."

"But I'm her boyfriend." Not officially, but close enough.

"Let the doctors do their job. They'll come out when they know anything," the nurse said. "What's her name?"

"Goldi Summers."

"Does she have insurance on her?"

"I don't think so. She should be covered under liability on my ranch." I got the card out of my wallet. "Here."

"Can you tell me her birthdate?"

"Not sure." I didn't even know the month. Wait. Maybe Peggy would know it from her application at the store. "I'll check with my sister."

I got out my phone and called. It went to voicemail, and I left a message. Reluctantly, I went into the waiting room.

I couldn't sit. I paced and paced and paced and practically wore a hole in the carpet.

A woman in a white jacket approached me. "Are you with Goldi Summers?"

"I am."

"Her breathing and heartrate are strong. But her pupils are dilated and that contusion on the back of her head is concerning."

"What can you do?" There must be something.

"I've ordered a CT scan. Other than that, let's just pray she wakes soon," the doctor's serious tone had me even more worried.

"May I see her?"

"Of course."

I walked into her room. She was hooked up to far too many machines, face a pale white, completely still.

I took her hand and rubbed circles along her palm. "I'm here, Goldi. Wake up, my little city girl. Please."

Minutes stretched into hours, but I refused to leave her side.

CHAPTER 36

GOLDI

Mark must have left the window open again because a bird kept on chirping. "Close the window," I rasped.

My fuzzy brain felt like it was wrapped in cotton. I squinted as I gazed around the room. White walls. A mounted TV. Silver rails lining both sides of the bed. What the heck?

A dark-haired man sat at the side of my bed, tall and broad-shouldered with a cowboy hat in his hands. "Morning, darlin'," the guy drawled.

"Who are you?" My hoarse voice didn't sound like me.

"Luke Wolfe." He squeezed my hand in a reassuring way.

"Luke?" I couldn't deny the flutter in my chest at his closeness, or the way his rugged features softened with worry. Except I didn't know anybody named Luke. My mind scrambled for memories, but they were elusive.

"You hit your head pretty hard and got knocked unconscious. I rode in the copter with you when we came here."

"Where is here?"

"Cheyenne General Hospital."

"This doesn't make sense. Why am I in Wyoming? I should be in California."

"You got hurt on my ranch." The stranger's eyes held mine with an intensity that almost felt intimate.

"I was on a ranch?" What in the heck was going on?

"Do you remember your car breaking down?"

"No. I don't remember anything." I put my hand on top of my head. A cloth wrapped around it. Probably a bandage.

"Let's not worry about that right now."

"But I'm freaking panicked." I tried to sit up, but the room spun.

The guy placed a hand on my shoulder, easing me back. "Rest, Goldi."

"Why are you here?"

"Someone's gotta watch over you." He spoke as if he should be there.

My throat got dry as fear lingered at the edges of my consciousness. "Am I going to be okay?"

"Yep."

They must've been giving me strong drugs because my world seemed muddled.

A nurse with cartoon horses on her scrubs bustled into the room. "Good morning, Miss Summers. It's good to see you awake." She replaced the IV bag.

"Can you tell me what happened?"

"Sure, hon." She offered me a glass of water with a bendy straw. "You have a head injury."

I tried to piece together the fractured memories. "How?"

"You'll have to ask him." She motioned to Luke.

"Well?"

"One of my horses reared up when you were inside his stall." Luke ran a hand through his thick hair. "And he threw you into a wall headfirst. I apologize for his manners."

"Oh, okay." This story kept getting more and more bizarre.

"Can I get you some juice, crackers, or Jello?" the nurse cut in.

"No, thanks." I wasn't the least bit hungry. "I better make a phone call. Can you get my cell out of my purse?"

"You didn't bring your purse, but we found your phone in your jeans pocket." She got out a plastic bag and rifled through it. "Here you go. How about I bring you some apple juice?"

"Fine." As long as it got the nurse out of the room.

I looked up at Mr. Tall, Dark, and Brooding. "If you don't mind, I'd like a little privacy."

He stood. "I'll get coffee."

I scrolled through the contacts. Mark. My fiancé. I remembered him. That's a good sign. His phone went straight to voicemail. I didn't have the energy to leave a message.

My mom's number showed next. Okay, how would I explain being in Wyoming when I didn't even know how I ended up here? Still, I pressed her contact.

It rang once.

"Goldi, I do hope you've given up this nonsense of staying on a ranch and you're coming home." Her tone came out snippy.

What happened to cause me to drive hundreds of miles away? "There's been an accident. I'm in the hospital."

Mom asked for the details and said she'd be on the first

flight she could get. When she hung up, I knew I should be relieved, but I wasn't. And I had no idea why.

Luke came back into the room.

"Why am I in Wyoming? It doesn't make sense." Chunks of my memory were missing. "I wish I remembered."

"It should come back to you." He wouldn't make eye contact with me.

A short woman in a white coat and stethoscope around her neck stepped inside my room. "I'm Dr. Lee." She held out her hand and I shook it. "I'm glad to see you're doing better."

"What happened?"

"Head trauma. You've been in and out of consciousness for hours. How are you feeling right now?" She flashed a penlight in my eyes.

"Okay, I guess. It's just I don't remember leaving Los Angeles." Talk about weird.

"Do you know what day it is?"

"Of course. It's July tenth."

The doctor's lips pinched together as she typed on her tablet.

"Am I wrong?"

"It's August twentieth."

"No way. You're joking, right?" I couldn't have lost over a month of my life.

She just shook her head.

"It's fine, darlin'. You've been through quite an ordeal." Luke took my hand, which somehow settled my nerves.

Dr. Lee asked, "Do you know where you are?"

"In a hospital in Wyoming. That's what Luke said."

"What's the last thing you remember?" She waited.

It hurt to think, but I did. "Waking up and getting ready for work."

The doctor asked where I worked and then asked a few more questions.

All the while Luke stayed at my side.

"Well, Miss Summers, you seem to have some memory lapses. It's not uncommon with head injuries. The MRI ruled out internal bleeding," the doctor said.

"When will I be able to leave?"

"As a precaution, you're staying overnight." She looked directly into my eyes. "Try to relax."

I must've looked terrified.

"I will be back to check on you after I do my rounds."

"Thank you, Dr. Lee." It had been ingrained in me to be polite, regardless of this fear struggling to take over.

"You're welcome." She walked out.

"See, you're doing great." Luke grinned at me, and my confused heart fluttered.

CHAPTER 37

GOLDI

I awoke with a start to the sound of rhythmic beeping. Where was I?

Right, a hospital. I'd hit my head.

I spotted a monitor. Blood pressure: 112/76. Oxygen: 98. Temperature: 98.7. All normal. Except for the fog in my brain. I sucked in a breath and my ribs smarted. Ouch.

That cowboy, Luke, dozed in a chair at my side with a Stetson on his lap. He had an angular face, strong chin, and a wide mouth. Handsome features. Supposedly I knew him, but thinking hurt .

"Morning." His eyes opened, holding mine. "How are you feeling?"

"Better, I think."

"That's good."

"I hate hospitals. I wish I remembered how I ended up here."

"It's best not to push." His muscular arms folded over a broad chest. "Your memory should come back to you in time."

Agitation galloped through my veins like a runaway horse. What a weird analogy. I shook my head and winced.

"Are you all right?" He scooted closer.

"Not really. You're frustrating me."

"I don't mean to." He swallowed hard.

The door opened and a dark-haired woman swept into the room. Relief flooded me when I immediately recognized her. "Mom!"

"Sweetie." She cleared her throat. "Your father and I have been worried sick about you."

"Where is he?"

"Out of the country. He'd be here if he could." Her eyes avoided mine. "But Mark came. He's parking the car and will be up shortly."

"That's great." With my fiancé here, hopefully everything would be normal again.

"That bandage around your head looks dreadful." She smoothed back a strand of hair behind my ear. "Are you in much pain?"

"A little." I suspected the drugs they gave me helped.

"How's my sweet sugar?" Mark strolled in looking every bit the successful lawyer and kissed my cheek.

Yes! Another familiar face. He was my fiancé. I lived with him. I belonged with him. "I'm better now that you're here."

"You look good." Mark took my hand and kissed it. "I'm so relieved. Who's your friend?" He motioned to the side of the room. At some point Luke had moved away from me.

My head throbbed as I figure out my situation. Two men, both striking in their own way. Mark, with his familiar confidence and sky-blue eyes. And Luke—taller, sun-kissed, with an easy smile.

"Name's Luke Wolfe." He stepped forward and the two shook hands. His gaze shifted back toward me, lingering for a blink.

"Are you the one who brought her here?" Mom asked.

"Yes, ma'am." Luke raked his fingers through his hair.

"Thank you for being with her. What happened?" Mark eyed Luke.

"She was in a stall with one of my horses when he got spooked. He kicked out, and… well…" His words trailed off. "She hit her head against the wall pretty hard."

My mom's face tightened as she processed this information, her lips thinning into a line that spoke volumes about her worry. "What an ordeal. You poor thing, Goldi."

Mark gave my hand a light squeeze. "I can't picture you on a ranch. Much less inside a stall."

He might be trying to lighten my mood, but his comment bugged me. "Why not? I've always loved horses. Someday I'd like to own one."

"You used to ride at camp," Mom said.

"I loved it. I wanted to take lessons with a friend, but you talked me into signing up for cheerleading instead." Which had been okay but not great.

"Let's not bring up the past now."

Mark glanced at Luke again. "So… you work on a ranch?"

Luke nodded. "That's right."

"How did you meet Goldi?

"Her car broke down, and I gave her a place to stay until the storm passed. I took her to town, but when the repairs were going to take a month, my family offered her a job to help my cook while it got fixed."

I should remember this. After all, I'd been there.

Mark leaned back in his chair and frowned. "I wish I'd bought you that Miata you've been eyeing at the dealer."

Actually, *he* wanted that car, but now wasn't the time to argue. "I prefer Nana's Camaro." Weird. Why did I remember Mark, my mom, even Nana, but I couldn't remember this nice cowboy?

"You always say that." His gaze softened. "You've got a sentimental side."

"Nana was special." My chest tightened from the bittersweet ache of missing her. "After all, she taught me how to bake."

Mom's expression barely flickered. She didn't say a word; she rarely did when Nana came up in conversation. She and her mom hadn't gotten along. Nana used to say they mixed as well as oil and water.

The door creaked open, and the doctor walked in. "I see you have company."

"Dr. Lee, this is my mom, and my fiancé, Mark."

Mark stood and extended his hand. "Pleasure to meet you."

"Same here." She turned to me.

"Is it okay if I share your medical information?" Dr. Lee asked.

"Sure," I said quietly. "It's fine." Truthfully, all I really knew was what I'd been told earlier—that I had a concussion and a couple of broken ribs—but even those facts felt distant, like they belonged to someone else entirely.

"Sir, could you give us some privacy?" My mom's tone came out polite but firm.

"Of course." Luke got up, his eyes guarded as he stared right at me. "I'll be right outside."

"Thank you." I watched him go. Ever since I'd awoken, he'd been kind.

"First off, Goldi has several rib contusions or bruises, but she's lucky there are no signs of fracture." The doctor pressed her hand against my right side, and I winced.

"Does that hurt much?" Mark asked.

"I'm fine."

"You'll need to take it easy for the next two weeks while you heal," Dr. Lee added.

"I'll try." It would be hard just lounging around the house.

"What about her head?" my mom asked.

"Goldi suffered head trauma and has a condition called retrograde amnestic."

Don't I know it.

"How can she have amnesia when she remembers us?" Mom remained composed.

"Since Goldi's hippocampus was not affected, she retained her long-term memory. Which is excellent. Some patients aren't so lucky."

"I should be thankful then."

"Definitely. Only your short-term memory has been compromised."

"That must be why yesterday I thought it was July tenth. I'm missing whatever happened between then and the accident."

"That's crazy." Mark patted my hand.

"Your MRI came back normal, which is common for concussions." She looked at me. "Still, given your injury, you most likely have minimal swelling in the temporal lobe which accounts for the memory loss."

"Will I ever get that month back?" The extent of my injury had just hit me.

"Possibly." She felt the back of my head and looked directly at me. "But it's the brain. Nobody knows for sure."

"I'll take good care of you, I promise." Mark threaded my fingers in his.

"Will I be able to bake right away?"

"Once you're feeling better. Give it a few days. Make sure you don't do any heavy lifting because of your ribs."

"I'll be careful."

"Dr. Lee, I appreciate you taking such good care of my daughter." My mom's voice was warm but tinged with unease.

"It's been my pleasure." She handed me a business card. "If you ever need to get ahold of me, call this extension."

"Thanks. You've been great."

"It's my job." The doctor smiled.

"When can I leave?"

"As soon as you sign your discharge papers. Will you be staying in town?"

"I'd rather go to SoCal."

"We live near L.A," Mark said. "Is it all right if she flies home?"

"I believe flying would be easier because it cuts down on the hours of travel. Being in a familiar place might speed up your recovery."

"I'm more than ready to go."

"That's understandable," she said with a laugh. "But take it easy. Rest isn't optional—it's mandatory."

"I'll make sure she listens," Mark told her.

"And schedule a follow-up appointment with your doctor."

"Of course," I said.

"Be patient with yourself." Dr. Lee stepped away.

"Just think. Tonight, you get to sleep in your own bed." Mark's words put me at ease.

"That sounds wonderful." No more getting woken up by machines or nurses taking vitals. "I'd like to say goodbye to Luke. He's been watching out for me ever since I got here."

"Sure, sweetie," Mom kissed my forehead. "We can tell him on our way to get coffee." She and Mark walked out.

CHAPTER 38

LUKE

Hospitals were places of too much waiting and not enough good news. Except Goldi was alive. Thank God. Still, it hurt that she didn't remember me or the moments we shared.

I texted my doctor cousin in Colorado.

Me: What can you tell me about head trauma and amnesia? My friend doesn't remember me.

I added details about what happened.

Kristy: You can't push her. Let her remember on her own.

Me: That's what Uncle Mickey said. I had called him yesterday while Goldi slept.

Kristy: Then why are you asking me?

Me: Because I hoped you'd give me a different answer.

Kristy: Sorry. Good luck with your friend. Gotta go. We'll talk soon.

Goldi's ex and mom walked up to me. "It was kind of you to

stay with Goldi while she waited for us." Her mom's eyes misted.

"It's no problem. I'm sorry she got injured."

The guy's grin rubbed me the wrong way. She picked his sorry ass over me—and there was nothing I could do about it. "I can't wait to get her back home."

"You're a lucky man." Who doesn't deserve her.

"I sure am."

"My daughter would like to see you before we go."

"Thank you, ma'am." I went inside and took the seat on Goldi's right. "Hey, darlin'."

"Hi." Her eyes searched mine. "Thank you for, um... keeping me company."

"It's the least I could do." Especially since I felt guilty about not being there to protect her. "If you need a place to stay while you get back on your feet, you and your mom are welcome at the ranch."

"That's kind of you, but we're heading to California." Her voice held a note of finality, drowning out the little hope I'd been holding onto.

"Sure, sure, I get it." I clenched my fists, wishing I could warn her about her supposed fiancé. "I'll swing by the ranch and grab whatever you left behind."

Her brow furrowed.

"It's no trouble."

"Don't worry about it. My phone and license will be enough for now." She offered a slight grin that didn't quite reach her eyes. "I doubt there's anything important."

"You've got your favorite skillet. And custom cowboy boots and matching Stetson." The details tumbled out of me.

"If only I remembered."

I should have asked her to stay yesterday morning. Although what good would it do now? "About your car."

I watched her fiddle with the edge of the hospital blanket, her fingers dancing over the cotton edges.

"I can drive your Camaro and leave it in the hospital parking lot. Save you the trouble of getting it."

"As much as I love that car, we're flying home." She bit her bottom lip.

"Oh." I fought to keep from frowning.

"Actually." She avoided my gaze, focusing instead on a spot somewhere near my left boot. "Would you mind leaving my stuff in the trunk? I'll arrange to have my vehicle shipped back to me."

That took me aback. I didn't like the idea of her car being loaded onto some stranger's trailer with her belongings boxed up. It felt final.

Silence stretched out for several seconds.

"Luke, did we... I mean, at the ranch, was there something between us?"

The question hit me like a stray bullet—painful and straight through the heart. Should I tell her the truth? After all, she asked.

The door swung open and the nurse, her mom, and Mark came in.

"Sign these and you're free to go," the nurse said.

"Guess that's my clue to leave." It killed me to say those words. "If you ever wanna visit the ranch, you've got an open invitation."

Her expression softened, a hint of the old Goldi peeking through. "That's really nice of you."

"Take care of yourself, okay?" I kept my eyes locked on hers as I backed away from the bed.

"I will. And Luke," she called out just as I reached the door.

I paused, half-expecting a miracle.

"Thanks for being my friend."

"Always." But she had been so much more than that. My lover, my girlfriend. I turned and stepped into the hall, my heart breaking into pieces.

CHAPTER 39

GOLDI

Honking horns echoed, mingling with a blaring siren and the chatter of voices from the street below. As usual, Mark had left the window open. The pungent aroma of exhaust fumes seeped in. I longed for crisp, clean air.

I padded to the window to close out the noise and got back under the covers. Rubbing sleep from my eyes, I glanced down at our silly dragon comforter with Mark's favorite anime character. It might not be my choice, but how could I refuse when he'd been so excited with his purchase? He was goofy like that sometimes.

I didn't get how I could recall inane details about this place but not a single detail about the last month. Freaking fudge cakes, this was frustrating. I took in several deep cleansing breaths to try and calm the chaos. It didn't work. Would this fog ever clear from my brain?

"Morning, sugar." Mark strode in, balancing a tray. "I made you scrambled eggs and toast."

"You didn't have to do that."

"Of course, I did. I want to take care of you." He set the tray on the nightstand. "How are you feeling?"

"Like I'm missing pieces of myself." The words slipped out.

His brow furrowed. "Does your head hurt?"

"Not so much." Except for the stupid missing memories. I got it, he was upset about the accident, but I wish he'd quit hovering. I humored him and took a bite of egg. They were good. "Did you add onions and a kick of chili pepper?"

"Is that okay? I mean, I'm not as talented in the kitchen as you." His eyes widened.

"It's perfect." I took another forkful and ate the toast. "You even added orange marmalade. You're the best."

"That's what I like to hear."

I didn't recall Mark ever cooking for me. What I did remember was we'd both been so busy with work that we hardly even saw each other.

"Have you called the restaurant and let them know I'll be out for a few days?"

"You've been gone more than a month. They told you that in the hospital."

"That doesn't seem possible."

"It's true."

"Did I get fired?" I'd never been fired in my life.

"Of course not. But when you didn't come back, I'm pretty sure you were replaced."

I picked up a pillow and threw it across the room. "This can't be happening."

"Relax, sugar." He rubbed my shoulders. "You weren't happy there, so I think it's for the best."

I glanced at the empty spot on my finger. "What happened to my ring?"

"I believe you lost it during all the confusion. If it doesn't turn up, we'll go shopping for another."

"Okay." But it wasn't. How could I be so careless with that two-karat rock? I had other questions. "How did I end up in Wyoming?" I pleaded, searching his face for clues to this puzzle.

"You went to the Pastry & Confectionery Expo. I begged you to fly, but you insisted on driving."

"Really? I finally got to go?"

He nodded.

"Why can't I remember that?" I hated my elusive mind right now. "I'm scared. What if my memories never come back?"

"Shh, it'll be okay." He wrapped an arm around my shoulders.

"How do you know?" I wasn't sure if I was asking him or myself.

"You are not only beautiful but resilient. That's one of the many things I love about you." The timer on his phone buzzed. He grabbed a glass of water and handed me a pill. "Here you go."

Knowing this drug would keep the edge off my pain, I swallowed it. "How much longer do I have to take these?"

"For a few more days. You'll be seeing your primary doctor on Monday, and a neurologist the following week. Don't stress. I'll be there with you."

I should be able to handle my own appointments. It irked me that he'd taken control, but with how much I'd been sleeping since we got home, I doubt I would have managed.

"You've missed so much work already. Isn't that going to be a problem?"

"You're more important."

His words were endearing, but they did nothing to ease the churning inside me. I wish I knew why.

"I'll be working from home as much as I can, but this afternoon, I have to go into the office. Your mom will stay with you."

"That's not necessary. I'm tired and plan to sleep."

"Please, Goldi. Otherwise, I'll worry about you." He gave me a quick peck on the lips.

He was both sweet and annoying. I yawned, my eyes getting droopy. "Fine." I didn't have the energy to fight him.

CHAPTER 40

LUKE

The sheets twisted around me as I reached for Goldi. Instead of warmth, my fingertips brushed cold cotton material and air. Cruel rays of dawn seeped through the curtains, revealing the brutal truth. She was gone.

For five nights running I'd had this damn dream of Goldi in my bed. For five mornings, I'd woken with her name on my tongue.

Her life's in California. I no longer existed in her memories, and that totally sucked.

Once again, I had stayed up far too late googling "traumatic brain injury" and "temporary memory loss" and came up with nothing substantially different than I'd already learned. I scrubbed a hand over my face. Charlie whined and rubbed his wet nose against my hand.

"You miss her too, boy." I brushed my fingers against his head.

As if agreeing, he yipped.

I swung my legs over the edge of the bed and glanced at the clock. Six a.m. Might as well get up.

My dog's nails click-clacked behind me as I headed down the hallway and stopped by the guest room where Goldi spent her first few nights on the ranch. I pushed open the door, hoping to see her stuff spread out on the dresser or get a sniff of her sweet fragrance. But the room remained as empty as I felt.

I started the coffeemaker and pulled out a clean cup from the cupboard. Of course, I'd pick her favorite mug with "Bakers do it better." Half-tempted to fling it against the wall and watch that ceramic shatter like my heart, I couldn't do it. I grabbed a black one with a cowboy boot on it. Much better.

My dog tapped his nose on the door handle leading to the yard. Maybe if I went outside with him, I'd feel better. Hot coffee in hand, I followed him as he sniffed just about every bush near the house before choosing one.

My stomach growled. I should head for the dining hall but couldn't bear the thought of Goldi's absence from the kitchen. Instead, I opted for PBJs which I ate without thinking and washed the bites down with milk.

"Wanna go to the barn?" I asked Charlie.

He wagged his tail.

"Who's a good boy?" I patted his head and moved toward the stables. Big drops of rain pelted the ground. I closed my eyes and tilted my face skyward, letting the torrent soak me to the bone as anguish and helplessness dug into me.

Thunder rumbled. Bolts of lightning danced across the brooding sky, briefly illuminating the empty cottage in the distance. Cascading, numbing rain continued. I used it as a distraction from the gnawing ache in my chest.

Shaking off the water, I trudged to the stables. "You think I'm nuts," I told Charlie. "And you'd be right." I got busy mucking out stalls. The monotony gave me far too much time to get inside my head. I'd kissed Goldi in this very building way too often. I punched the wall, barely feeling the pain in my hand.

I saddled Stormy and went for a ride, but galloping for miles didn't improve my mood. I was brushing Stormy when Pete walked up to me.

"Have a nice ride?" His sharp eyes scanned my face like he tried to read me.

"Yep."

"Hey." Chase appeared beside Pete, his hands shoved into his jeans pockets. "How ya doing?"

"Just dandy."

"Liar. Goldi really did a number on you." Pete stepped closer then, his hand landing on my shoulder.

"I'll get over her soon enough." It was easier to tell the lie, than accept the truth.

"You know, you could go after her." Chase's lips twitched up.

Anger snapped inside me. I whirled on my brother, fists clenched tight. "I've thought about it. But she's with her ex. End of story."

"Alright." Chase held up his hands in mock surrender. "Point taken."

Pete shifted uncomfortably, rubbing the back of his neck. "How about we go out for beers tonight? You deserve a night out, Luke. Hell, we all do."

"Come on, it'll be fun," Chase chimed in.

I hesitated, my gaze flickering between my brothers. Part of me almost told them to leave me alone and let me wallow in peace. But another part knew they wouldn't take no for an answer. And maybe they were right.

"As long as it's the Sunrise Tavern." The bar was right around the corner.

"Deal," Pete said with a grin.

"Give me a chance to shower."

"Pick you up in thirty," Pete said.

I headed home, my dog trailing next to me. "Might as well check the mailbox."

Charlie barked. He liked going anywhere I went.

The mailbox creaked as I tugged it open. Inside, a single package rested against the back, clearly addressed to me. The return address came from an unfamiliar leather shop I didn't recognize. "Wonder what this is?" I hadn't ordered anything.

Charlie barked, his tail wagging faster now.

I scratched behind his ears before heading toward the house, Inside, I kicked off my boots and slit the package open with my pocketknife. The paper tore with a satisfying rip. I pulled out a beautifully tooled leather wallet with the initials LW stamped into one corner. A folded piece of paper fluttered to the floor.

For the man who has everything except a decent wallet.

Love,

G.

My eyes drifted to the order date at the bottom. The day before our relationship fell apart.

"Dammit, Goldi." I clutched the wallet tightly, knuckles going white. "How in the hell can I go on without you?"

If ever I needed whiskey, it was tonight.

CHAPTER 41

GOLDI

Back at the apartment after my doctor's visit, the x-ray of my ribs showed they were just about healed, and I should take pain meds as needed. My memories weren't back, which sucked, but at least the swelling had gone down.

"I'm gonna check out jobs today and see what's out there." I sipped the latte we'd gotten at a drive-thru.

"Wouldn't it be better to wait?" Mark didn't look up from his computer. "You're not supposed to do any heavy lifting."

"There's no harm in looking."

"You don't have to work. Relax and enjoy being home."

Couldn't he see I was going batty sitting around here? "Did you ever hunt down the owner of the building down the street from your office?" Mark had promised to help me with the lease's terms.

"That one didn't work out. Sorry."

"Let me guess. You got too busy and never bothered

contacting the owner." I recalled that happening with a different location.

"I hate to upset you, but someone came in with a better offer while you were out of town."

My life was like a recipe gone wrong, with my lacking memory the missing ingredient.

"We'll find another property when you're better." He reached for my hand.

Maybe it'd be best to wait. I should be a hundred percent when I started my business.

"You know, you could work on that cookbook you've talked about creating."

"That's not a bad idea." I might even include some of Nana's recipes.

"If you're really bored, you can plan our wedding."

"My mom can take care of that. That kind of thing is her forte. I'd much rather bake."

"Speaking of our wedding, what if we get married in Seal Beach where we met?"

"I like that idea." I'd been taking a run along the trail, and he'd come up behind me on his bicycle. He had stopped me and invited me to coffee. The attraction had been immediate, at least on my side. I mean, his light blue eyes were the color of the sky.

A month later, I introduced him to my parents. When my dad learned he'd just passed the bar and had graduated at the top of his class, he had Mark come in for an interview. Dad hired him on the spot. Which worked for both of us.

"Great." He came over to me and dropped to his knee.

"Goldi Summers, will you marry me?" He pulled out a ring box and opened it to reveal a massive rock.

"Of course." I loved him.

He slid the band on my finger. I held it up to the light and practically got blinded by the large stone surrounded by dozens of smaller diamonds.

"I saw it online a few days ago. The jeweler delivered it to me yesterday."

"That was sweet. But it's a bit flashy."

"You deserve the best." He pulled me toward him and kissed me, long and hard.

"I love you so much."

The three little words I should repeat stayed choked in my throat.

"I hate to leave you now." He cupped my face in his hands. "But I really have to go into the office today. Are you okay being alone here?"

"Of course. Making junior partner requires putting in the work."

"How 'bout I take you out tonight to celebrate? You pick the place—anywhere you want."

"I'd like that."

He gave me a chaste kiss and headed out the door.

As soon as it clicked shut behind him, the stillness of the kitchen settled around me. He hadn't left me alone since that one afternoon. I didn't ever recall him being so attentive. My injuries had really shaken him up.

I should call my sister.

No, I'd better not disturb her now. I think Mom said she

was in New York for a family law conference. She was probably in a meeting.

All my friends would be working.

What else could I do? Now that the swelling had gone down, my brain should be able to handle a little social media on my phone.

Where was my phone? I had it when I left the hospital. I opened the nightstand. Bingo. Plugging my cell into an outlet, it powered up and notifications started pinging. Missed calls, texts, emails.

A message beeped from my sister. She had sent me a picture of an ice cream sundae with the caption: *Best lunch ever.*

Me: Hey. You busy?

Sis: I'll be free once I finish my last bite.

Me: Smiley face.

My phone rang a few minutes later.

"Finally, I get to talk to you. How are you doing?"

"Better. I'm determined to stop taking the pain meds. They make me loopy." I paused. "And no comments about the last part."

"You've never been loopy before. A little crazy, maybe…"

"You've got that right. I wish my brain would quit being fuzzy."

"It'll come."

I wanted to believe her.

An announcement sounded in the background.

"My session is starting back in a couple minutes. Gotta go. I'd call you later tonight, but I'm going out with friends. I won't get back 'til Wednesday. Let's catch up. I'll take you to dinner."

"Sure."

"Talk to you soon." She hung up.

Darn it. I didn't get a chance to tell her about the ring. I should send her a picture, but it could wait.

My email folder said there were over a thousand unread emails. Figuring most of them would be junk, I decided to tackle them tomorrow.

I scrolled through mindless entertainment on social media. Kittens freaked out over a cucumber. Penguins slipped on ice. A horse jumped rope.

My phone rang. Area code 307. Wyoming.

"Hello."

"Is this Goldi Summers?" A deep voice with a slight drawl asked.

"Yes, how can I help you?"

"This is Timber Wolfe's Auto Shop."

He might be one of Luke's relatives.

"I've been trying to get ahold of you for several days. Your transmission is fixed. Luke mentioned you'd like your car shipped to you."

"That would be great."

"Is 7555 Fifth Street in Stardust, California, where you'd like it sent?"

Why had I given my sister's address? I corrected him.

"Okay. I'll schedule a transport. It won't be until sometime next week."

"That's fine." As much as I would like my car, I could wait.

"It'll be fifteen hundred for the tow. Luke paid for the repairs."

"He did? Why?"

"He said it was compensation for working at his ranch."

"That's really nice of him." A huge kitchen with picture windows came to mind. Where'd that come from?

"My nephew has his moments."

I gave the man my credit card info.

"I'll call you once everything is arranged."

I thanked him and hung up.

Then I opened my photos. This might help fill in the missing pieces. The first one showed Luke and me taking a selfie with the ranch in the background. I looked happy.

I kept scrolling. Another photo of Luke and me at what appeared to be a country bar.

Why didn't I remember this? My head hurt with all this craziness.

I took several deep breaths and thought about being outdoors. Normally, I'd picture the beach, the sun warming me, but today I ended up in the mountains with a view of a beautiful valley. I breathed in fresh air and the scent of pine.

Could this be Wyoming? Come on brain, give me more than this little tidbit.

I was tired. So, I took a nap.

Knocking woke me. Looking through the peephole, a woman held a long rectangular box. I opened the door.

"These are for Goldi Summers."

"That's me." I brought the box to the table and opened it to a dozen yellow roses. I picked up a single flower and smelled the sweet scent. What a nice gesture.

I read the card.

I'm so sorry, sugar. Can't do dinner tonight. I promise I'll make it up to you. Big case at the office. Don't wait up, I'll be late.
Love you always,
Mark

DARN IT. I'd been looking forward to going out on a date with Mark. Oh well.

My stomach grumbled. A slice of pizza from Eddie's Pizzeria would be divine. I headed out the door for the two-block walk.

CHAPTER 42

LUKE

I collected eggs in the henhouse while Charlie waited outside the gate for me. Someone else could do this job, but it kept the memories of Goldi alive. Roostifer pecked at my boots. The hens acted more skittish than usual, which might be why I only gathered seven eggs instead of over a dozen. They probably picked up on my sour mood. "Come on, Charlie. Let's head back."

I set the eggs on the counter, grabbed a beer, and plunked down on the couch. My dog nudged my hand, and I ruffled his ears.

Bootsteps sounded from outside. Charlie rushed to the door whining like he'd done ever since Goldi left. Yep, even my dog missed her.

Someone knocked.

"Come in." I didn't bother getting up.

"Hey." Chase strode inside with his Australian Shepherd

puppy trotting behind him. Both dogs greeted each other by sniffing and wagging their tails.

"What's up?"

"We're going riding. Grab your hat." My younger brother wore that easy grin of his.

"Where to?" I asked, reaching for my Stetson.

"Does it matter?"

I shrugged. "Not really."

As Chase and I saddled up, Pete rode up on his stallion.

"Let's go." I urged my horse into a gallop. The thud of hooves against earth grounded me.

We didn't talk as we barreled through the fields, crested a hill, and found a quiet spot by an old ash tree. Dismounting, I slumped down, my back against the rough bark.

"Man, Goldi really did a number on you." Chase plopped beside me.

"It's not her fault she can't remember. I just wished she hadn't gone back with that cheating bastard. She deserves better than him."

"Damn right, she does," Chase said.

"Have you tried to call her?" Chase nudged me with an elbow.

"I sent a text to her last night, but she hasn't replied."

"Are you gonna give up on her like you did Rachel?" Pete eyed me.

I shrugged.

"Goldi's not like Rachel. Your ex had big dreams of becoming a star," Chase said.

"Goldi belongs in the city."

"Says who? You? Well, you're wrong," Pete growled.

"Maybe, maybe not."

"Do you miss her?" Chase eyed me sideways.

"Hell, yes." I longed for her every minute of the day.

"Then fight for her." Pete crossed his arms over his chest.

"I would, but she's with someone else," I squinted at the sun.

"Are you in love with her?" Chase fiddled with a stick on the ground.

"She was only at the ranch a little over a month."

"Like that matters. From the moment she arrived, you couldn't take your eyes off her. Plus, dumbass, you smile more when she's around." Chase's hand clamped my shoulder, bringing me back to the present. "See if she's happy. If not, make her fall for you all over again."

"You won't know unless you try." Pete nodded.

"It's not that easy."

"I'm pretty sure Goldi's car is still at Uncle Tim's complex." Pete gave me a smirk.

"I figured someone from her family already made arrangements to get it."

"Nope. I saw it there yesterday. Uncle Tim's looking for a driver." Chase grinned at me. "What do you have to lose?"

"My pride. Plus, if I run into her fucking cheater fiancé, I'll most likely knock him out."

"Doncha worry, little bro. If you get arrested, we'll bail you out." Pete puffed up like the older and wiser brother.

If there was even a sliver of a chance she would remember, it would be worth the risk. "I'll do it. I'll take the car to California."

"Yes." Chase punched the air with his fist.

And for the first time in days, hope surged through me.

CHAPTER 43

GOLDI

"How are you doing today?" Mark asked. He grinned at me and went back to shuffling through his briefcase at the table. He was handsome in a bookish kind of way.

I was making raspberry pancakes at the stove. "I'm going stir-crazy, so I decided to cook." I handed him a plate and took the spot across from him.

He poured a generous amount of syrup and took a bite. "These are delicious. Just another perk to spending Saturday morning with you."

"It is nice." My phone rang.

Timberwolf Auto Center.

I answered it and spoke with the owner. "That's great news. I'll be home all day." I hung up.

"What was that about?"

"My car's done and getting dropped off on Tuesday. I owed the shop money, but Luke picked up the bill."

"It's the least he should do. You could sue him. The ranch was negligent for allowing you to go into a horse's stall."

"It was an accident. If I recall, you thanked him at the hospital for giving me a place to stay."

"That day, I had been under duress and was happy to see you. Now that I think about it, you deserve compensation. Honestly, you almost died." He put his hand over mine. "I can draw up papers today."

"No way. As you can see, I'm fine." I fought the agitation bubbling up in my veins.

"Are you really? Chunks of your memory are gone."

"This sounds like something my dad would say."

"Well, he did bring it up to me at work."

"It figures." I got up and looked out the window. "I'm better and more than ready to get my car back."

He stood behind me and wrapped his arms around my waist. "Let's not argue. I hate it when you're upset."

"Then don't piss me off."

"That was never my intention. Don't be mad." He tucked a strand of hair behind my ear.

"Do you have to go into the office?" I hoped he'd stay with me today.

"Not for another hour." He leaned over. His lips crashed into mine with a desperate need.

"Mark," I breathed, my voice shaking.

Then his phone rang, and he pulled away. "I've gotta take this," he said, his voice tinged with reluctant frustration.

And just like that, the moment shattered. Work would always come first for him.

CHAPTER 44

LUKE

I'd been on the road two days now, only stopping for gas and to grab shuteye at a rest stop in Utah. Vegas and State Line hadn't been too bad, but once I hit the split off for the Cajon Pass, drivers acted plain loco.

The 10 Freeway turned out to be even more crowded. People were assholes, in a rush, cutting me off and giving me the bird as they zoomed past me. Could I help it if I liked to drive the speed limit?

I squinted in the rearview mirror, catching a glimpse of Goldi's Camaro. It would be at her doorstep soon enough. The thought stirred up a mix of longing and nerves. Would she remember me?

I just hoped that asshole of a fiancé wasn't around. What if she already married him? It was too late to change my mind, and I really did want to make sure she was doing okay.

After what seemed like forever, I reached the city limits of

Stardust, California. Following the GPS, I took the next offramp. This was it. Do or die, so to speak.

The narrow streets were crammed with parked cars. Some city slicker's sports car zipped around the corner. My grip tightened on the steering wheel as I stomped on the brakes, horn blaring.

Spotting a sign for 5th Street, I read the numbers on the gutter and let out a long breath when I found 3996. Goldi's apartment building.

Luck was on my side when I found an opening out front that looked just wide enough for my truck and trailer. I tucked it in and waited for my pulse to slow. My gut twisted. Part dread, part anticipation.

Rubbing the back of my neck, trying to ease the tension, I got out and walked down the sidewalk. My hands fisted at the thought of that fucking lawyer. But I would keep my calm around him—maybe. Here goes nothing. I got out my phone.

"This is Luke from Timber Wolfe Auto."

I heard a brief pause on the other end. "Luke? From the hospital?"

"Yes, ma'am." I tried to keep my tone professional even though just hearing her voice made me feel like I'd been sucker-punched. "I have your car. I'm standing in front of your building."

"I'll be right down."

The glass doors swung open, and there she was wearing jeans and a T-shirt that hugged her frame, golden hair piled up into a messy bun.

My hands got clammy, and I ran them along my pants. I longed to pull her into my arms, but dammit, I had no right.

"Hi."

"Hey. How've you been?" I said, trying to remain calm when all I wanted to do was pull her into my arms and kiss her.

"Not bad." She walked up to her car and ran her hand against the hood. A huge rock on her finger glittered in the sunlight. "I've missed you, Old Red."

I swallowed hard against the words clawing their way up my throat. I'd missed Goldi. But I couldn't say it. Instead, I managed to get out, "Give me a minute to get your car down. Is there anywhere in particular you want it parked?"

"The street is fine."

I hated this awkwardness between us. As I used the hydraulics, my eyes kept drifting toward hers.

"I'm surprised you're here. Aren't you busy with the ranch?" She glanced at me curiously.

"My two brothers, Pete and Chase, are there." I paused a second to wait for recognition, but her expression didn't change. "And the hands can pick up the slack."

"You have a lot of support. It must be nice."

"It is." I hesitated before adding, "Do you remember meeting any of them?"

She shook her head. "Sorry, I don't."

"It's not a problem." Except that her memory loss tore me apart inside. Once I parked her car, I'd better say something before I lost my chance with her. "I was wondering if you'd like to get coffee—or soda—or whatever." I winced inwardly at how ridiculous I sounded.

"I'm buying as a thank you for bringing my car back."

"You're on." At least I'd get to be with her.

"There's a café just down the street. Do you mind walking?"

"Not at all." And suddenly my world became brighter.

Goldi

Seated in a café with a window view, I sipped my iced latte. This man knew me. Why didn't I remember him?

"Are you okay?" His voice broke through my thoughts.

"Yes, of course." I blinked and forced myself to meet his eyes, soft brown with flecks of gold. "Actually, that's a lie. It sucks having amnesia."

His expression softened. "Don't push yourself, darlin'."

"I'm tired of hearing that." Frustration bubbled up inside me. "Would you mind telling me what I did on your ranch? It might spark something—anything."

Luke studied me for a moment before nodding. "We went horseback riding. You took a liking to Honey. She's one of my gentler mares. Sweet as sugar for the most part." His lips curved up as if the memory brought him some kind of joy.

I frowned, trying to grasp onto something tangible. "That's odd because… in my mind… I haven't ridden in years." I closed my eyes trying to slow down the agitation making my pulse race. "What else did I do?"

He considered my question for a moment. "Well, you cooked for me and some of the other cowboys. You baked dozens of chocolate chip cookies. Used up a whole heap of flour."

"I did?"

"Yep."

"What else did I make?" Cooking was my go-to whenever I needed to relax.

"Apple pies. They turned out delicious even though you used a bag designated for horses."

"That can't be true."

"Scout's honor." He held up three fingers.

"This is infuriating. Over a month of my life is gone. I really hoped talking with you would jog my memory. What if I never get it back?"

"Fretting won't do you any good."

"It's not that easy to do." In fact, it had become unbearably difficult as the days went on. "Are you heading home soon?"

"Not for another week or so. I'm going to check out a few horses while I'm here."

"I love horses."

"I know." He gave me a devilish grin. "Maybe you'd like to join me tomorrow? Could use the company."

"Sorry. I can't." As much as I'd like to get away, it wouldn't be right spending time alone with him. After all, I was engaged to someone else.

"Of course." He handed me a business card. "Here's my number just in case you have more questions."

"Thanks." I took it and typed his info into my phone. I couldn't lose my only key to the missing month.

"That's a beautiful ring."

I held it up, allowing the diamonds to catch the light, the facets glinting like tiny stars. "It's new. My other one got lost during my trip. Did you ever see it?"

Luke's eyes flicked to the ring, his jaw tightening just a fraction. "Can't say I have. Sorry, ma'am." His voice sounded steady, but a bit restrained.

The waitress brought out the bill, and I paid it.

"We'd best head back," I said.

We strolled along the sidewalk toward my apartment.

"Do you like living here?" he asked.

"I do." I glanced at his big biceps. "We're close to L.A. and not far from the beaches."

"I plan to at least dip my toes in the ocean while I'm here."

"You should try paddle boarding or take a surfing lesson." I was blathering, which wasn't like me.

"I might just do that."

When we reached the front of my building, the moment felt heavy.

His expression was unreadable, but something flickered in his gaze, something uncertain. "If you ever want to talk, give me a call."

I doubted I would.

"Goldi." He hesitated, just long enough for my pulse to trip. "Take care of yourself."

"I will."

He nodded, then turned and walked away, his broad shoulders tense, his stride purposeful. I watched him go. This might be the last time I ever saw him.

That thought settled onto my chest like a weight.

CHAPTER 45

LUKE

My reunion with Goldi had been an utter disappointment. Based on that huge rock on her finger, she was staying with the damn lawyer. As much as I wanted to tell her about the cheater, everything I had read said it was best to let the person's memories come back on their own.

Last night, my sister had said to give Goldi space.

She took my number. That had to be enough for now.

Around eight a.m. I merged onto the freeway. The sea of brake lights was a stark contrast to the open roads of Wyoming. I inched forward, the truck's engine grumbling as if sharing my frustration. I'd rather wrestle a rattler than be stuck in California traffic.

Once I hit the 15 Freeway, the road opened up. My radio played rock which reminded me of Goldi. I longed to call her. Bad idea. Let her remember me on her own.

A sports car cut in front of me, missing my bumper by inches. How did people commute in this? I continued driving and finally arrived at the Silver Spoon Ranch, a headache brewing behind my eyes. Popping an aspirin and downing it with water, I got out. If luck were on my side, I'd add a couple of Tennessee Walkers to our stables.

The owner greeted me and led me to a lanky sorrel with shifty eyes. He pranced in place, tossing his head and snorting. "Blaze has good bloodlines, plenty of spirit."

I stepped closer, trying to get a better look. The horse immediately sidled away, nostrils flaring.

"Spirited, huh?" I muttered, narrowing my eyes. All flash. Tons of nervous energy. No substance. "How does he handle under pressure?"

The man shrugged. "He's young. Still learning." Blaze pawed at the ground, ears twitching at each little sound.

"Look," I said, crossing my arms. "I want a horse that's reliable. Something tells me this one would bolt if a leaf blew by."

His jaw tightened. "He just needs a firm hand, that's all."

I snorted. "No thanks. Got anything a little more... solid?"

Disappearing into the stables, he emerged leading a striking black gelding. The horse moved with a quiet confidence.

"This is Thunder."

The animal was impressive. This trip might not be a total waste after all. "He's got good conformation," I stepped forward to get a better look. The second I got within arm's reach, Thunder's ears pinned back flat against his head. His lips curled, revealing teeth. That horse was a definite no.

After seeing three more horses, none of them matching my needs, I said, "I appreciate you taking the time with me, but I think we both know this isn't going anywhere."

We shook hands. And then I was once again driving on the damn freeway for a couple more hours. My stomach growled, a stark reminder that disappointment didn't curb hunger. I pulled into a drive thru.

"Welcome to Burger Bonanza, can I take your order?" A tinny voice crackled through the speaker. I ordered a double cheeseburger.

At the window, a teen said, "Were you in a rodeo?"

It must've been my hat. I had yet to see anyone else wearing a Stetson in town. "Just looking at horses all day." I took the bag and ate in the parking lot. The bright lights and the constant hum of traffic made me long for the endless sky of Wyoming.

CHAPTER 46

GOLDI

After coming in late last night, Mark promised he'd be home for dinner at six. I'd made his favorites. Duck a l'Orange, garlic roasted potatoes, braised red cabbage, and a Chocolate Grand Marnier Cake for dessert. I'd gone all out to show him how much I loved him.

The clock said it was five. Light from the window shone on my diamond ring. It looked pretty.

I glanced out the window and spotted Mark on the street, chatting with our neighbor, his stance straight, his shoulders locked. Jenny mirrored the intensity, arms crossing and uncrossing. He ran a hand through his hair, gripping the back of his neck before dropping his arm in defeat.

Jenny hesitated, shifting on her heels, and stepped closer to hug him. It wasn't one of those friendly, 'Oh hey, buddy' hugs. Her hands slid down his back, slow and deliberate, stopping just above his butt.

And Mark? That jerk didn't even flinch. He just stood there, letting her press her breasts against his chest.

I frowned, my fingers gripping the window frame so hard I thought I might leave permanent fingerprints in the wood. Something about it felt off—not wrong, exactly, but... unexpected. Like when you're watching a movie, and the plot just twisted. I trusted Mark. Or at least, I thought I did.

But then his arms came around her, and he kissed her full-on, tongue-down-her-throat, while his hips moved in a rhythm against her.

I wanted to look away. I really did. But I couldn't. My eyes were glued to them, watching every stupid detail like a voyeur. Her hand moved to his zipper. I thought she might pull it down right there on the street. But Mark broke the kiss, his lips grazing her neck as he whispered something in her ear.

And then—bam. A memory slammed into my brain. Mark. Naked. In our bed. With our neighbor.

The image was so vivid it made my stomach churn. The rustle of sheets, the sound of her moaning his name, the sickening gasp that tore from my throat when I walked in on them. It was all there, playing on a loop in my head.

I swayed where I stood. The room tilted, and my vision blurred at the edges. My legs buckled. I practically collapsed into a chair, gripping the table for stability. My heart pounded hard.

I stared into space. This couldn't be happening to me. I'd always been a good person. I treated Mark well. And he does this to me.

Breathe, Goldi. Just breathe.

Every kiss. Every promise. Every 'I love you.' Lies.

My fists clenched in my lap. White-hot fury crashed over me. I trusted him with my heart, and he shattered it. I blinked back the sting of tears, refusing to let them fall. He didn't deserve them.

But the rage? Oh, I drowned in it.

And for once, I wouldn't hold back.

The door creaked open. "The food smells delicious." Mark wore a brimming smile as he walked into the kitchen. Then he spotted me. "Sugar, what's wrong?"

I couldn't speak. Just stared at him like a zombie.

He placed his hands on my shoulders. I flinched.

"Did something happen?" He pulled a chair next to me.

That snapped me out of my fog. "It sure did." I flashed him a smile. "I was thinking about the reason I left. You know, the conference. It's funny, but I can't find any pictures on my phone."

His shoulders squared, back rigid, his usual smug confidence dimming just enough for me to notice. "You broke down on the way there." The more he talked, the deeper the hole he dug.

"Right. Of course I did."

"What are you getting at?"

"I saw you talking to our super friendly neighbor. Don't you think she's nice?"

His face fell for a quick second before his lips twitched up. "She's alright."

"I noticed the two of you from the window before you came in."

A muscle in his jaw ticked. "She's upset because her boyfriend broke up with her."

"Which makes total sense why your lips were dueling. You cheated on me," I kept my voice even. Calm.

"W-what are you talking about?" He averted my eyes.

"You were with her. That's why I left."

"It's not true."

"For weeks, you've acted like we had a strong relationship."

"Believe me, it is."

"Your right eye's twitching. I know you're lying."

He groaned.

"Memories are funny. I know better than most about that. Admit it. I deserve the truth."

"Fine. I slept with her. It meant nothing." He attempted to reach for my hand, but I moved it under the table. "I promise it won't happen again."

I laughed.

He remained quiet.

I folded my arms and glowered at him.

"Sugar, please don't be like this. You know we belong together."

"Meaning if I marry you, you'll make partner quicker in my dad's law firm." Things became crystal clear. He'd been with me to help himself.

He blinked at me in surprise. "It's not like that. I love you. I always have."

"You only love yourself." Placing my phone into my pocket, I rushed into the bedroom and grabbed my rolling suitcase from the closet.

"Come on." He moved closer and grabbed my arm. "Don't leave. I love you."

"Like you even know me. I went along with whatever you wanted. I supported you even when you worked long hours. I did it because I thought I needed a man to survive." Haphazardly throwing clothes into my luggage, I added my medication from the end table just in case I needed it. "But I don't need you. I don't even like you."

"Don't be like this," he pleaded.

I huffed.

"HEY. There's an empty storefront on Main Street that would be perfect for a bakery. We can look at it today."

Now he came up with a bakery option. Typical. "As if I'd ever own anything with you."

I opened one of my drawers and added underwear into my suitcase. "Now I get why I ended up in Wyoming." Although that memory had yet to come back. "Driving for days to get the image of you two in our bed out of my mind."

The ring snagged on one of my thongs. I took the band off and slammed it on the end table. "I'm done."

An image of what I did with the first ring came to me. "You lied about the other ring. I threw it at you. Jenny picked it up off the floor and slipped it on her finger. You've been with that woman the whole time."

"It's not like that."

"What kind of a fool do you think I am?" I zipped up my suitcase. "It's best that I move out. I'll come back for my stuff another day." Holding my head high, I turned to him. "Just so you know, you'll be hearing from my dad soon."

His jaw dropped.

I strode down the hall, texted my sister to say I'd be coming over, and got into my car.

CHAPTER 47

GOLDI

Since Hayley wasn't home, I used my key to her place. It came in handy when I fed her cat.

As soon as I walked in with my suitcase trailing behind me, the little charmer rubbed against my legs, begging to be picked up. Leaving my luggage where it landed, the two of us snuggled on the couch.

"You're such a sweetie, Snickerdoodle." I petted her, finding comfort in her ultrasoft fur. She purred for a few minutes, then hopped down and stood by her bowl in the kitchen. "Are you hungry, sweet kitty?"

She meowed.

I poured kibble into her bowl.

The front door shut. "Hey, Goldi. I see you got your car back?"

"Luke brought it yesterday. He's the guy who took me to the hospital in Cheyenne and stayed."

"That's a long drive. I hope you thanked him."

"I did." I told her about having coffee with him. Then I said nonchalantly, "I left Mark."

"Good for you." She came over and gave me a bear hug. "I never liked him."

I blinked at her. "Wait—what? Why didn't you say anything?"

"I tried. But you were in love." Her expression softened. "I've been there before with my ex."

"Did he cheat on you?"

She hesitated for half a second before nodding once. "That—and cleaned out my savings." She gave a short laugh. "I got it back eventually, thanks to Dad. But still, it was a stupid stage of my life. I'm smarter than that now."

"Looks like we were both fooled."

"Let's sit on the couch." She motioned over her shoulder. "I've got Praline Pecan ice cream in the freezer. It's therapy in frozen form."

"Works for me. I hope you don't mind me crashing here." I flopped onto the cushions.

"Never." She handed me a spoon. "Did you get you memory back?"

"Just the part where I caught dillweed in bed with our neighbor."

She winced. "I'm sorry."

"It's not your fault."

"Umm..." She fiddled with her spoon. "You have no idea how much I wanted to spill. Especially when you moved back in with Mark. But you were already there when mom told me about the accident."

My brain felt like it might explode. "You should have told me."

"Your doctor said not to push you. I hated the idea, but I didn't want to chance making things worse." She sighed.

"I see." I didn't really.

"I came by when Mom was there and tried to talk with you. You were pretty out of it." She shook her head. "Mom said you were healing and doing well, so I believed her. I told Mom she should be staying with you, but she said you were comfortable and happy. I tried to tell her about what Mark did, but she wouldn't listen. You know her. She thinks Mark is practically perfect."

"True enough."

"It's probably for the best. Mom probably would have blurted everything out and you might have gotten worse. I think everything happens for a reason."

"You could have called."

"I did. Countless times. When you finally texted me back, I'd been out of town and decided it would be best to tell you in person."

"Okay. I get it. That doesn't mean I like it." I clenched and unclenched my hands.

"I'm sorry for all you've been through." Her eyes got soft. "How are you feeling now?"

"Much better."

She smiled at me in that way of hers that made me relax and want to talk. "Can you believe Mark said I went to Wyoming to attend a baking expo?"

"I'm not surprised. To be fair, he lied for his own self-preservation." She scrunched up her nose. "Enough about him. Do you remember being at the ranch?"

"Little things like riding in the hills and looking out these huge picture windows when I baked." I tried to think but nothing else came

"What about line dancing?" She tilted her head.

"I wish I could remember it." I scrolled through my photos and found one with me in a saloon. "Luke has a really nice smile." Staring at his mouth in the picture, it hit me. "The first time we kissed we were in the stables." As a barrage of memories hit me, I slumped back into the couch. "It's too much."

"Take deep breaths. In and out," my sister said. "That's it. Keep on breathing. This is why the doctor wanted you to regain the memories on your own. It's overwhelming. I'll get you some water."

"I'm struggling to make sense of the fleeting images bombarding me."

Hayley handed me a glass. "Take slow sips."

I did. My head stopped spinning. "I'm better now."

"Do you want to talk about it?"

"Luke and I were lovers." I picked up my phone, opened the attached holder on the back, and spotted his card. "This is his number. Should I call him?"

"Yes."

"I'm not sure what to say." My hands shook as I stared at his name: Luke Wolfe, Sunrise Ridge Ranch.

"Have him come over." She squeezed my hand.

I pressed his number.

"Hello," a deep voice answered.

"This is Goldi… Summers."

"It's good to hear from you. Is everything okay?"

"Not hardly." He didn't know the half of it. "What are you doing tomorrow?" I deserved answers now, but knew it'd be better to sleep on it.

"Checking out a couple of potential horses for our ranch. Wanna join me?"

"I'd love to." I couldn't help grinning.

CHAPTER 48

LUKE

My beautiful gal sat next to me in my truck. Not exactly my gal, but I could work with this. I packed us a lunch. Even picked out a park for our way back. After all, people have to eat. And if today happened to remind her of Wyoming, of us, well… I wouldn't complain.

We drove past a fenced-in pasture. She pointed to a cluster of red cattle. "Are your cows similar?"

"Those are Red Angus. We have Black Angus. Herefords. And a mix of the two called Black Baldies."

She got out her phone. "Yours are much cuter. The white makes them look innocent."

I laughed. "Only you would say that."

"What?" She held up her phone. "You have to admit this calf is adorable."

"If you say so, city girl."

"That better be a compliment, mister."

I smirked. God, I'd missed this. "I like it when you're riled.

Your cheeks get all pink and your eyes turn a darker green." Sexy as hell. Whoa, there, I told myself. Because my druthers longed to pull over to the side and kiss her senseless.

"You're teasing me."

"Yes, ma'am."

She pressed a hand against her forehead.

"Are you okay?" I slowed down. "I'll pull to the side if you need it."

"That's not necessary." She paused for a few seconds. "My ex cheated on me." Her voice was tinged with both anger and hurt. "I left him—that's why I had you pick me up at my sisters."

"It's about time." Hope surged inside me. "Do you remember us?"

"You kissed me in the stables."

I laughed. "I sure did."

"How serious were we?" she asked quietly, as if uncertain of the answer.

"I was all in." Not that I ever told her that.

"And I wasn't?"

"You liked me well enough." I attempted to keep the conversation light. "I can be quite charming."

"Confident, much?" she asked.

"Where you are concerned, not in the least."

She worried her bottom lip. "I'm a little confused. I made a ton of chocolate chip cookies at your house, you took me to town to get my car fixed, and I stayed at a hotel. But then what happened?"

"The ranch ended up hiring you because it would take weeks to fix your car."

"That makes sense."

"Ask me anything. I don't mind."

Her gaze returned to the window. "This memory thing is pretty taxing."

"I can't even imagine."

"At least things are coming back. Be patient with me."

"Always." She was here. That's what mattered. The GPS directed me to turn right and we drove up a long driveway.

"It's pretty out here."

"It is," but I glanced at her. I parked by the stables and hurried to help her out. Damn, she looked good in that tight fitting pair of jeans and a sparkly tank top.

A stocky man in a baseball cap walked up to us. "You must be Luke."

We shook hands and I introduced Goldi.

"The stallion you're interested in is in the second stall. His name is Devil."

"That's the roan I saw on his website," I said to her.

We followed him inside a spacious stable.

I asked, "How does he ride?"

"Loves to run. Often have to hold him back."

I went inside the stable and ran my hand down the horse's legs, feeling for swelling, heat, or old injuries. Then I lifted each hoof, checking for wear or cracks. Finally, I opened his mouth. Everything looked good. "Think I could take him for a ride?"

"Yes, sir. If you'd like I'll saddle up a horse for you too, miss. There's a nice trail behind the house."

"I'd love that."

I whispered to her. "Are you sure you're up to it?" It had been a little over a month since her accident.

"I am." She pointed to her tennis shoes. "It's too bad I didn't bring any boots."

"I have a pair in the truck that should fit you." I kept the cowhide ones just in case.

"Perfect"

"I'll get your horses ready. What kind of a rider are you, miss?"

"Okay. I usually rent horses from a local stable."

The man smiled. "Sunshine should be perfect for you. She's fairly calm."

I handed Goldi the black and white cow print boots.

She studied them for a second. "Did these belong to your sister?"

"They did. You remembered." I wanted to shout yippee but didn't want to upset her.

"Yes. I like Peggy. She's nice." She wrapped her arms around me, and I held her.

"You're doing well—for a city girl."

"I used to call you cowboy, right?" Her eyes widened.

"Yes, ma'am." She might not remember all our time together, but I was with her, which mattered a whole hell of a lot.

The ranch owner brought us the horses. After mounting, we walked down the trail. I insisted Goldi wear a helmet and planned to take our ride at an easy pace.

"Race you to the creek." She took off.

I wasn't sure if she should be doing this, but how could I stop her? She had her own ideas. I galloped full out to see what Devil could do. In several seconds, we passed Goldi. I slowed to let her catch up and we walked side by side.

"I've missed riding." Her cheeks were flushed, her smile wide. "Did we race to a water tower?"

"We sure did."

"I got another memory back." Her eyes were bright. "One day I might even feel normal again."

"To me, you're perfect just as you are."

"Aww. That's sweet."

"I aim to please. Let's head back."

"Are you buying that stallion?"

"Yep. And your mare too if I can. She'd make a good horse for Peggy's girls when they get a little older." I'd give the mare to Goldi if she wanted. Or she could have Honey. We walked our horses.

With a contract signed and the horses being shipped next week, we drove off.

"I packed us a lunch. Would it be okay to stop at Heritage Park before I take you home?"

"Why not? I've got nowhere else to be."

In about ten minutes we were sitting on a blanket overlooking a pond. I hoped maybe the water would bring up memories. It had been hard, sitting so close to her and not being able to kiss her all day, but I could wait until she was ready.

CHAPTER 49

GOLDI

After a wonderful time with Luke, today I had to face family dinner with my parents. My stomach churned with dread. What I had to say wouldn't be easy.

Hayley navigated her SUV along the 5 Freeway and took the third turn-off. "It'll be fine. You're telling mom and dad Mark is your ex, aren't you? They deserve the truth," she insisted.

I closed my eyes as if that would block out the inevitable. "I can't."

"I'll be right there with you."

"Fine." I gave her a reluctant surrender.

"How'd it go with Luke yesterday?" she asked, steering the conversation into safer territory.

"Not bad. We looked at horses, and he took me on a picnic afterwards."

"It sounds romantic. Did he kiss you?" A teasing grin spread across her face.

"No. I wish he had." I sighed. "The cowboy's being respectful."

"Taking things slow for now is probably a good thing."

We pulled into our parents' driveway and I took a deep breath. "Okay." My voice was steadier than I felt. "Let's do this."

I stepped into the foyer, nervous energy buzzing through my veins.

"Hayley. Goldi-locks!" Dad wrapped us up in his arms. "You're just in time to hear the big news!"

I hugged him back, guilt twisting in my stomach. "What news?"

"We just closed the Hendrickson deal. It's the biggest account the firm's landed in a decade."

"That's... that's great, Dad," I managed, my voice sounding hollow even to my own ears. My sister just smiled.

He didn't seem to notice our reactions, launching into a detailed explanation of profit margins and expansion plans. I nodded along, my mind racing. How could I shatter his good mood?

"Dinner's ready. Let's talk in there." Mom ushered us to the dining room.

My brother, Will, barely looked up from his phone, his fingers flying as he textcd.

I sat next to him. "Busy, huh?"

"You don't know the half of it." Will scrunched his eyes.

Dinner went on, and I tried to eat but mostly swirled my fork through the noodles while Dad continued to talk about his news.

"We'll be doing contracts, mergers, and acquisitions for ten new offices."

I got it. This client was a big deal for him. But did he have to be so cheerful when my insides were churning with worry about what I was about to say?

"Mark has been instrumental in our research." Dad stopped. "By the way, why didn't you bring him with you tonight?"

The name hit me like a physical blow. I flinched.

"Sweetheart?" His brow furrowed. "Are you alright?"

I swallowed hard, feeling Hayley's supportive presence next to me. It's now or never.

"About him… We're through."

"What happened?" Mom's eyes searched my face with laser-like intensity.

I took a deep breath. "Mark cheated on me."

Dad's face reddened. Mom's hand flew to her chest, her eyes wide with disbelief. Will's phone clattered to the table, work emails forgotten in an instant. I almost saw the gears turning in his head, recalculating every interaction he'd had with Mark at the firm.

And Hayley smiled. Thank goodness for her.

Sipping wine and grateful for something to do with my hands, I forced myself to meet my father's blazing eyes. "I caught him with the neighbor. That's why I left town and ended up in Wyoming." The words tumbled out, each one a sharp reminder of the betrayal that shattered my world.

Hayley spoke up, her voice steady. "She's living with me while she figures out her next steps."

Dad appeared to struggle processing this information. It must be hard to reconcile the man who worked for him with the one who'd broken his daughter's heart.

"I'm sorry," Mom whispered. "We had no idea..."

I nodded, not trusting myself to speak. The lump in my throat threatened to choke me.

Dad's fist crashing on the table made me jump. Silverware rattled, and Mom's delicate china teacup clinked against its saucer. "I hired that son of a bitch. I trusted him." His voice blazed with fury. "And I'll make sure he never works in this town again!"

Will rubbed his temple. "Dad," he started, his voice strained, "I know you're angry. We all are. But maybe we should think about this before—"

Dad cut him off, his voice rising. "There's nothing to think about. I can't tolerate a cheater."

"I never liked him," my sister said, crossing her arms over her chest. "Always thought he was too slick, too perfect. Guess I was right."

I shot her a grateful look.

"Hayley, that doesn't help." Mom narrowed her eyes.

"What can I do for you?" Dad asked, his voice gentler than I'd heard it in a long time.

The question caught me off guard. "I don't know."

I looked up to see Mom's eyes fixed on me. "You've been through so much with the accident and now this. We just want you to be okay."

"I'm better now that my memories are returning." I thought about riding yesterday with Luke. The wind in my hair, and not a care in the world. I caught an image in my mind of racing through wildflowers at Luke's ranch.

"What are you going to do next?" Will asked.

"I'm not entirely sure," I ran my finger along the rim of my wine glass. Whatever it was, deep down I hoped it would include Luke.

CHAPTER 50

LUKE

Goldi had been busy yesterday, so I visited a saddle company, a bit and spur manufacturer, and spent the afternoon at a local trail barn. Those horses were worn ragged, but the visit gave me ideas for the dude ranch Chase talked about.

Waking up at six, my fingers twitched to text her. Except this was the crack of dawn. So I ate breakfast downstairs and snatched a flyer with local attractions, amusement parks, and museums. In my room, I was searching for options when my phone buzzed with a text.

Goldi: Are you busy today?

Me: No plans.

Goldi: I'm going to the beach. Wanna come with?

Me: Yep.

Goldi: What hotel are you at?

I texted her the address.

Goldi: Pick you up in 30.

I dialed Peggy's number.

"What's up, bro?"

I told her about the texts.

"It's all good. Let her take the lead."

"Yeah, sure." Like that would be easy for me.

Less than an hour later, we arrived at Venice Beach. Goldi seemed right at home, those big green eyes lighting up like fireworks. "What do you think of this place?"

"It's interesting. There are more people here than the state of Wyoming."

"Come along." She wore a spark of mischief in her eyes.

"Yes, ma'am."

She tugged me toward one of those touristy shops and bounced from one cluttered area to the next. She slipped on a pair of giant purple sunglasses. "How do I look?"

"Funny."

She shoved a wide-brimmed monstrosity covered in fake flowers and feathers at me. "Your turn, cowboy. Model this one for me."

My first instinct was to grumble. Instead, I shoved the hat onto my head with as much dignity as I could muster. "Happy now?"

"Very." Goldi doubled over, shoulders shaking, and I ended up chuckling despite my mock irritation.

We drifted along. Up ahead, flames danced. "What the hell is that?

"A fire juggler."

A guy twirled blazing batons through the air.

"If you ever get tired of baking, you should try that."

"Sure." Her arm linked through mine. "Look. A photo

booth." She yanked aside the curtain and ushered me inside a clunky box.

It was a tight fit, our shoulders brushing as we squeezed in.

"Okay, big guy." Her fingers poised over the start button. "First one has to be normal, deal?"

"Yep." I played along with a resigned shrug.

The camera flashed.

"Now act silly." Goldi crossed her eyes, and I just gazed at her.

I leaned in close and kissed her cheek for the third snapshot. By the fourth shot, we were laughing hard.

"This is going in my scrapbook." She added it to her backpack. "Oh, look. Pizza. I'm starving. How 'bout you?"

"I could eat." We snagged a table with a red and white checkered tablecloth.

Goldi opened the box. "Bon appétit, cowboy."

It didn't take long for the two of us to finish.

We came to the beach. Goldi ran toward the water, and I followed her. She dropped to the sand near the shore, sifting through shells and rocks. "Pick a shell. It's good luck."

I nabbed the first one I found. "Will this one do?"

"As long as it chose you." The corners of her mouth quirked up. "Close your eyes and make a wish."

I wanted her to come back to Wyoming.

"What'd you wish for?" she asked.

"I can't say. That might jinx it."

"Fine. Then we're building a sandcastle." She got on her knees. "

I sunk down onto the warm sand.

"Been a while since I built one of these." Her tone came out wistful. "It's nice to slow down and enjoy being outdoors."

"Do you like living in a city?"

She shrugged. "I like the beach."

"What are we making?"

"A birthday cake. It's going to look like a crab."

"Interesting. How can I help with your sand creation?"

"You could make the oblong body."

I did as she asked. She shaped it. I attempted to make pinchers. "Are these okay?"

"Sure." She evened them out, added eyes and a mouth, and 'Happy Birthday' on the top of his head. "What do you think?"

"It's different. If this guy were real, I'd definitely avoid his pinchers. But I like his smile."

"I think he's cute."

"If you're happy, that's all that matters." I could tell she was based on her wide grin. I'd love to make her smile like that every day. I gazed into her eyes. "Do you still want your own bakery?"

"It's my dream—someday."

I'd make it happen in Wyoming, if I could.

"It's a beautiful day. I'm going swimming." She took off.

I ran after her. When she kicked up an arc of foamy spray that splattered right at my face, I yelped, more in surprise than any real protest. "Hey!"

She giggled, "Oops, my bad."

"Is that how you wanna play it?" I captured her by the waist and tugged her close.

She brought her lips against mine and kissed me. "I remember us. I remember everything."

"It's about damn time." I kissed her again.

"Luke. I'm glad you didn't give up on me."

"Never." She was mine now.

She nodded. "But you live in Wyoming."

"We'll figure it out together." I'd have to talk her into moving in with me later. "For now, you're coming back to my hotel room."

"Works for me. I hope you're as good in bed as I remember, cowboy." She smiled at me.

And my cock came to attention.

CHAPTER 51

LUKE

After an incredible night of sex with Goldi, I wanted her in my life more than ever and would do my best to show her she belonged with me. But getting her to come to Wyoming had to be her choice.

Heading to meet her sister for lunch, I fidgeted with my hat. "What's Hayley like?"

"Wickedly smart."

"Like you."

"Not really." Goldi gripped the wheel. "She can be like a dog with a bone when making a point. That's what makes her a top-notch family law attorney."

"Does she work for your dad?"

"No, much to his dismay. But my brother joined him in corporate law."

"You've got quite a family." Now I understood why Goldi had been with a lawyer.

"We're here." She easily parallel parked the car into a spot on the street.

"Where'd you learn to do that?"

"My nana."

"From what you've said, she sounded like one special lady."

She gave a wistful sigh. "Unlike my mom, who can be a touch dramatic, Nana was chill. I think she would have liked you and your ranch."

We walked inside. The tangy aroma made my nose twitch. It wasn't unpleasant, just different.

Folks sat at the sushi bar, watching a cook slice up raw fish.

"There she is."

A woman with long chestnut hair waved us over to a table near the back. "You must be Luke." She stood and shook my hand. Green eyes that matched Goldi's seemed to size me up. "I've heard a lot about you."

"Same here." I held out the chair for Goldi and sat next to her.

"You ever have sushi before?"

"Can't say I have." I poured myself some tea.

The waitress set bowls of soup in front of us.

"I ordered the variety platter. Hope that's okay?" Hayley looked directly at me.

"It's perfect," Goldi said. "You'll get to try a little bit of everything."

"Sounds good. What is this?" I motioned to the soup.

"Try it first, then I'll tell you."

All eyes were on me as I took a spoonful. "This is delicious."

"It's miso soup. Tofu, seaweed, and green onions," Hayley added.

"Do you think your brothers would like it?" As of last night, Goldi remembered them.

"It's hard to say."

"You have brothers?" Hayley asked.

"Pete and Chase. They're both single, in case you were wondering."

"Do you have any pictures?"

I got out my phone and showed her one from my sister's wedding. "I also have a sister name Peggy who's scarier than hell. Pardon my language."

"Actually, she's nice."

"You worked with her for a couple of days, didn't you?" Hayley asked.

Goldie nodded. "Just so you know, I remember my time at the ranch."

"That's great." Hayley eyed Goldi sideways. "Did it have anything to do with what you did yesterday?"

Goldi's cheeks flushed. "What? We went to Venice. Ate pizza. Walked along the beach."

"And didn't sleep in the guest room last night." Hayley tilted her head, watching her sister.

"Guilty as charged, counselor."

"You're happy. That's all that matters." Hayley turned to me. "How much longer will you be in town?"

"Another week. Maybe two." Would I give up all I knew to live here? Hell, no. But where would that leave me and Goldi?

"You know, you could go back to Wyoming." Hayley pointed at her sister. "You loved it there."

"I wouldn't mind," I said.

The waitress dropped off the platter with several plates, saving Goldi from having to answer.

"Just to warn you, the jalapeño-topped nigiri has quite a kick." Hayley put some fish on her plate and added sauce that I assumed would be spicy.

"I'll try that next time."

Goldi added a golden log on a plate and handed it to me. "The California roll is pretty mild."

It was delicious. So were the sashimi and hamachi rolls.

The waitress brought out the bill. Hayley handed over her credit card. "This is my treat. It's not every day I get to meet a real live cowboy." Her phone buzzed. "I'd better get back. Luke, it was a pleasure meeting you."

"The pleasure is all mine. I can see where Goldi gets her spunk."

Her sister grinned. "I hope to see you again soon." She left.

"I think that went well. I like your sister."

"Good to hear. She's my best friend." Goldi quirked a brow. "Hey. It's only two pm. How do you feel about Disneyland?"

"As long as we go on the Matterhorn and Space Mountain." I'd seen a couple of videos of those rides.

"You're on."

CHAPTER 52

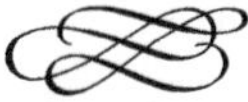

GOLDI

It was a perfect day for a picnic in the park. Mid-seventies. My sundress blew in the light wind. A smattering of clouds floated above. Our bench tucked under a tree overlooking the bay.

I'd never dated anyone like Luke. He listened to me, kissed like the devil, and holy moly, the sex was amazing. My core heated thinking about what he did to me last night and then again this morning.

"Keep looking at me that way, city girl, and we'll be heading back to the hotel."

"Would that be so bad?"

"I'm trying to woo you right now. Is it working?" He kissed my cheek.

"I'm not sure." I teased, keeping my voice light, though my heart was anything but.

"How about this?" he hummed. His lips brushed against my

jaw, feather-light, trailing soft, slow kisses along the curve of my neck.

I tilted my face toward him. Our lips met. The world melted away as we kissed. My hands found his chest, feeling the steady thrum of his heartbeat.

He pulled away and met my eyes, his gaze dark and searching. "To think I'd been leery about falling for another city girl." His thumb brushed against my cheek, tender, reverent. "But you're worth it."

"Did someone hurt you?" I needed to know.

He exhaled, shifting slightly, his fingers grazing the collar of his T-shirt. "Rachel."

"What was she like?"

"Different from you. Dark hair. Brown eyes. Played the guitar."

A pang of jealousy hit, and I tamped it down. After all, Luke traveled hundreds of miles to be with me. "How'd you meet?"

"In high school my junior year. She moved to town, and I fell right from the start. We dated all the way through senior year. Anyway, I saved the money I made from doing chores and drove to Cheyenne for a ring."

"Why not get one in town?"

"I wanted to surprise Rachel."

I placed a hand on his shoulder and massaged it with my fingertips.

"A week before graduation, I took her out on the lake in a boat, thinking it was romantic. She complained about the bugs." He let out a slow, controlled exhale. "Anyway, I asked her to marry me. She laughed, saying she refused to stay in this town, and once she had her diploma in hand she'd head to Nashville. It turned out I was just a guy to pass the time."

"You're better than that."

"I get it now." He gave a half-hearted chuckle.

"But I did the same to you and went back to the city."

He gazed into my eyes. "You're nothing like her. You're determined, hard-working, and don't back down from a challenge."

"You make me sound like a cattle dog."

"A cute one." His fingers brushed along my arm, slow and deliberate, sending a shiver racing down my spine.

"Aww. You're sweet."

"I do my best." His gaze dropped to my lips.

A slow heat spread through my chest, pooling low in my stomach. Given we were in the middle of the park, I should have said something lighthearted to break the spell. But I didn't.

"Goldi." His fingers tilted my chin ever so slightly. His lips met mine, testing, exploring, savoring. I leaned in, tilting my head, deepening the kiss. When he finally pulled away, just an inch, it left me breathless. His forehead rested against mine, his thumb tracing the curve of my cheek. "I love you, Goldi."

"You do?" My heart soared.

"Sure. What do you say you move back to the ranch and give us a real chance?"

I couldn't speak. Tears welled in my eyes.

"I get it. You can't leave the city." He looked down at the ground.

"I didn't say that."

"No?"

"I'd love to live in Wyoming with you." I kissed his cheek. "That is, if the cottage is still available."

"You'll be living with me." He yanked me onto his lap and kissed me long and hard.

"I suppose that works," I said, panting. "Holy fudge sticks. I have to break the news that I'm leaving to my parents."

"I'll go with you."

"I need to handle this on my own." Which I would do. Tomorrow. Maybe.

"Fair enough."

"Thanks for understanding." I settled into his arms and said, "I love you, cowboy." A memory niggled in my mind. "I can't believe we made love against a stable wall."

"Yep. And in other places too—like the kitchen and under the stars. You asked. How could I refuse?" He tugged me closer, giving me a lopsided grin.

"Smooth move, cowboy."

"What can I say? You're mighty distracting."

The kiss that followed proved I wasn't the only one who could be distracting.

CHAPTER 53

LUKE

Tomorrow, I'd be heading back to Wyoming with Goldi. My visit to this big city turned out great. I purchased five horses from three different ranches. Found a new dealer to buy bridles and bits. And visited Disneyland, Universal Studios, the Griffith Observatory where we stargazed, and a ton of restaurants and shopping malls.

But I was more than ready to go home. "I'm glad you're driving. You're good at it," I told her.

"Then why do you have a death grip on the seat?"

"Because I don't trust other people. From what I've seen here drivers are loco."

"I get it. These freeways take getting used to."

I took her hand. "Where are we off to?" I knew it would be a beach trip.

"Pacific Shores. It's way less crowded than Venice. We'll just chill and watch the sunset."

"I'm all for that." I patted the zippered pocket of my swim trunks for the small square box, finding it in place.

She parked and popped the trunk. I snatched two oversized towels.

"Love your shoes."

"Thanks. Think I'll replace my boots with these?" I held up one foot showing the blue crocs Goldi talked me into buying at a shopping mall. They might look like hell but were kinda comfortable.

"They wouldn't be practical on the ranch. Come on."

"You're bossy." I said as I watched the sway of her hips in the short yellow sundress she wore.

"Only with you."

We made our way down to the sand and set the towels not too far from the shore.

She peeled off her dress, revealing a hot pink bikini. "Wanna go for a walk? Get our feet wet?"

I managed to hide my desire as I took off my shirt and shoes. The sand felt cool between my toes. "Lead the way."

We strolled along the shore.

"You're awful quiet." Goldi nudged me with her elbow.

I cleared my throat. "Just takin' in the view, darlin'."

She scooped up water and splashed me.

I ran after her, caught her in my arms and kissed her. Waves splashed against our ankles. The weight of the ring box felt heavy in my pocket.

It was now or never.

I led her a few steps away from the water's edge, grabbed a piece of driftwood, and started writing in the sand.

"What are you doing?"

"Patience, city girl." As I finished the last letter, I heard her sharp intake, turned to face her and sank to one knee.

"Luke," she whispered. Her hand covered her mouth.

I pulled out the box, my hands a bit shaky as I opened it. "I know we haven't known each other long, but we're good together. Damn well perfect."

"We are." Her eyes misted.

"Marry me?" I blurted quickly.

The silence stretched, filled with my own thundering heartbeat. I waited for her answer. The seagulls cawing above seemed to be mocking me. "Well? What do you say?"

"Yes! Yes, I'll marry you!"

"Took you long enough to spit it out." I slipped the ring onto her finger, pulling her on my lap to kiss her deeply. "You had me scared there for a second."

"I'm in shock. This feels like a dream."

"I know what you mean. Never thought I'd be proposing on a beach, of all places."

"Neither did I." Goldi rested her head on my shoulder. "Remember when we first met? You were set in your ways and kind of a grump."

"And you were determined to get back to the city."

A wave crashed onto the shore and kept on going, soaking us both. We scrambled to our feet, our suits wet.

"I think the ocean is trying to cool us off. You were looking at me pretty intently there," her voice came out low and sultry.

Caught red-handed. "Can't help it. You're my sexy fiancé." I liked the sound of that.

We walked along the shore, hand in hand.

"I love you." I pressed my lips to hers in a tender kiss that quickly grew more passionate. When I pulled away, I asked, "What do you say we get hitched today?"

"No way. When we say our vows, it will be on your ranch with our friends and family. Maybe in May or June."

"I guess I can wait that long. As long as you're sleeping in my bed." I kissed her again.

"Yes, please."

"What will your folks think about us?" I should have asked her father for her hand, but I didn't want to chance him saying no.

"It doesn't matter. I belong with you."

"Still, we should tell them the news in person. It's the least we can do."

She bit her bottom lip. "How about later tonight?"

"Okay. Are your parents happily married?" I asked, curious.

"More like co-existing." She rolled her eyes. "Dad expects Mom to support all his decisions and to entertain his clients. Mom loves Dad's prestige. Otherwise, they basically live separate lives. I don't want that with us."

"Me, neither."

"What were your parents like?" she asked.

"Dad used to yell. At my mom. At us." I sucked in a deep breath. "When I was six, he left."

"He walked out?"

"Yep." This topic wasn't easy, but she deserved to know. "He hated ranch life. One day, he packed his bags."

"That's awful."

"Yep. My mom would cry in her room late at night. I think he broke her spirit for a while, but I didn't understand."

"How would you? You were so little."

"Looking back, he did us a favor. He wasn't the nicest person." I took her hand. "You know, I've never said that out loud. Dad's leaving is a sore spot for all of us."

"Then it's been a long time coming. What was your mom like?"

"The best. Patient as all hell, especially with three rambunctious boys." I hadn't talked about her in years. "She taught English at the high school. Grammy said she was the godsend that her son never appreciated."

"What happened to your mom?"

"Coming home late one night a car plowed right into her." I sucked in a long breath.

"I'm so sorry." She pressed her lips to my cheek. "Here I thought you had the perfect childhood."

"It wasn't bad. I had my grandparents, aunts, uncles, and half the town to watch out for me and my siblings."

"I'm glad you had them."

We'd both opened up to each other and it felt damn good. I kissed her for the longest time.

EPILOGUE

GOLDI

Sunset Ridge Ranch, nine months later

I opted to get ready in the little cottage so Luke wouldn't chance seeing me before the wedding. Normally I didn't believe in superstitions, but why tempt fate?

"Stop fidgeting." Tiffany pulled my hair with a curling iron to add in spirals.

I sat in the kitchen and tapped my nails on the table. "I can't help it. I'm excited." Happy butterflies flittered in my belly.

Hayley set a glass of water on the table. "Drink up. You have to stay hydrated. We wouldn't want to chance you passing out at the altar."

"You're right. Soon I'll be marrying my hot cowboy."

"From what I've seen so far, all the men around here are quite nice. I should have visited months ago."

"You're here now, which means a lot."

"Keep your head still, hon," Tiffany said. I sat at the kitchen table as she fiddled. "We're almost there."

My hands twisted the edge of the silk robe embroidered with "Bride" in swirling gold letters. This day was finally here.

Tiffany reached for the pearl combs my sister bought for me. "These are gorgeous." She held one up for me to see before sliding it gently into my hair. "Delicate but elegant—just like you."

"Elegant?" I laughed, careful not to ruin her work. "Have you ever seen me chase chickens in cowboy boots and a sundress?"

She giggled. "Maybe it's not every day, but today you're the epitome of a blushing bride. Luke won't know what hit him."

Her words sent warmth through me. She added the second comb and held up a hand mirror. "What do you think?" she stepped back to admire her handiwork.

My curls cascaded down, soft and romantic, framing my face. I tilted my head. "This is perfection."

She spritzed hairspray, "Done. Time to get that dress on."

I got up and followed my sister into the bedroom.

She unzipped my dress from the garment bag. "How'd you talk Mom into buying a strapless gown with only a foot long train?"

"It's designer—which is all that matters to her." I allowed her to shop with me with the caveat that I had the final say. "Honestly, I would be happy in jeans and a tank top."

"And miss the look on Luke's face when he sees you in this?" She placed the gown over me, laced up the back, and pushed me toward a full-length mirror. "Look at you."

Smoky eyes met my reflection. The beaded bodice sparkled and danced in the light.

"Twirl around."

The airy tulle skirt fluttered around me. "I hardly recognize myself."

"You're exquisite." My sister's eyes misted.

"Thanks. You look amazing." She wore a hunter green dress with capped sleeves and a slit up the right side.

"That's because you let me pick out my dress—trusting my judgement." She'd narrowed it down to five styles and colors before she decided on this one.

Someone knocked.

"Got it," Tiffany said from the kitchen.

Auburn strolled into the bedroom in a hunter green gown matching my sister's. "You look beautiful."

"So do you."

She'd pulled her hair back into a chignon with tendrils of red falling. "It's one of the few colors that doesn't wash out my complexion. Sometimes being a redhead sucks."

"If you ever decide to become a blonde or brunette, I'm available," Tiffany called out.

The three of us laughed.

Peggy strolled inside with her daughters. The girls ran toward me.

"Hold it right there," my soon to be sister-in-law commanded. "No hugging Auntie Goldi until after the ceremony. We can't chance wrinkling her dress."

"Yes, Mom." They said in unison and perched on the bed, their legs swinging back and forth.

"I saw Luke earlier today," Peggy's said.

"Is he okay?" My stomach twisted for a second. What if he changed his mind?

"He's wearing a goofy grin, so all's good."

"I love that grin." I loved him.

"Hurry up. girls. Let's get you dressed," Peggy said.

"I'm on it." Hayley snagged their gowns from the closet, and I headed for the living room.

Another knock sounded on the door.

"I'll get it."

Mom came into the room wearing a mint green chiffon dress with a V-neck that showed off her jade and diamond necklace. Classy but a bit overdone for our country setting. "You look absolutely beautiful, sweetie."

"It's the dress."

Mom puffed up. "I knew it was the one when you tried it on."

Not exactly true. She preferred the mermaid style one, but it wasn't me.

"I love shopping with you." Her eyes lit up. She loved spending all day looking for the perfect outfit. "You'll have to come back to L. A. soon so we can do it again."

Yeah. Right. Not if I could help it.

My mom held a long black box in her hand. "This was your great-grandmother's." She opened the case to display a pear-shaped diamond pendant. "It will count as something borrowed."

"Thank you." I checked to make sure the emerald earrings that Nana gave me for my twenty-first birthday were in place. At least a part of her would be here with me today.

Mom clasped the delicate chain around my neck. "It's your special day. I just wish you had the grand wedding you deserved." Meaning she longed to show off for her elite society friends in California. She tried to change the venue three times. I held my ground. After all, this was my wedding.

Peggy strolled in with her daughters wearing frilly dresses and flowers in their hair. "We have to go. Are you girls ready for that wagon ride?"

They gave high pitched yesses.

"Let's get going." Auburn and Tiffany left, arm in arm. "See y'all at the wedding."

That left me alone with my mom and sister. A knock sounded at the door.

"That must be your father."

I stepped outside.

"My little girl's all grown up. You look beautiful, Goldi-locks." He placed a kiss on my cheek. "Are you sure this is what you want?"

"Yes."

After what Mark did, Dad transferred my ex-fiancé to an office on the East Coast, figuring it was best to have him living on the other side of the country. I found a new respect for my dad after that action. He might not understand me, but he loved me.

My parents had been a bit leery about me getting engaged so fast. Luke came with me to California when I looked for my dress. He asked my dad for my hand, saying he should have done that earlier. Dad had traditional values, so I think Luke impressed him.

"Very well then." Dad nodded, offering me his arm.

An open-aired carriage waited outside attached to two Percheron draft horses. Since I didn't recognize the animals, I assumed they belonged to one of our neighbors.

"What a classy ride." Hayley said. "I feel like we're royalty."

"It's Luke's idea," Will said.

"Just another reason to love that guy." Hayley smiled at Mom.

"He's the best." I sighed.

Mom's lips twitch up for a second.

Will helped Mom into the seat facing backward. As I moved onto the soft leather seats, my sister adjusted my dress to make sure my train was in and sat next to me. Dad took the spot by Mom.

"See you at the wedding." My brother popped his head inside, looking happier than usual. Then he hopped on top next to Sam.

My sister raised a brow. "Can you believe him?"

"He's cowboying up." He seemed at ease on the ranch. What if we had that in common?

"Maybe he'll fall for one of the locals here?"

"One can hope." I laughed.

Mom actually harrumphed.

"That would never happen," my dad chuckled. "He's a city boy through and through."

Which could change. I mean, look at me.

"How can you stand living out here in the middle of nowhere?" Mom asked. "I'd perish without having restaurants, shopping, and entertainment close by."

"I've never been that way. I've always loved being around nature."

"You used to cry when you had to come home from camp." Thank Hayley for having a quick retort.

"I hated leaving Chantilly." I looked straight at my dad. "I loved that horse."

"You wrote about riding in your letters." Mom said.

"When you begged for a horse, I thought it a waste of time and money. Maybe if I'd given in to you, you might not be moving so far away." His eyes squinted like he couldn't quite figure me out.

"Things happen for a reason. I'm where I belong now."

"Are you happy?" Mom asked.

"More than ever." Which was the honest truth.

I gazed out at the spectacular view of the valley. The river meandered through the property. Horses and cattle grazed on the hillsides plush with grass and wildflowers. The weather cooperated with blue skies and a scattering of thin, wispy clouds.

"Who thought of shuttling people here?" Hayley asked.

"Luke. Too many cars would ruin trails." People parked near the old barn where the reception would be held.

"Smart man. You should marry him," Hayley said.

"I might just do that."

The carriage stopped in front of a white runner that led to the arbor where Luke awaited. My heart sped faster.

As soon as I stepped out, I noticed all the people lining both sides of the aisle. Pete escorted my mom and brother to a seat in the front.

I caught a glimpse of Luke's white Stetson. He'd gone all out for today.

A friend of the family sang, "Love Wins," because it fit our journey.

Rose petals were thrown by my serious-acting, soon-to-be nieces. Hayley gave me a quick hug before she marched along the aisle followed by Peggy and Auburn.

"You're stunning. You remind me of your mother on our day."

"Thanks, Dad." I kissed his cheek.

"Just yesterday you were looking for four-leaf clovers with your sister. Where has the time gone?"

"I wish I knew."

"The Wedding March" played and everyone stood. My pulse quickened as Luke's eyes met mine.

I walked up the aisle. Charlie barked. Knowing him, he wanted to run up to me to get a dog biscuit. Yes, I brought him one. I insisted he be part of the ceremony because that sweet animal had been with us through our whole journey. He looked adorable in his faux black and white vest with a black bowtie and white buttons.

"You and your animals," Dad chuckled.

"He's part of the family."

My dad brought me under the arches.

"Who gives this woman to be married today?" Mabel asked.

"Her mother and I do." Dad handed me to Luke. "Take care of my little girl."

"Always." Luke drew me into his hands.

"You sure look handsome, cowboy," I whispered.

"And you're gorgeous."

"Are you ready?" Mabel said softly from her spot at the altar. Her sequined floor length gown suited her. She'd been ordained to do the ceremony.

I struggled to listen as she droned out the words and my eyes fixed on my cowboy. I couldn't believe we'd found each other and were getting married.

"Luke and Goldi have made up their own vows. Luke, would you begin?" Mabel asked.

He cleared his throat. "I'm a cowboy set in my ways. When you broke into my house, I wasn't exactly friendly. I'm right sorry about that."

"It's fine," I whispered. My attention remained fixed on him.

"Somewhere along the way I fell for you. You own my heart, darlin', now and forever." He let out a long sigh.

I heard oohs and awws while I gazed into his beautiful eyes. My cheeks hurt from smiling so hard. I sucked in a deep breath and exhaled. "I never thought I'd fall in love with a cowboy in the middle of Wyoming. But I did." I paused, blinking away tears. "You've given me the courage to be true to myself and believe I can do anything. You are the best man I know. I vow to make you strawberry crepes or chocolate chip pancakes for breakfast on the weekends, ride by your side, and be your partner for every sunrise and sunset."

"I'm counting on it," he whispered. "I love you."

"Back at you."

We exchanged rings. And then we were kissing. Not just a little peck, but a full-on deep kiss that sealed our promises.

"Folks, I'd like to introduce Mr. and Mrs. Wolfe," Mabel announced.

The crowd hooted and hollered. Charlie barked and wagged his tail.

We rushed down the aisle hand in hand. "We did it, cowboy."

"My city girl turned country. Who'd have thought?"

We stopped at the entrance, and he pulled me into a kiss that proved just how much I meant to him.

The End

TIME TO SAVE A COWBOY

Time to Save a Cowboy

If you enjoyed FIREBRAND'S CUPID, you might want to read TIME TO SAVE A COWBOY from my Western Time Travel Series.

The Cowboy Doesn't Deserve to HANG

Captivated by the story of a cowboy hanged as a horse thief in 1890, Mia Kellogg travels back in time with only thirty days to save an innocent man.

Dusty Mann is determined to buy his own ranch.

He doesn't need a modern, straightforward woman to barrel into his life or knock his plans off track.

But Mia steals his heart—and then says she's from the future.

Read the first chapter from TIME TO SAVE A COWBOY

CHAPTER 1

Present Day, Old Town Rialto, California

The sepia photograph of a cowboy in the antique shop's window drew Amelia Kellogg closer. For the moment, she shut out the clamor of people and the bustling noise and stared at the man in the dark Stetson. His bronze complexion. His square chin shadowed with dark stubble gave him a handsome rugged quality. His lips pinched together as if he tried to stay serious. And failed.

Her cousin's floor-length skirt swished as she stepped next to Mia. "What are you looking at?" Birdie tilted her head. The pink ostrich feather in her old-fashioned knob-shaped hat quivered.

"This guy's gorgeous." Mia did a Vanna sweep of her hands to the picture. His direct gaze mixed with playfulness and confidence "It seems like he's staring right at me."

"You do realize it's only a picture."

"Way to ruin my fantasy." Mia let out an exaggerated sigh. Underneath her long taffeta dress, the corset pinched her waist. Her cousin had cinched her strings so tightly Mia could hardly breathe, while insisting their costumes looked authentic for their trip on a turn-of-the-century steam locomotive.

"You need to get out more."

Birdie had a point. For the past few years, Mia's career came first, ruining her last few relationships. She didn't need a man to be happy, but she definitely needed this mini vacation on a nineteenth century steam locomotive.

Her focus drifted back to the photo. What kind of life had this cowboy led? She imagined a hint of longing or heartache in his expression. *Crazy. Now I'm making up a life story for this guy.*

Antique bottles and glassware were placed on shelves below the picture in the window. It made her wonder about other treasures the shop might have inside.

"Let's go in. I want to check it out." Birdie pushed open the door and bells chimed.

"We'll miss our train."

Birdie glanced at the time on her phone. "It's only quarter to one. We have forty-five minutes before the train even arrives."

"All right, ten minutes." Mia strolled inside the cluttered room, fingered a hand-blown glass vase, then picked up a porcelain cat figurine. "Too bad the paw broke off. It's cute."

"I suppose." Birdie scrunched her nose. "This room smells like dirty socks and moth balls." The scent didn't stop her cousin from wandering toward a pile of children's books, grabbing one, blowing off the dust and leafing through the pages. "Look, an original *Dick and Jane.*"

"Nice." A text-message beeped. Mia grabbed her phone.

Congrats. You're in charge of the Cashmere Kitty website.

The account came with an ultra-demanding client. She stifled a groan.

"What's the matter?"

"A work thing." Mia shook her head. "But we're in partying mode. No stress for the next forty-eight hours." She clicked off her cell.

Birdie rested her hand on Mia's shoulder. "It's about time you relax and have fun."

"Fun?" Mia's upper lip twitched.

"You know, being amused, happy, entertained."

"Sounds kinda familiar." Mia giggled. "I'm gonna see if there's any jewelry."

"Go ahead. I'll meet up with you." Birdie waved her on.

As Mia strolled into a long musty room, a current of mystery stirred the air. On the wall, a variety of coiled ropes hung on horseshoe nails. She passed a saddle on a stand and headed for a glass display case. Incandescent light gleamed off shiny trinkets. A rusted pistol, knives sheathed in leather, spurs, a silver belt buckle, gold-hooped earrings, a cracked cameo. Nothing of interest.

An older gentleman popped up from behind the counter. "May I help you?"

She jumped, and her pulse warped to fast lane speed.

"Sorry to have startled you." He twisted the silver ends of his mustache. "I was busy cleaning out a bottom drawer over there. Thought I heard footsteps."

Still a bit spooked, she fidgeted with her purse.

"May I help you find anything in particular?"

"You have something to go with my ruby earrings?"

"I may have just the thing for you. This ring came in yesterday." He reached behind on a shelf and produced a small black box with a fancy golden latch. His long fingers carefully opened the container, as he moved it over for her to see. "The previous owner said the ring has been in the family for several centuries. Supposed to fire up the heart for love," he said in a quiet voice.

"I don't believe in superstitious things." Although she liked watching paranormal movies.

"It makes a fun story. We get all kinds. A man brought in that rusted gun; said it was cursed. People say just about anything to try to get a better price."

"I can imagine." She couldn't blame the seller. When money's tight, you do what you can to survive.

"Would you like to try the ring on?"

"Yes, please." She slipped the thin gold band shimmering with inlaid rubies on her finger—it fit perfectly. Then she turned the case over and saw the price. Hmm … two hundred dollars was a steal but only if the stones were real. "Do you have a certificate of authenticity to prove it's ruby?"

"No. I'm going by what I was told. Our appraiser won't be in 'till next week."

She held it up to the light and noted the deep red color. "It's garnet, not ruby." Taking the ring off, she placed it back in the case. She didn't need the ring, but wanted it, and asked, "Would you take a hundred?"

"One twenty-five's the lowest I can go."

She'd consider it a souvenir from this trip. "Okay, I'll take it."

"Excellent choice."

The superstition behind the ring would make a great tale to tell her friends.

The man carried the box to the front and rung up the sale. On the counter, a frayed scrapbook lay open to a newspaper clipping with an etching of a cowboy. She edged in close enough to recognize the same man from the window photo.

The clerk handed her the purchase, and she slipped her ring inside her purse.

"Interesting article. The same person with your ring brought in this scrapbook and the photo in the window."

Hesperia Weekly Press, July 6th, 1890
Local Foreman, Dusty Mann, Hanged as Horse Thief.

Her heart saddened at the caption.

Los Flores Ranch, Hesperia, California, 1890

The horse's long shadow against the flat desert landscape signaled the last speck of day. Dusty's gut gurgled, telling him to hurry back to the ranch's dining hall or there'd be nothing left.

Fifty yards away a calf struggled, his leg caught in a barbed wire fence. Dusty dismounted, untangled the wounded calf, and slipped a noose around the frightened animal's neck. It kicked, nicking Dusty's shin. "Ouch."

The calf's eyes rounded, and it let out a bleat.

Ignoring the creak in his knees and the twinge in his back, he bent down. Today, he'd only chased maybe fifty cows, yet his twenty-eight-year-old bones crackled as if he were sixty. Every weary muscle on his six-foot frame ached, but the poor critter needed tending, and he wouldn't sleep without helping it.

"Gotta clean this. If you cooperate, we'll both get sleep tonight." He tied the rope around a Joshua tree and used his bandana to wipe off the worst of the blood.

Walking to his saddlebag, he grabbed supplies. His canteen clicked against his belt buckle embedded with a quarter-sized garnet. The silver heirloom once symbolized a future filled with happiness. He ran his fingertips over the inlaid stone. Today, the blood-red garnet symbolized the loss of his family ranch.

Ten yards away to the east, a blonde woman gathered wildflowers. Where'd she come from? A lone woman didn't belong in the middle of the desert.

He stepped toward her and waved his hat. "Howdy, miss."

The young lady didn't see him. Her colors faded as her shape became transparent, and she vanished.

"Where'd you go?" He rubbed his eyes. Sagebrush, plenty of sagebrush and nothing else. *Must be seeing things.*

The calf bawled, bringing him back to his task.

"Quit complaining." Holding the dang animal between his legs, he cleaned the cut while thinking about the bonus from tomorrow's roundup. With what he'd saved, it might be enough money to buy a ranch. He applied a generous amount of smelly salve to the calf's leg. "Easy there, we're 'bout done."

By the time he finished, the sun had set. A full moon led him along the trail. Certain dinner would be gone, he snatched jerky from his saddlebag, and took a bite and pretended he was biting into a juicy steak. Pulled out hardtack and pretended he was eating fried potatoes. Pretending never worked.

Thirty minutes later inside his cabin, he stretched out on a goose-feathered mattress and drew his ragged patchwork quilt to his chin. His shin throbbed. Damn calf.

Exhausted, he needed sleep, but his mind whirled. *Check the creek for strays. Remind Ace to ride lead. See if the holding pens are sound. Stop fretting and get some shut eye.*

He counted. "One cow, two cows, three cows—a whole dang herd."

Quit being a fool and go to sleep. He eyeballed the ceiling and counted one million cows.

His eyes closed, and he envisioned the blonde. Why'd she keep popping up, making him question his sanity? Maybe a dozen times in his life, he'd see a vision of a blonde. She was always in the distance, never close enough to see her face. It usually happened when he was overly tired.

He'd obviously been too long without a woman.

It couldn't have been more than an hour, and the old red rooster crowed his greeting. He yanked back the covers, stumbled out of bed, and dressed. What happened to his other boot? It took getting down on his knees to locate the object under the bed.

Slamming the door, he stomped over to the main house in a sleep-deprived, cantankerous mood. The already warm morning meant the day would be a scorcher.

"Howdy." From under the eaves by the dining hall entrance, the cook flipped flapjacks on a cast iron stove.

Dusty gave a cordial don't-bother-jawin'-to-me-nod and went inside. A dozen cowboys sat in mismatched chairs and ate at long wooden tables. They jabbered, forking food in their mouths. Full mouths didn't cease their conversing. The men were noisier than a wagon on a frozen road.

He headed for the sideboard, filling his dish with scrambled eggs, crisp bacon, flapjacks, and fried taters. Holding a cup of thick Arbuckle coffee, he slunk into a vacant chair on the end of a table.

Reynolds and Slick sat in the corner. Their loud voices jangled Dusty's nerves. Reynolds' chuckling turned to snorting. Slick's chortle could pass for an enraged bull.

The ranch owner's nephew on his wife's side, Reynolds, touched the brim of his hat, and called, "Mornin' boss," to Dusty.

Dusty would bet his boots and saddle Reynolds brewed trouble. His sly glares kept Dusty wary. Yesterday, Dusty had found his cinch snipped, making him wonder if the incident had been intentional.

Dusty's friend, Trevor, took the chair next to him. The skinny wrangler had to be pushing forty; still, he could ride and rope like a man in his twenties. "You okay?"

"Yep." His problems were none of the cowboy's concern.

Trevor wore a goofy grin. "Hard to reckon freedom comes tomorrow afternoon."

Dusty smiled. "No cow punching or chores for three days. Can't wait for that room at the Hesperia Hotel." He planned a hot bath, a stiff drink, perhaps the company of a woman.

"Can't stop thinking about the cowboy, Dusty Mann," Mia said, standing next to Birdie at the depot's wide-open platform.

Dusty didn't look like a criminal. His eyes seemed bright, not dull like the men on internet mugshots.

"Dusty Mann?" Birdie laughed. "What kind of name is that?"

"Be nice. The poor guy hanged." Mia held her hand against her throat.

Birdie made a pretend noose motion. "Hanged, as in from the highest tree death?"

"Now you're making fun of him."

"If you're interested in cowboys, I'll set you up with one of my brother's friends."

Mia rolled her eyes. "No more blind dates."

"We'll see." Her cousin's smirk meant she'd be persistent. She reached in her purse and handed her a delicate floral tapestry coin purse. "Found this in grandma's attic last week and added three silver dollars to commemorate our trip."

Mia hugged her cousin. "You're so sweet." She tucked the items inside her purse, deciding to check out the coins when they were seated on the train.

Directly in front of her, a barbershop quartet harmonized an old love song. Their red striped vests, straw hats, and handlebar mustaches added to the ambiance.

No surprise, Birdie knew the lyrics.

Auntie Mickie walked up and pulled Mia inside a lavender-scented hug. "I'm glad you moved back."

"Me too." Mia didn't mind housesitting for her grandparents, especially since she didn't have to pay rent for a year. She didn't mind her relatives—but would miss hanging out with her friends in the city.

"Something bugging you?" Auntie Mickie asked.

Darn intuitive aunt.

"Nope." Mia had to fight to keep from clenching her teeth.

"Uncle Al's old west cookout sounded fun," Birdie said. "Why didn't you go with him?"

"Riding horses for hours and sleeping on the hard ground has absolutely no appeal for me." Her aunt fidgeted with the netting on her Knobby hat.

"I'm with Auntie." Mia tugged a capped sleeve down. "Last time I camped, I stepped in a gopher hole and twisted my ankle. Now I'm more into resorts."

"Well, I'd do it. Must've been quite a trip." Her cousin made a wanna-be-a-cowgirl lasso in the air.

Auntie Mickie tapped her pointy black-and-white boots and laughed.

The train's horn blasted from a distance. Voices buzzed. Everyone crowded the gate as Mia edged forward. The steam locomotive chugged, hissing and billowing steam clouds as it stopped.

Birdie posed by one of the car's wheels. "The rims are taller than I am."

Mia grabbed her phone and took a picture. "That's not saying a lot."

Birdie stuck out her tongue.

The conductor flipped open his pocket watch. "Welcome to the California Southern Railroad. You'll find traveling on this fifty-thousand-pound wonder a step back into the year eighteen-ninety."

Dusty may have ridden on a train like this. Birdie was right; Mia had to stop thinking about the darn cowboy.

Auntie Mickie led them up grated metal steps and into the gaming car. Half a dozen men in period black duster-coats, tooled leather boots, and dark Stetsons leaned against a mahogany bar, drinking beer out of glass mugs. To her left, gamblers played cards at a felt-covered table. A redheaded man winked at her.

She flashed him a smile, rushed behind her aunt, out the vintage train door, and into the passenger car. A lady held a young girl on her lap; both wore matching periwinkle dresses and bonnets.

Auntie Mickie pointed two rows ahead to a middle-aged woman with tangerine glasses. "Let's sit over by my friend."

Mia took the window seat next to Birdie, facing her aunt.

Birdie crossed her right leg and leaned over to Mia. "Can't wait for the Daggett Western Shindig tomorrow night."

"Remember those crepe-papered high school dances in the gym?" The high school gym where Mia initially danced with her cowboy crush, Craig.

"Sure. They were a blast."

The server handed Mia champagne. She sipped. Bubbles tickled down her throat. A giddiness filled her for the first time in months.

Her cousin lifted her glass and toasted, "To adventures."

After far too many hours staring at her computer screen, Mia was more than ready for an adventure. The whistle blared, and the train jerked forward. She lazed back into the plush seat. A gentle breeze drifted in from the open windows as the car rolled along the tracks. Its wheels clickety-clacked.

"You double-crossing son of a polecat," a raspy voice came from a bearded man, less than a foot from Birdie, blocking the middle of the aisle. He wore a dirty, red-checkered shirt, a weathered cowboy hat, and his lip twisted into a glower.

At the opposite end of the train car, a man, resembling Wild Bill Hickok, fingered the handle of his gun and kept his eyes on his opponent. "It's a mistake to draw first."

The other man pulled out his six-shooter and squeezed the trigger.

Fake gunfire boomed. Wild Bill's opponent fell to the carpet.

Even knowing they were actors, Mia flinched and told her heart to chill. She glanced at Birdie. Her eyes fixed on the still body as her fingernails dug into the seat's padded arm.

The conductor squatted beside the body. "The man's dead!" he shouted to Wild Bill.

"If you don't want to die with your boots on, let that gun lie!" Wild Bill's voice projected the famous line to the audience.

"Bravo." Her cousin whistled, her face shone, and her eyes sparkled. "Wild Bill's hot."

"Probably married," Mia whispered.

The actors stood, bowed, and headed into the next car.

Mia stared out the window. The train rolled past a stand of eucalyptus trees as they wound through the foothills and ascended to a plateau. Creosote bushes and Joshua trees scattered along the dry ground. She found the desert's simplistic beauty calming.

Auntie Mickie pushed her head out her window. "We're climbing the Cajon Pass." The train meandered east and crossed under the freeway. "Summit Valley's over that hill."

Birdie nudged her. "You got any gum?"

Mia moved her valise onto her lap and took out her purse. "In here somewhere." She pulled out a small black box. "I forgot about this." Flipping the lid open, she put the ring on and admired the gemstones. "Got it at the antique shop."

"Let me see." Birdie's green eyes glittered.

Mia lifted her hand up so her cousin could get a look at her purchase.

"Nice."

"The Hesperia Airport's around the bend. Ellen and Sally said they'd be waiting by the tracks." Auntie Mickie pointed. "There they are, right by the bridge."

The metal band felt hot against Mia's finger. She twisted and pulled on the ring, but the thing didn't budge. Her heart raced. "Birdie, do you have lotion … anything to get this ring off? It's burning my finger."

"I'll check."

Mia's vision blurred. Vibrant colors rotated like a hyper kaleidoscope. Dizzy, she shut her eyes.

A whistle shrilled, the train stopped, and her valise thunked to the floor.

She opened her eyes and turned to Birdie. "Hey—" An unknown woman slept in her cousin's place. "What the heck?"

In her aunt's spot, an older man smoked a hand-rolled cigar. An icy wave shivered up her spine. This couldn't be right. The combination of her tight corset and lack of oxygen must've caused her to hallucinate.

The man puffed smoke in her direction. A gray haze curled around her face. Her eyes watered, fumes went up her nostrils, and she coughed.

Fresh air, she needed fresh air. She hurried along the center aisle to an open doorway and stopped, catching her breath.

COWBOY'S CUPID

If you enjoyed FIREBRAND'S CUPID, you might want to read COWBOY'S CUPID from my Love's Magic Series.

A Forbidden Love

When Cupid's arrow accidentally strikes the wrong cowboy, she's supposed to fix her mistake—not fall for the alluring mortal.

Cami Calypso receives her first assignment just in time for the Valentine season. As a newbie Cupid Archer, her life is perfect until her arrow accidentally strikes the wrong man. She has sixty days to secure a job as his housekeeper on a ranch and find the cowboy his soul mate—not keep him for herself.

Rhett Holloway needs a housekeeper and cook.

He doesn't need an adorable blonde to distract him.

He doesn't need her to fix his love life.

But here she is, and he finds her irresistible.

Rhett had a strange feeling in his gut during dinner. Cami kept checking her watch. He'd asked what bothered her, but she said everything was fine.

After a long day, he helped her clean up the dinner dishes, and they walked to her apartment. Her stance was rigid, her body tense. She didn't shift toward him as he strode with his arm around her shoulder.

"What's wrong?"

"I need to tell you something." She shrugged but wouldn't look at him.

They'd only known each other close to two months, but his heart was all in. He unlocked the apartment door. Seated at the edge of the couch, Cami put a distance between them and avoided eye contact.

"Go ahead." He stood by the kitchen table and waited for a response.

"We were never meant to be together," she said, still not looking his way.

His chest tightened. She was breaking up with him.

"I've got a secret. When I show you, I hope you'll still love me."

"Whatever you've done in the past doesn't matter. We'll get through it." He'd made his share of mistakes.

She extracted a glass vial from her pocket. It sparkled and shimmered. "It's not what I've done, it's what I am."

"What are you?" He didn't even see a flicker of a smile.

Her lips tightened into a grimace. "Please listen carefully to what I say."

"All right. Spill." He tapped the side of his pants.

She licked her lips and took a deep breath. "I told you I was a Cupid when you took me to the archery range."

"Okay."

She folded her arms. "I live in Zeus' Kingdom up in the clouds."

His teeth ground, as he sat next to her and said sarcastically, "Of course you do."

"You've seen my archery skills. Even said I was talented." She lifted her chin and blew out a breath. "I am a Cupid, a real live Cupid."

"That's crazy." Maybe she was crazy. His primal instinct told him to leave, but he couldn't move.

"My occupation is an archer." Tears pooled in her eyes. "I'm telling you the truth."

"If you're leaving me, say so, and quit making up this lame story."

"I don't want to go anywhere." She twirled a curl around her finger.

"You don't? And here I thought you were breaking up with me."

"If only things were different. I've got to return home." She looked at her watch.

"So, you are leaving me? Why?" He was confused.

"I don't want to. I'm happy here." Her body slumped, her chin dropped. "My whole life I've dreamed of being good enough."

"But you are good enough." She was the best thing to ever happen to him. "You're perfect for me."

"Don't make me cry. Please let me finish." Her eyes softened. "I've dreamed of visiting Earth and infusing humans with arrows of love. When I got my first earthly assignment, I hit the wrong man, namely you."

Those blue eyes. "You shot me with your arrow of love?"

"It was a mistake. My assignment ducked, and I hit you instead. I was sent to rectify my mishap and set you up with your soulmate. We were never supposed to fall in love."

"You love me." His spirits soared.

"Yes."

"'Bout time you admitted it." He moved closer, but she backed up, out of his reach.

"Will you accept the real me?"

"What do you mean? The real Cami's right in front of me."

"Watch." Rocking back and forth on her heels, her cheeks flushed to a rosier red.

His eyes riveted to her hands.

She unscrewed the glass vial and poured out a glittery

substance. Iridescent pink dust swirled and surrounded her. Her body shrunk to the size of a doll, dressed in a shimmering gown. Iridescent wings formed at her shoulders. She flew up midway between the floor and the ceiling.

"Holy shit!" He stared, not frightened, confused.

"I'm a C-Cupid." Her words came out broken.

He froze, became immobile. "This can't be happening."

"I love you, always will." She hovered close to him, and he felt her lips kiss his cheek.

"It's unreal."

"Tell me about it." Her eyes were wide. Wary.

"You really are a Cupid?"

"Yes. Do you still love me?"

He didn't know what to think. "It's too much." He turned his back to her, put his head in his hands.

His girlfriend—a ruler-sized pixie. It couldn't be true.

Except he'd seen her.

DEAR READERS

Dear Readers,

Thank you for COWBOY'S CUPID.

I hope you enjoyed my story as much as I enjoyed writing it. Won't you please consider leaving a review? Even just a few words will help others decide if the book is right for them.

Best regards and thank you in advance.

Niki J. Mitchell

I look forward to hearing from my readers.

Visit me at https://nikimitchell.weebly.com/

Follow me on FaceBook at Author Niki Mitchell

Twitter: Niki Mitchell@NikiMitchell7

Instagram: NikiJMitchellAuthor

Tiktok: https://www.tiktok.com/@nikimitchellauthor

GOLDI'S GRUMPY COWBOY is dedicated to my friends and family who always support my crazy ideas, and to my readers for supporting me.

ABOUT THE AUTHOR

Niki Mitchell writes children's books along with contemporary, fantasy, and historical time-travel romance. She was born in Chicago, Illinois, and moved to Whittier, California in first grade. With a houseful of books and a local library located a few short blocks, her love of reading began at a young age.

Married for over thirty years and a romantic at heart, she enjoys writing about strong female characters in unusual settings. When she isn't playing with her cats, she enjoys reading, taking walks, water aerobics, photography, and traveling.

KURIOUS KATZ AND THE BEST CHRISTMAS EVER

FOSTER CATS: ARTEMIS AND HER SNEAKY
BROTHER HERCULUES

KURIOUS KATZ AND THE FOURTH OF JULY

KURIOUS KATZ AND THE VALENTINE SURPRISE

KURIOUS KATZ AND THE SNICKERDOODLE STORY

PRECIOUS PUPS: BREEZY, THE LABRADOR RETRIEVER

AMAZING ANIMAL GROUPS

www.ingramcontent.com/pod-product-compliance
Lightning Source LLC
Chambersburg PA
CBHW060629310726
48982CB00003B/716